Settlers

Steve Denison

Copyright © 2024 Steve Denison

Settlers

Steve Denison

Yet all experience is an arch wherethro'
Gleams that untravell'd world whose margin fades
For ever and forever when I move.

Ulysses, Alfred, Lord Tennyson

Chapter 1

Ben looked out the window at the crack in the street. Ten feet wide and raised three feet on the far side, it ran as far as he could see in both directions up and down the street. He remembered the headlines: "Scientists learn to control gravity. Bending gravity waves will capture greenhouse gasses, lower sea levels." There was a car in the crack that hadn't been there yesterday, and he wondered when someone would pull it out. He wiped out his bowl and put it in the sink, took a last drink from his cup and looked out the window again. The sky was a lighter orange today but there was always the drizzle. Lighter orange meant you could go outside but still for only a few minutes and always with your skin covered. He put on his jumpsuit and picked up his backpack and opened the door. Turning right out of the door, he walked four blocks to the end of the street. Rows of buildings all made of the same gray composite material: blocks of condensed carbon dioxide from

Carbon capture that were supposed to lower greenhouse gasses but like everything else it was too little too late. He looked down the street as he walked at the crumbled buildings, brought to the ground by too much gravity, and tried to remember what they had looked like before. His mother had worked on the sixteenth floor of one of them. He turned left at the end of the street and walked two more blocks.

He stopped at a metal door and entered some numbers on a keypad. The door opened and then shut as soon as he walked through. He closed his eyes as a mist filled the small room. As the cloud cleared, a second door opened and he walked through that one. He put his backpack and jumpsuit in a small recess, which closed with a sucking sound as he walked away then got onto a bicycle and started pedaling, nodding and smiling to the man on the bike next to his.

"You know," he said, "there was a trope, before, that in the future we would all just be batteries, or generators, for a super intelligent computer." Wolfie looked over. "But it's not that bad really." They both smiled.

Chapter 2

"With my crossbow, I shot the albatross." Anna read aloud and then looked up, thinking about the poem, written now over three hundred years ago, and about the situation they were in now. Like the Mariner in the poem, humans were certainly expiating for the way they had treated nature. Nature. This is the book I'll take with me, she said to herself. Water, water everywhere, nor any drop to drink. There were times when she thought her life had been like the poem's author's life. The doubt and uncertainty. She had put certain of her beliefs in abeyance until further notice. There was no such thing as conservatism anymore. At other times, she felt her life had been more like that of the author's friend, Wordsworth, with his steady conviction and sense of vocation. She felt like of the two, Coleridge was a more likely comparison as nature, so important to Wordsworth's writing, was in very short supply. She wished that wasn't the case.

She remembered when the first Settlers were sent back, about two years ago, as a way of escaping the present earth with too little food, too much pollution, too much cancer. She wasn't sure who first realized that although bending gravity waves put too much strain on the earth, that it created a way back in time, an arch through time.

Chapter 3

Ben put his pack up, got on his bike and started pedaling. Wolfie was already there. "Did you ever wonder," Ben said, "why anyone really would want to go back in time and live with dinosaurs? To settle?"

"Look around," said Wolfie.

"Right. But wouldn't most people rather take their chances with the Orange, than face a Tyrannosaurus rex?"

They looked up at Settler's TV, the screen on the wall. Video images of Settlers' lives came back from cameras that were part of Settlers' kits. The images travelled at the speed of light, which was thought to be the reason they could travel forward, through some residual time anomaly, even though nothing else could. People were understandably fascinated at the video clips of people's lives twenty, thirty, even eighty million years ago. Encounters with dinosaurs didn't usually go as badly as most people thought they would; the dinosaurs, even the big carnivorous ones, usually ignored them.

Settler's kits cost five thousand dollars, and Wolfie had made almost enough money pedaling to buy one. He was planning to go back to the Oligocene, about twenty-five million years ago. No more dinosaurs. The images had confirmed for paleontologists many things they had suspected about dinosaurs. They did indeed have feathers and were brightly colored. In one video image, a Settler stood transfixed as behind him what looked like a giant chicken appeared to be making a deafening roar. The sound, however, would still be left to the imagination of viewers, as sound did not travel with the images. Birds are the only dinosaurs I ever want to see, Ben had thought to himself.

"So what do you do when you get there, to the Oligocene?" Ben asked.

"You know, start making a new life."

"With what?"

"The things in your Settler's kit," said Wolfie.

"Things like what?"

"There's a saw, nails, a compass, water purification tablets. Then you start making things. Like it all happened before but faster because you know what's going to happen. You find ore and melt it and make nails. Then you make things to make nails faster and go from there."

"Sounds great."

"Look around."

Ben got off his bike.

"Also one book."

"Have you decided which book?"

"Euclid's Elements."

"Geometry? To help build things?"

"No. I just like it. The abstractions have a certain charm. An independent world created out of pure intelligence." Ben looked at Wolfie who had started pedaling again.

"Or maybe a drawing pad. And some paints," Wolfie said. "A tabula rasa."

Ben nodded.

Most of the electricity generated by pedaling was used to run the enormous web of quantum computers, Qweb, that ran almost everything. "Web" was an apt description, Ben thought, as it suggested the importance of the computer to the ecology of everyday life but also had a certain elegiac meaning. Like a spider's web.

Ben pressed the water button. Pressure was lower today. Qweb had lowered the pressure here, diverting it to some place where it was needed more. The same for the protein mix. Fewer packets on the shelves. He looked at the latest avatar of Qweb on the wall: a circle with wires radiating out of it, kind of like a sun, with a simple, smiling face in the center, and then removed his electrodes.

He had pedaled for an hour, generating one tenth of a kilowatt hour. The attendant handed him back his chip after adding ten credits. Wiping his forehead with a towel, he removed his backpack and jumpsuit from the locker. Zipping up the suit, he went through the double doors and out onto the street.

Anna was waiting for him outside. They smiled then hugged and she gave him a quick kiss. "What can ail thee knight at arms, alone and palely loitering?" she said. He looked at her and smiled. "The sedge has withered from the lake and no birds sing," she finished and looked at him. They sometimes found it funny that people were still going to college and that you could still major in something like literature. "People in a Triassic Utopia someday may need to learn Shakespeare," she had said one night. "Or Thomas Moore," she added with a laugh. They were sitting on a bench by the river, and he turned his head to look at her. "So you're getting a Settler's education?" he said. She didn't say anything.

Chapter 4

Bill Wilson ran his fingers along the hieroglyphs, translating a few of the symbols then glanced at the Egyptian and Greek and wiped a cloth across the stone. Curator of Antiquities, he said to himself. Being Curator was not much different from being a janitor, which he had been just before. When the last Curator died, of glioblastoma, they asked him. I don't know much about antiquities, he had said. You know how to clean, they said. Most but not all of the air was kept out so most of his time he spent wiping down the artifacts. People still go to museums, he thought to himself.

He walked to the end of the hall, past stone lions, anthropomorphic animals, and up the stairwell, looking at Roman mosaics. Now walking past rows of Greek vases in glass cases, he stopped to look at one. A satyr was grabbing at a woman's gown who looked back at him. What maidens loth? He walked into the Parthenon gallery and looked at the friezes. Some had been destroyed and some had been brought here. If they were outside today, they would not last very long. Men on horses, women carrying amphora, a procession for a goddess. He walked slowly along the length of the gallery, looking up. Most people today, he thought to himself, probably look at these and just think about how clean the air was back then. Then he saw it, small and partially hidden behind a chariot. A car. He thought maybe a Toyota Corolla. He stared at it for a few minutes trying to make sense of it.

"Someone has broken the fiver," he said out loud.

Five thousand years. "A Fiver." This was how far back you had to go, to Settle, to not affect our timeline. Five thousand years before that to not affect that one. You couldn't break this rule. The Fiver was determined accidently. Historians were the first ones interested in the Arches, wanting to go back to witness key events in history, like the signing of the Declaration of Independence. When they went back, records of the Declaration started to disappear. Go back to the Bronze Age though, and nothing here is affected. Scientists thought it had something to do with how advanced civilizations were. Messing around with the Indus Civilization in Asia didn't change anything. Go back to watch the Colosseum being constructed and we might not have airplanes.

"Someone," Bill said out loud again, "has broken the fiver."

Chapter 5

Anna's mother and brother were already sitting at the table when Anna came through the door. She hung up her jumpsuit and walked to the sink. The dust outside was dense today and she washed her hands. Her brother's violin was on the coffee table, out of its case. He had been practicing. They had finally gotten new strings for the violin; the old ones had corroded too much to play. With her father gone, her mother's brother had made sure that Sam could continue to learn to play, saying that someday he could join an orchestra although there weren't any to join.

Anna's uncle Al was in the military, which meant he worked in security at the Arch. He was coming over for dinner tonight and just then there was a knock on the door and Al walked in. He was carrying a bottle of wine, which he handed to Anna's mother who stood up and walked over and hugged him.

"Hello," he said and then turned to smile at Anna and Sam. "You've been practicing! Good!" he said picking up the violin. "I wish I'd kept playing," he said, running his fingers lightly over the strings. "Al," Anna's mother said quietly, "do you think it's a good idea to encourage him like this? I mean, who is he going to play with?" Al smiled and handed her a chip for the player. She inserted it and the opening notes of a symphony, Beethoven's Pastoral symphony, started to play.

Dinner was spaghetti and meat sauce. The meat sauce was made from greenhouse soy. Lab-grown meat tasted better but it was more expensive, and they only had it every other week or so.

After dinner, Sam played his violin and then hugged his mom and Al and went to bed. Al washed the dishes and handed them to Anna's mother who put them away. They were sitting at the table again and Al drank from his wine glass.

"Did you ever think," he said turning to look at his sister, "that there is something dialectical about our situation?"

"How so?" she said.

"Well, the Arch presents an obvious way to fix our problems, but we can't go back too recently or we might make things worse than they already are."

"OK. And?"

"Well, maybe there is a way after all," he said. Anna sat quietly, swirling the wine around in her glass but not drinking it.

Chapter 6

Settlers went back in groups of five hundred. Each group included certain specialists: engineers, doctors, mechanics. People with unusual skills suddenly found themselves in demand: brewers, candlemakers, herbalists, mycologists. Others, like Wolfie, were just regular people. The organization of groups was based loosely on military principles, and military terminology was used. There was backup and redundancy. When something had obviously gone wrong with a group of Settlers, that was a Charlie Foxtrot. Each group had leaders but once through the arches, people were under no obligation to stay with the group and groups could elect their own leaders.

It was assumed that groups would not make the same mistakes that had gotten the world into the situation it was in now, but groups were free to do what they wanted. This was laissez faire time travel. Settlers had been seen on Settlers TV making crude iron instruments and copper kettles that might have been boilers or stills. Other groups seemed to be living in clusters of small huts made of an adobe material.

"The Romans basically had a better quality of life than we do," Wolfie would often point out. "Heated floors, spas, plenty to eat. Clean air."

The first group of Settlers went back to the Ordovician period, around 460 million years ago. The scientists wanted to send them as far back as possible to not affect our timeline. The Cambrian period, just before the Ordovician, did not seem as inviting. Land plants had not yet evolved and no one wanted to eat a trilobite, the dominant marine life form of that time. Fossil evidence indicated that by the Ordovician, however, the land was filled with plants and the climate was mild. Settlers would find themselves on a large supercontinent, Gondwana, near the South Pole. The arches allowed you to choose the time and place to which you would travel, and this is where they went. An abundance of cephalopods, snails and primitive fish ensured that there would be enough to eat.

Settlers had been going back now for two years and there was proof that children were being born at different times in the past. Images showed people holding babies and walking with babies in slings. An image from a group in the Permian period showed a Settler holding a dragonfly about the size of a dachshund that seemed to be wearing some type of collar, like a pet.

Some Settlers preferred to go back to a time when there was some human civilization. Because of the Fiver though, that meant going back to the early Bronze Age, when most historians believed civilization was just beginning. One group, about which there was much interest, went back to the Archaic Period of Egypt, 3000 BC, close to the most recent time you could go back to. Scholars watched for video from this time as it was an important time in the history of Egypt. King Menes was thought to have united the two kingdoms to become king of the first dynasty and historians closely watched for clues. Most Egyptians then were thought to have lived in small farming communities and this was confirmed by images from Settlers' cameras. The dark, shadowy past was coming into sharp focus for these scholars.

Chapter 7

Ben was pedaling and read the headline on his phone: "Ask member arrested near Arch facility." The Ask was a group who saw the Arch as an obvious way of fixing earth's problems. They were thought to have a "hit list" of people in the past, mainly scientists and engineers, to prevent the problems their inventions had led to. People like James Watt and Henry Ford. Other targets were early pioneers in computers and artificial intelligence.

They wore orange masks to hide their identities and being the Ask was another thing you could get arrested for. The consensus was that, apart from the ethical concerns of going back in the past to kill someone, that the effects on our timeline would be too great, too unpredictable. Most people thought the Ask wanted to take the risk.

The Ask were motivated not just by the desire to fix the world, but by some personal tragedy, a family member who died as a result of the pollution. Most people had thought that infectious diseases would increase with warming, but it turned out bacteria and viruses didn't like higher temperatures any more than we did. But the pollution, the chemicals, the metals all combined to cause cancer in more people. In fact, you could almost count on it. Their grief made the Ask single-minded.

Ben finished pedaling and left the pedaling center and started walking. He turned right instead of left to home. He needed to pick up his mother's medicine and thought he would spend a couple of credits on something to eat. He passed a cooling station and stopped for a few minutes to stand in the mist. He had some protein mix in his bag but wanted something different. From the small, covered market, there was the aroma of cooking and he walked past stalls selling clothing: masks, hats and gloves to keep out the dust. Phone cases. He nodded at the woman behind the counter and passed her his credit chip. She swiped it and handed it back to him along with a plastic bag. He sat down and started eating a soy taco. Across the street, a few children were kicking a soccer ball. Sports had mostly been moved inside and after a few minutes, they went into the building next to the playground. Ben looked up at the Settlers TV monitor.

The video clips were random. You couldn't predict which Settlers' feeds were broadcast when or for how long. You might see someone standing next to an ancient temple and a few seconds later someone standing with a Stegosaurus in the background. It was hard not to cheer when you saw a Settler standing with a spear next to a dead wooly mammoth. Some people watched the channel occasionally, some a lot, especially people wanting to Settle. There were screens here and there in the cities and people would stop to watch at lunch or just whenever, like Ben was doing now. He was watching what he thought was the Ordovician group. Briefly, a small group of people could be seen sitting in a circle. Their clothing looked worn, and they were eating things with shells that looked like clams. A baby could be seen in the background on a bed of some type of plant. The video feed quickly switched to a picture of the sky in some other time period, impossible to know which one. The video still showed the sky when Ben got up. Maybe a Charlie Foxtrot, he said to himself. He picked up his backpack and started walking.

Chapter 8

Anna first knew she had to settle when she saw the ASPM Chimps for the first time. Scientists had genetically engineered ASPM Chimps to express the human ASPM gene, resulting in larger brains. Mutations to that gene a couple of million years ago had resulted in larger brains in humans and researchers found that expressing the human version of the gene in chimpanzees gave them larger brains. The resulting genetically engineered chimps were about as smart as an eight-year-old human, smart enough to help with cleanup in Level Five Orange Sites. Ethicists argued about whether they were enhanced chimps or attenuated humans, and the public outcry of seeing them working in the Orange was too much, and the program was eventually shut down. The remaining chimps were made sterile with genetic scissors and lived out the rest of their lives in a curious community. It was interesting to see them building simple huts and preparing food, mostly ignoring the people who came to see them.

Scientists tried other genetic techniques for fixing problems caused by climate change. Mammoths were brought back to redevelop habitats they once occupied but they didn't do much and appeared confused and out of place. This program too was shut down and the remaining mammoths lived in a zoo in Iceland. The chimps provided researchers with a kind of window to our evolutionary past, as they were thought to be similar in some ways to human ancestors of about two million years ago. Now of course researchers had a better, actual, window through which to view that past.

Anna wondered if she would encounter our ancestors. She was hoping to join a group of Settlers going back to the Pleistocene. How would they react to seeing us? Could we join their communities? Did they have communities? She was pretty sure her family would understand why she wanted to go back but less sure that Ben would understand.

Settlers had gone back to the late Pleistocene, about 40,000 years ago, a time when Neanderthals were still around. Since the discovery that human genomes contain Neanderthal DNA, meaning that modern humans and Neanderthals had interbred, people wondered what Neanderthals were like and what interactions between Neanderthals and our ancestors had been like. What traits did we inherit from our Neanderthal ancestors? Settlers TV had provided some information. Neanderthals could be seen living in hut-like structures, though it was possible that the Settlers had shown them how to build the structures, and others were seen sitting and making some type of jewelry. Praxis and poiesis.

Chapter 9

Ben didn't say anything at first but just looked at Anna. "I knew you would probably go eventually but," he finally said. He knew why she wanted to go back. Nature. She needed to see the nature that she read about, to be under its habitual sway. "It's the indifference of earth too," she had once said. "Its calm obliviousness to our struggles. It slowly subsumes everything we do and it will still be here when we're gone." Ben understood this as a specific representation of her general grief.

They were walking along the river, whose banks now were much wider than they had been.

"Have you told your family yet?"

"No, just you. Ben, you could come with me."

"You know I can't. My mother," he said looking down while she looked up.

They had first met in college, five years ago, in their senior year. They had both put off taking Introduction to Psychology and sat next to each other in the lecture hall. They got coffee after class one day.

"Why is it so important that the dog salivated? When it heard the bell," Ben asked.

"It has something to do with free will, I think," Anna said.

"Maybe like with other things. Genes. Newton. Determinism."

"So I didn't really choose to order this Latte?" Anna said and laughed.

The air was still clear enough to be outside for a few hours and during finals week they would take long walks along the river. Sometimes Ben would bring a blanket and a picnic, and they would sit by the river and eat cheese and bread and drink wine. They would watch the rowers passing them in their long, skinny boats.

"Better them than me," Ben would say.

Sometimes they would just lie back and look up at the clouds.

The semester ended and it was Christmas break. It was over break that Ben's father got sick. His mother worked and there was no one else to take care of his father so Ben didn't come back in the spring.

There was an open house the next day at the Arch for prospective Settlers, kind of a meet-and-greet with the space-time continuum, Ben had joked. Anna could bring one person and Ben said he would go.

Ben stopped to look at a small pile of white feathers on the ground. It looked like someone or something might have killed a bird, which was illegal. Birds had remarkably survived the changes to the environment, showing great resilience. They were after all the only dinosaurs to survive the extinction at the end of the Cretaceous. Birds were now symbols of hope and groups of Settlers were given bird names: Osprey, Swallow, Swan. Ben picked up one of the feathers.

That night they had dinner with Ben's mother, Beth. Ben was cooking when Anna arrived with a grocery bag, which she set down on the counter. Steam rose from the pot Ben was stirring. She gave Ben a kiss, smiled at Beth and reached into the bag. She took out a box of chocolate substitute and some flour, opened the flour and measured some out into a cup.

"How are you feeling today, Beth?" she asked.

"Fine."

But Anna noticed she had not gotten up and now had her eyes closed.

Now Anna measured out the chocolate substitute and added some water, pouring the mixture into a pan, which she put into the oven. Ben put some pasta and soy protein sauce on the plates and set them on the table then sat down between Anna and his mother. The news was on the TV and Beth muted it. The CEO of Quantco was being interviewed about a recent announcement that he planned to run for President.

Quantco was one of several companies responsible for building and maintaining Qweb. The interviewer had just asked if he planned to remain CEO of his company if he were elected President when Beth turned off the sound. A few minutes later an ad for Qweb came on, with an animated version of the avatar Ben had seen, its wire-like rays undulating and its eyes blinking and looking from side to side. Ads for Qweb were really unnecessary, as its invisible hand controlled so many things; a force acting everywhere like the indiscernible forces that produce mountain ranges or new species.

After dinner they sat looking out the window at the sun setting. The Orange produced some wonderful colors at sunset: red and deep purple. Sometimes green.

Anna cut the cake she had made into squares and gave one to Ben and Beth then sat down with her plate and cut the cake with her fork.

"This is good," Beth said.

Leftovers went into the refrigerator; they were careful not to waste any food. Food availability was a concern for everyone though scientists had taken some steps to solve the problem. Sunlight and carbon dioxide were two things that there was no shortage of, and scientists developed the technology to allow people to photosynthesize some of their food in the form of carbohydrates. "Synths", as they were called, were usually a pale green color. One of the women Anna worked with was a Synth. She never ate lunch but sometimes complained of vibrations in her arms. Anna considered at one point having the procedure but decided she would rather deal with the mild worry over food. There was some concern that Synths shouldn't try to have children.

Anna got up and walked over to the cabinet and pulled out the Scrabble board. Ben watched her as she unfolded the board and put the letter tiles back in the small bag. They each drew letters and Anna played the first word. Anna was winning and Ben put an R on the end of Piece.

"Piecer," he said.

"What's a piecer?" Anna asked.

"Someone who puts pieces together?"

Anna looked at Ben's mother who shrugged.

They finished their game and put away the board. Anna said goodnight, and she and Ben kissed.

"Goodnight, Beth," she said.

"See you tomorrow," she said to Ben as she closed the door behind her.

Chapter 10

Anna had asked for the day off work and she and Ben started walking and then got onto a bus. The bus started moving and after a few minutes stopped in front of the Arch building, and Ben and Anna and a few other people got off. The door made a squeaking sound as it closed, and the bus drove silently away.

The building was a long tan brick building with a larger, raised central cupula-like structure. It was surrounded by a tall chain link fence and two soldiers in blue uniforms stood at the gate entrance. There were no other defenses visible, but Ben guessed there must be other, hidden levels of security. They walked to the gate and one of the soldiers asked them their names and began flipping through pages on a clipboard he was holding. He looked at them and then looked down at the clipboard and asked to see their IDs. He scanned the cards with a hand-held scanner, held the scanner up to his face to read it and then nodded to them. He was wearing a pistol and a beret that was tilted slightly. The other soldier opened the gate and they walked through.

Once through the gate they saw that the Arch building was just one of many on the base. There were many smaller brick buildings, identified only by plaques with numbers on them, and larger buildings that looked like apartments. Farther away, a plane was landing on an airstrip, appearing to move very slowly. Another plane flew low overhead and there was a taller building with a spinning antenna on top. They were walking along a sidewalk with bushes planted on either side and a soldier was pointing the direction they were to walk in. They had been given badges at the gate to wear around their necks that didn't have any writing on them but were red, which must have told the soldier they were going to the Arch viewing area. Blue-suited soldiers were walking in different directions, some in small groups walking in order and others more casually, talking and gesturing with their hands. The roar of a plane, this one louder, as they walked through a door that opened as they approached and into the building.

Inside the large room, fifty or so people were standing around talking. A long table held drinks and food and some people were holding plates or cups. A man walked up to Ben and Anna and introduced himself. He, like most of the others, was hoping to join a group in three months going back 60,000 years to England. This group of Settlers was being called Peregrine, and a picture of one of these birds was hanging on one wall. This would be the next group of Settlers after today's group to the Cretaceous. This group, Hummingbird, was going back one hundred million years to what is now Nebraska and some of the group members could be seen through the viewing window in the part of the building underneath the cupula.

Anna walked over to the wall and looked at the picture of the Peregrine falcon. She hadn't told Ben she wanted to join that group, but he knew and watched her looking at the picture. She turned to look at him and he tried to smile.

They walked over to the viewing window. The Arch room was about one hundred yards long and maybe fifty yards wide and the only things in the room were the two large magnets that produced the Arch. Each consisted of a large metal ribbed box and a taller, dactylus pole next to it. The base of each was covered in pointed glass pieces that looked like bottles, each with a wire connecting it to other bottles. Much of the wall was covered in pointed foam panels, like soundproofing material. When activated the two magnets would bend gravity to create the arch through which the Settlers would travel. Only Settlers were allowed in the Arch room, and most were still saying goodbye to family and friends in the room next to it but now more of them were starting to come into the room. They were scheduled to start going through the Arch in twenty minutes.

Now something was happening near the table with the food. A man was stepping up to a lectern and reached out to adjust a microphone. Anna recognized him as the Arch Director and now a second man walked up beside him, and Anna was surprised to see that it was her uncle. Voices were dying down as people stopped talking and turned to look at the two men. "Good afternoon," the Director said. "It's great to see you all here today as we wish our Hummingbird group well on their journey to the Cretaceous and begin planning for the Peregrine Pleistocene group, which some of you will be part of." People applauded and looked around the room. Anna looked at Ben who was looking straight ahead. "I want to introduce today our new Arch Director as I step down after five years in this important position." Anna and Ben looked at each other and Anna raised her shoulders slightly to say she was as surprised as he was. "I think everyone would agree that the Arch program has been a great success. We have sent Settlers back to begin new lives thousands and millions of years ago. These people are now living on an earth without the pollution and damage that has created the problems we are now living with. They are enjoying the clean air and water, the beautiful scenes and abundant resources that we all dream of. Video feeds confirm that they are happy and healthy and starting new families." Ben thought that was true for most, but probably not all of the groups. "As conditions here and now worsen, we expect there will be more and more groups of Settlers." "Now, however," he continued, "it's time for me to turn the program over to a new Director who can continue its success and continue to move the program forward. Please let me introduce that man to you today, Colonel Al Paris." Anna looked at Ben and mouthed the word "Colonel" with a look that said I didn't know.

Anna's uncle stepped up to the microphone and shook the outgoing director's hand and began to speak into the microphone. He reiterated the successes of the program and talked about opening up more time periods to meet the requests to settle. He thanked everyone for being here today and stepped away now to applause and picked up a bottle of water and his eyes met Anna's.

A few minutes later as people were moving towards the viewing window, Anna got a text. It was from her uncle: "We need to talk." He was no longer in the room and Anna saw the outgoing Director walking through a door that her uncle must have gone through a few minutes earlier. Anna and Ben were at the viewing window now and there were several hundred people in the Arch room. Some were talking excitedly, and others were standing and looking at the space between the magnets. Anna could feel a vibration now in the floor and the tall columns of each of the two magnets began to glow a pale blue color. More Settlers began joining the group and Anna could see what some of them were carrying. There was a limit on what settlers could bring with them having to do with interactions, a ratio, between organic and inorganic materials, which also prevented larger pieces of equipment from going through. She knew that each carried the same things in their bags, including the compass and knife and a book, but many also carried other things; one man had a guitar, another a bow and arrows. A woman was carrying what might have been a tent and another had a duffel bag which Anna thought probably contained tools. The vibrations in the floor were now getting stronger and a blue arch began to appear between the poles. All of the people in the viewing room were now against the window looking through it. Most of the Settlers now were standing and looking intently at the arch, trying to catch a glimpse of what would be their new home. There was a suggestion or adumbration of trees, maybe some mountains. Some dark shapes and some light shapes, as if in a mountainous region mists allowed only a dim prospect. From the crowd of Settlers a few began to form a line. Settlers had to go through individually and couldn't be too close to each other. Ben reached and took Anna's hand. Now the first Settler walked towards the Arch. As the man walked, his shape became less and less distinct and he seemed now to be merging with the mist until all that could be seen was the mist. It was like watching an object sink slowly beneath the surface of the water until you can't see it anymore. Then one by one, the other Settlers followed. After about ten minutes, all of the Settlers had gone through the Arch and now the room was empty. The blue arch faded until it was gone, and the magnets shut down and the vibrations stopped. Most of the observers continued to watch after the last Settler had gone through. The effect was profound, like when a child spins around exulting with arms outstretched looking up at the sky. Stopping and laying on the ground, looking up, the sky continues to spin until gradually the child realizes it has stopped but doesn't remember it stopping and all is now tranquil as the sea. Some went back to the table with food for something to eat or drink or started talking with someone but most slowly made their way to the exit, thinking about what they had seen. Ben and Anna walked outside to the bus stop, passing several soldiers on the way.

Chapter 11

The next morning at the coffee shop, Anna ordered at the counter and then sat down. As the waiter was setting her coffee down at the table, her uncle walked in. He smiled at her and went to the counter to order a drink then walked over to Anna's table. Anna stood up, and they hugged and then they both sat down.

"Al, when? How?" Anna said.

"You mean how did I get to be Director?"

"Yes, I knew you were in the army, but had no idea you were that closely involved with the Arch."

"Well, I am an engineer."

"OK. But Director?"

"Let's just say the outgoing Director was a friend of mine and leave it at that for now. Anna, we need to talk."

"OK."

The waiter set another cup down on their table and walked off.

"Anna, someone has broken the fiver."

Anna knew that this meant someone traveled back to a time less than five thousand years ago, which was not allowed because of the effects it would have on the present time.

"How? How do they know?"

"The Parthenon Friezes."

"The Elgin Marbles? What about them?"

"Someone went back in time and changed them, or changed them from what they used to look like. The Curator discovered it."

Anna had seen the Elgin marbles, years before when travel was easier. Keats' poem about them was one of Anna's favorites and, she thought, one of the most Romantic. Keats saw the sublime artifacts for the first time with their detailed depictions of life in ancient Greece and could only think of himself: "My spirit is weak."

"Changed them how?"

"Well, behind one of the chariots there is now a car."

"A car?"

"A Toyota Corolla."

She looked at him for a few seconds with her mouth open. "But shouldn't they have disappeared? Isn't that what is supposed to have almost happened with the Declaration of Independence?"

"Well," Al said, "the story there might be a bit different than we first thought. That person who went back might have actually been trying to keep the Declaration from ever being written."

"What? Why? Why would anyone want to stop the Declaration of Independence from being written?"

"Well, it turned out OK for us, but not for the British."

"So, you're saying someone from Britain went back in time to make sure the Declaration of Independence was never written so that Britain would still own the American colonies?"

"Well, maybe not exactly, but there are some fringe groups out there with some pretty strange political ideas. Maybe they wanted a different Declaration."

"OK, so it started to disappear because someone was trying to keep it from being written, not just because someone watched it being signed."

"Basically."

"So that would mean that you could go back to more recent times if you were careful?"

"That's what some people now think."

"And maybe even change something?"

"Maybe."

On the muted TV, a reporter was interviewing the Quantco CEO. They were standing in front of the Quantco building and as he talked, he turned his head and gestured at the building, making a point that Anna and her uncle could only guess at, probably something about the planned expansion. The other screen in the room was showing Settlers TV. They could see a marshy area and a person very far away in the background, too far to tell what he or she was doing.

"Anna, are you thinking about Settling?"

"Yes."

"Maybe you should wait."

"Why?"

"Well, maybe you just should. You know your brother and mother would miss you."

"OK, probably. And I would miss them. But what kind of life can I really have if I stay? The things I study, the things I love, they aren't here anymore."

Al nodded and took a drink of his coffee.

"Anna, they may need someone to help. With looking at the changes to the friezes. And there may be other changes."

"What do you mean?"

"Well, the curator doesn't have a background in antiquities. But some other things may have changed too."

"I have a master's degree in Greek antiquities, but my Ph.D. is going to be in Romantic Literature."

"How many other people do you know with master's degrees in Greek antiquities?"

"A few. How many do you know?"

"Just one. You. What was your master's thesis on?"

"Greek life as depicted on Grecian vases. Grecian urns."

Al nodded.

"Are you saying there may have been some changes to those too in the museum?"

"They think maybe."

Anna took the last drink of her coffee and sat back in her chair. She had spent hours in the British Museum galleries of Grecian urns working on her thesis. Her primary interest was religious ritual depicted on the urns and she knew many of the scenes very well. It was while doing this work that she first became interested in Romantic poetry, through Keats' Ode on a Grecian Urn. The answer to Keats' question in the poem, "To what green altar, O mysterious priest, Lead'st thou that heifer lowing at the skies, And all her silken flanks with garlands drest?" turned out to be the answer to an important question that scholars had been trying to answer for decades, and she had answered the question by finding a series of urns depicting the story.

"So, you want me to go to London and look at Greek vases in the British Museum for anything different about them?"

Al nodded. "Is there someone that could go with you?"

Chapter 12

Anna was waiting outside when Ben and Wolfie walked out of the pedaling center wearing their jumpsuits and masks, which they usually didn't wear but the air was worse today.

"Hi," Anna said giving them both hugs. "How was pedaling?"

"Good," said Wolfie," I'm only a few hundred credits short. It looks like we might be settling together." He smiled. "Tell me about the Arch."

"Well, it's big," said Ben. "And impressive. And blue. And there's free food." He added, grinning.

"We watched the Cretaceous group go through. And my Uncle Al is the new Director," she added, looking at Wolfie.

"What?" said Wolfie, stopping and turning around to look at them.

"Yep. I was as surprised as you are. And something is going on."

"OK. And," said Wofie.

"They think someone might have broken the fiver and somehow managed to change something."

"But isn't that supposed to kind of change everything?" They had just arrived at the coffee shop and went in.

"Yes, but they think they may have had that wrong."

"What did they see?"

"A car. In a twenty-five-hundred-year-old Greek carving."

"A car."

"Yes. A Toyota."

"Well, I guess they know that ancient Greek's didn't have Toyotas so someone must have done."

"Wait, look," Ben said pointing to one of the TV screens.

Several people wearing orange masks were begin arrested outside of the Arch building. One was being led out of the gate with his hands behind his back.

"That's where we were," said Anna. "It looks like some of the Ask have been arrested and one made it in through the gates."

"Can you please turn that up?" Ben said to the waiter who pressed a button on a remote control and now the announcer's voice could be heard.

"...arrested yesterday for trying to break into the Arch facility. Some of those arrested were carrying packs as if they were trying to travel back," the announcer was saying. He continued, "Arch Director Al Paris was quoted saying security at the Arch would be increased to prevent further security breaches."

On Settlers TV, there were some people from the Cretaceous group that Ben and Anna recognized from the Arch room. Their packs were in a small pile on the ground, and they were standing in a semicircle. Now the picture changed to show the ocean with sand in the foreground, as if the camera were sitting on the beach.

"Wonder where. When. That is," Wolfie said.

Anna looked away from the TV screen and at Wolfie. "They think there might be more things changed, there at the museum."

"The British Museum."

"Yes."

"And they want someone to go check it out?"

"Yes."

"And I'm guessing that's you."

"I told my uncle I would think about it."

"By yourself?"

She turned to look at Ben, but he didn't say anything.

"Ben, I can look in on your mom." Both of Wolfie's parents had died within a year of each other, of cancer. Wolfie spent most of his time pedaling now.

"She takes her medicine twice a day," Ben said.

"I remember. Remember?"

Ben looked at Wolfie and nodded.

Chapter 13

"When would you go?" Anna's mother asked and looked at Anna.

"Tomorrow," Anna said.

They were sitting at the table, which still had a few empty dishes on it. Anna's brother was playing the violin. Ben and his mother were also there.

"And Ben you would go too?" she asked.

Ben nodded and looked at his mother who also nodded. There was a knock on the door, and Sue went over and opened it and Wolfie walked in wearing a green t-shirt and jeans and carrying his backpack.

"The gang's all here," he said and sat down next to Ben's mom.

"Wolfie, you need a haircut," Anna said.

"Al, what do you think about the arrests at the Arch? The Ask?" Sue asked

"They didn't get very far," he said.

Everyone thought they knew someone who might be a member of the Ask. No one was sure how organized they were, but this latest break-in had taken some coordination. Mostly they protested and held rallies and stunts to promote their goals. They liked to put orange masks on public sculptures.

"What do you think they were doing?"

"Well, they say they want to clean up the earth by preventing some things from ever starting. AI, electric vehicles, the industrial revolution."

"And that would mean?"

"Breaking the Fiver. But of course, it looks like someone may have done that," Al said. "All of this is new of course. But the interesting thing is we remember what they looked like before. The Friezes."

"Instead of the change not really being a change, just the way it has always been?"

"Yes."

"Why isn't the Arch the best solution? Keep sending Settlers back?" Sue asked and then looked at Ben's mom and then looked away.

"Do the math," Al said. "We can send five hundred people back every three months. That's two thousand a year. In five years, that's only ten thousand people. In fifty years, they think we might not be able to live here anymore."

"Unless you're underwater," Anna said.

The Ask was probably responsible for some video footage that was recently posted to news sites of an underwater city. There had been rumors of such a city for the ultra-wealthy - wealthy mostly from technology - but no real evidence. Many of these people had lived for a while, a few decades ago, in an orbiting, satellite city. You could visit the city, but it was very expensive. The only problem was to produce enough oxygen, which could be done catalytically. Cancer was less common there. The orbiting space junk that destroyed the orbiting city was known to be a risk, but most didn't think it could completely destroy the city. Now it seemed as if the rest of the rich had gone underwater.

"And what about this footage? Did you know about the city?" Sue asked Al.

"We knew they were building a residence of some sort underwater but weren't sure how big it was. Apparently, it's pretty big. The orbiting one. That was supposed to be it."

"But the space debris got it," Sue answered. "How many people?"

"Thousands. I'm not sure."

"You went there once didn't you Al?"

"Once. Right after I enlisted. On my way to the moon station."

"What was it like?"

"It was beautiful. Expansive, arching spaces. Green. Buildings and people walking around. Working. The air was clean. Manufactured air. And the earth, looking at it from there. It looked fragile and resilient at the same time. Of course, you couldn't see what it was really like from there."

Anna remembered seeing it in the sky at night. Without a telescope, it looked like a tiny ring but through a telescope it looked like a beautiful, frosted donut.

"Why did they close the moon station?"

"It was really just there for the metals. And when they found out there weren't that many metals on the moon there wasn't really any need. It wasn't like a lot of people could live there."

"How is it that these people keep getting so rich? Those people living underwater." Ben's mother joined the conversation.

"When the world runs on AI and batteries, whoever makes the AI and batteries is going to get rich," Wolfie answered.

In their publication, "A Short History of Screwing Up the World", the Ask pointed out that whereas solar and wind energy, as earth moved away from fossil fuels, was seen as a panacea for the environment, batteries were needed. As the metals used in them became harder and harder to find, more toxic metals and compounds were used. More toxic, harder to get rid of. Most batteries now were based on chemical reactions of Arsenic salts.

"Why not build more arches so more people can go back?" Ben asked.

"We wouldn't be able to do it much more than we are now. The gravity waves interfere with each other. Some of the waves are very large," Al answered. "You can open it more often occasionally but there are risks. And each time it gets riskier."

"Wolfie, there's some food left on the stove if you want some," Sue said.

"Thanks, don't mind if I do," he said and picked up a plate. He went into the kitchen and then came back out and sat next to Ben's mother.

Chapter 14

The next morning Sue had breakfast on the table and Anna and Ben sat down to eat. Ben poured coffee for them both.

"Off to England?" Sue said.

"Looks like it," Anna said raising her eyebrows.

Ben's mother walked over and kissed Ben on the forehead and sat down. Ben poured her a cup of coffee.

"Good morning," Al said as he walked in. "Everyone ready for our trip?"

After breakfast, they picked up their bags and went outside. A black SUV was waiting for them, and Al opened the door for Ben and Anna, who got into the back seat. Ben pulled the door and was surprised at how heavy it was and at the muffled sound it made when he closed it. Al got into the front seat and shut the door and looked at the driver.

"Let's go," he said.

They drove to the highway and then went south for twenty minutes and exited. They drove up to a gate and the driver rolled down his window. A soldier looked in and nodded and the gate opened. They drove towards a large metal building and went around it and pulled up behind it and stopped. There was an airstrip and there were several planes outside the building.

Al led the group out the door and onto the tarmac. The military plane they were walking towards had four large jet engines and an odd egg shape in cross section. He walked first into the plane. They entered by walking up a ramp at the rear of the plane; there was no door and no jetway. He pointed to a rack where they could put their bags and then looked towards the front of the plane to indicate the seats. There were seats on either side and two rows of seats in the middle, each with a seat harness. The interior of the plane was unfinished and gleaming silver and rivets. A few red cargo nets were fastened to the wall.

"No in-flight entertainment for this flight I'm afraid," Al said.

A jeep was parked on one side and strapped to the wall next to what looked like a small folding helicopter. There was a forklift and several boxes and near the front of the compartment was a rack with guns. Several soldiers had already boarded the plane and were buckling their harnesses.

There was a smell of gasoline and Anna could see a fuel tank outside the window and a hose leading up to one of the plane's wings. A few more soldiers got on and dropped their duffle bags on the rack and sat down. They all had short hair and their blue uniforms had some darker spots in a camouflage pattern. One of the soldiers turned his head and smiled at Anna. The ramp at the back of the plane slowly began to close and then the sound of the engines starting.

The big breakthrough in AI came when engineers realized that neural networks had a fractal arrangement, that they were similar at any scale. Newer, bigger AI networks, designed based on the Mandelbrot equation, were more general in their abilities and were considered now by many to have obtained a level of consciousness. The Oxford scientists about thirty years ago who made the breakthrough were inspired by the Dover coastline and its fractal nature as their flight approached London's Gatwick airport. On their way to the airbase, Al told Anna and Ben that the recent decision for Qweb to take over security for the Arch may have been as much Qweb's decision as the outgoing Director's.

"What did you mean Qweb may have decided to take over security for the Arch?" Anna asked as the plane taxied to the runway.

"It has a certain autonomy," Al said, "It monitors and adjusts things as necessary."

"Like resources," Anna said. "Yesterday there was no water at the house."

"Yes. Water."

The plane was now at the end of the runway. There were no flight attendants and no safety briefing and Ben joked that he wanted some peanuts. The plane accelerated and started moving down the runway. It seemed like it was going too slow to take off, but in a few seconds left the ground and climbed quickly. Al said there would be one stop on the way.

"Monitors what?" asked Ben.

"Everything. The news, data from sensors and cameras. Cell phone data."

"Cell phone data?"

"Yes, probably knows who you talked to yesterday. Read your texts."

Ben tried to remember what he had said in his texts yesterday.

Al closed his eyes and put his head back.

They had been flying for about half an hour and the plane had leveled off. Anna took a book out of her backpack. The compartment was lit now only by red, dome-shaped lights overhead, but Anna thought it would be enough to read by.

"For your dissertation?" Ben asked.

"Yes," she answered and began reading aloud from the book:

> What happy fortune were it here to live!
> if a thought of dying, if a thought
> Of mortal separation could come in
> With paradise before me, here to die.

She was still reading aloud softly, and Ben opened his eyes and realized he had been asleep. She closed the book and set it down and Ben saw the title, "Home at Grasmere." Wordsworth.

"Now to the business at hand," she said and picked up another book, this one with a Greek vase, an urn, on the cover.

On the urn was a painting of a man standing in a chariot holding reins, which led to several winged horses which seemed to be straining and their feet and the wheels of the chariot were lifting off of the ground.

Ben leaned closer and looked at some of the pictures in the book. On one of the urns, two men were holding shields and fighting.

"They really didn't like to wear clothes," he said.

Ben turned to look at Al, who was wearing glasses now and also reading a book. He saw Ben looking over and closed the book. Ben saw the title, "A Short History of Artificial Intelligence."

"Do you think an AI can feel emotion?" Ben asked.

"Well, it depends on what you think emotions are," Al said. "When an AI is trained initially, when it is still a tabula rasa, it's given massive amounts of data. Text, say, and then looks for patterns in the texts. It then begins to arrange and rearrange, recursively, the letters, symbols really, based on those patterns until they make sense to us." Anna now looked over. "Similarly with emotions, I think. If patterns could be recognized in certain basic emotions or passions, an AI could assemble an emotional response."

"A grandeur in the beatings of the heart," Anna said, looking up.

"This move by Qweb to protect the Arch is interesting," Al said. "It's almost like it's trying to protect itself." He turned to look out the window.

"How so?" Ben asked.

"Well, if someone went back to prevent certain developments in technology or AI, the Oxford fractals for example, Qweb wouldn't exist."

Now the plane seemed to be descending and it was getting lighter outside. "Iceland," Al said. "We're leaving a few things and a few people here. We'll be here for about an hour."

Outside the window, Anna could see some land jutting into the ocean and an inlet of water. The plane banked sharply and a few minutes later they were on the ground.

The back ramp was lowered, and everyone stood up. A few of the soldiers walked over to the jeep and unfastened it from the wall. Two men that weren't in uniform unfastened the folding helicopter. One of the men was wearing a green John Deere hat and he started pushing the helicopter so that it was facing the rear door. The other man drove over with the forklift, which he positioned in front of the helicopter and the forks moved forward and underneath the pallet that it was sitting on. Soon the forklift was moving down the ramp with the helicopter and a soldier was driving the jeep behind it. The forklift returned and started taking the crates off the plane.

"Don't go far," Al said to Ben and Anna as they walked down the ramp. Outside there were several large buildings, each capable of holding one or two planes like the kind they were on. It was cooler here and Anna smiled. They walked towards one of the hangars, but the posture of a uniformed soldier told them they probably shouldn't go any farther. Inside they could see several helicopters and a smaller plane that looked like a drone. Al was standing next to their plane talking with an officer in a dark blue uniform. The officer looked at the wing and pointed and Al nodded. A fuel truck drove over, and a man attached the hose to the plane and held up his hand. Ben and Anna walked to the end of the buildings and could see a mountain in the distance.

"Probably covered in snow a few years ago," Anna said.

A few minutes later, Al waved to them that it was time to get back on the plane. Inside, soldiers were loading crates onto the plane and securing them to the wall. They took their seats and a few minutes later were in the air.

"There. You can see the coast of Scotland," Anna said excitedly an hour or so later. They were approaching the UK from the Northwest. Their flight path would take them south down to London. "That means we'll pass over the Lake District," she added, smiling.

"It's crazy to think I could be back here in a few months, in the Pleistocene, but it would look so different. No Ireland. No English Channel." Al and Ben looked at each other but didn't say anything. There were clouds, but as they passed over the Lake District, they could see mountains and valleys and lakes. Soon the plane started to descend. They would be landing at a military airstrip near Gatwick. There were very few overseas commercial flights anymore; most planes were powered by batteries and had a shorter range, and Anna had wondered a few years ago if she would ever see England again. Ben and Anna took their bags from the rack and walked off the plane. This base was smaller and there was only a single hangar.

"Just wait here a minute," Al said and walked into the hangar.

When he came out, he was not wearing his uniform but was dressed in jeans and a plain black t-shirt. "We're going to try to not draw attention to ourselves," he said. "We're tourists visiting museums." He smiled.

A car drove up and Ben could see it was a self-driving car. The trunk popped open, and Ben put his suitcase in and then put Anna's in. Al sat in the front seat and Ben and Anna slid into the back seat. There was a steering wheel in the driver's side, and it turned by itself as they drove. The drive to their hotel on Gower Street near the British Museum took about an hour. There were not that many cars on the motorway and most of them were self-driving. In the backseats, people were reading newspapers, sleeping. The car drove up in front of the hotel and stopped. Al tapped a solid black card on the meter and stepped out. Ben took his and Anna's bags out of the trunk. Al had only a small handbag. Ben wasn't sure what he would see inside the hotel as he walked up the steps, a person, a check-in kiosk, but was happy to see a man standing behind the check-in desk.

"Good morning," the man said cheerfully, putting down a newspaper.

I haven't seen a newspaper in a while, Ben thought to himself.

"Good morning," Al said. "Al Paris. And Ben and Anna, checking in for two nights. We have two double rooms I think."

"Ah yes, here you are sir. May I just see your passports?"

They handed the man their passports and he looked at each of them, flipping a few pages, and then handed them back and then gave them each a key. He printed out a piece of paper, which he gave Al to sign and then said, "Breakfast is at eight AM tomorrow morning. I hope you enjoy your stay. There's tea and coffee in there," pointing to the dining room.

Their rooms were on the second floor, and they turned and walked towards the stairs.

"No lift," Ben said.

"Meet down here in an hour?" Al said.

"OK," Anna said and carried her bag up the stairs followed by Ben. They unlocked the door to their room and went in and set their bags on the floor and lay down on the bed. Neither of them had slept much on the way over and they both fell asleep.

Chapter 15

They awoke to the sound of Ben's phone ringing.

"What time is it?" he asked. He looked around at the rose patterned wallpaper and the two chairs by the window. After a few seconds, he picked up his phone.

"Hello," he said.

"Ben," Wolfie answered.

"Wolfie. Everything OK?"

A few seconds of silence then, "Well. Not really."

"What?" Ben asked

"Your mother."

"What about her? What happened?"

"She fell and they think it may be the cancer. Maybe metastasized."

"You took her to the hospital?"

"An ambulance."

"Where are you now?"

"We're at home. Your house."

"How is she?"

"She's sleeping. They say she's stable."

Anna came over to Ben's side of the bed and sat down beside him. "Your mother?" She mouthed the words silently. Ben nodded.

"Well, I don't think we can come home any sooner," he said.

"No," Wolfie said.

"Everything else OK?" Ben asked

"Well, there hasn't been any water, so I've been bringing it in. Otherwise yes."

Anna looked at her watch and said, "We need to get going probably."

Ben nodded. "Is she awake?"

"No, they gave her something."

"OK. As soon as she wakes up, tell her I said hi and we'll be home soon."

"How was the flight?"

"It was fine. I'll have to tell you more later. We have to meet Al. Thanks, Wolfie," he said. "I appreciate it," he added then hung up. He looked at Anna, took a deep breath and breathed out.

Al was waiting downstairs, looking at some brochures from a rack. The Tower of London, Westminster Abbey. No one else was in the lobby.

"Hi," he said, putting a folded brochure back in the rack. "Your room OK? We're going to the British Museum tomorrow morning but there's something else I want to see today."

They walked out of the hotel and turned right and then right onto Store Street and went into a coffee shop. Al ordered an espresso and looked at Anna and Ben who nodded and then he ordered two more.

"Hungry?" he said.

"A little," Ben answered.

"Can I also get three of those?" he said pointing to a glass case with pastries.

The coffees were in small paper cups, and they went out the door and turned left towards Tottenham Court Road. Al handed them each one of the pastries. The underground system was out of use most of the time because of flooding and so they walked to a bus stop and waited. Across the street, someone walked out of a bookstore carrying a bag. A few minutes later, a red bus stopped, and they got on. The bus had two levels, a double-decker, and they walked up the stairs and sat down.

"Where are we going?" Anna asked.

"The Science Museum."

The bus went a few blocks and then turned right onto Oxford Street. Most of the Christmas decorations had already been taken down but there were still a few stars hanging on wires over the street. The sidewalks were crowded with people walking and carrying bags. A man was selling bags of nuts from a cart. Traffic was light, mostly self-driving taxis and they passed several now unused tube stations: Oxford Circus, Bond Street. They turned left at Marble Arch, and they could now see Hyde Park on their right. They turned right at Hyde Park Corner and now they were driving through Knightsbridge. A red sports car stopped beside them at a light. A woman walked out of Harrods carrying a bag and it seemed to Ben that the rich were somehow immune to many of the things they were facing. They continued to South Kensington and the bus stopped in front of the Natural History Museum.

They walked down the stairs and off the bus and Anna stopped to look at the museum. Anna loved this museum with its fanciful animal carvings and colored bricks.

"There's a skeleton of a blue whale hanging in there," she said.

"We'll have to see it next time," Al said, walking past it towards the Science Museum.

There were several groups of school children in the museum, carrying backpacks and wearing loosely tied ties. Al nodded at the woman who let them in and continued walking to a large red wheel, about half of it under the floor level. The cogged wheel was turning slowly, and several straight pistons were moving back and forth beside it. On the top a small cylinder with two bent arms was spinning.

"Steam Engine," he said. "There's a boiler outside providing steam which turns the wheel which moves the pistons."

There was something elegiac about it, Anna thought.

"It's big," said Ben.

"Before about 1780 they couldn't do much," Al said. "Not efficient. But then there were a couple of improvements which paved the way for the Industrial Revolution. Improvements made by him," he said, pointing to a display case.

"By the early eighteen-hundreds they couldn't keep them running. They needed more fuel. More coal. They dug coal mines, canals to transport the coal."

"It was the beginning," said Anna.

Al nodded and walked over to the display case. Inside the case were some metal tools, wrenches of different sizes and on the front of the case a picture of a man. Underneath the picture, it said "James Watt 1736-1819." And underneath that, "The founder of the Industrial Revolution."

Next to the case was a black metal ball, mostly inside a low brick edge, with rivets all over and a pipe leading from the top to the wall. They walked over to it.

"A boiler," Al said. "To produce the steam. Steam power. That's what the coal was needed for."

Then they walked over to an exhibit of Victorian goods mass-produced in factories with steam engines, including Wedgewood china.

"The Victorians liked to collect things," Anna said. "I guess there were a lot more things to collect after the steam engines."

They walked into another gallery and there were airplanes and spaceships. Cars and tractors. It was afternoon now, and they hadn't eaten, and they walked back to the exit and out the door. They turned left and started walking towards Hyde Park. They stopped now to wait for the light to change so they could cross the street. On their right, a dome-shaped building of orange brick and across the street some kind of statue or memorial.

"Albert Memorial," said Anna. Crossing the street now and walking towards the memorial, they could see the gold statue of Queen Victoria's husband and at each corner evidence, symbols, of how far the British Empire stretched. A woman riding an elephant. A man kneeling.

They walked into the park on a sidewalk lined with bushes. In the distance to the left some ducks and geese were floating on a pond. The air was pretty clear, and some children were kicking a soccer ball. It rolled over to Ben and he kicked it back to them. A little bit later, they were on the other side of the park and on a bus heading back down Oxford Street in the direction they had come.

They got off the bus and walked a few blocks and went into a pub called the Museum Tavern. The British Museum, closed now, could be seen just across the street. They walked up to the bar and ordered three pints of ale and sat down.

"Cheers," Al said, and they took a drink. Al walked back to the bar and ordered three fish and chips, the fish not really fish but a flaked type of soy protein. The waiter came over to their table and gave them each a fork and knife wrapped in a cloth napkin and set a few condiments on the table. A few minutes later, she returned with the fish and chips and they started eating.

"Not bad that," Ben said taking a bite and smiling. He got up and went to the bar to order another round and brought the beers back to the table. The pub had a video screen showing Settlers TV and Al and Anna were looking at it. It was nighttime wherever the camera was, and the camera was showing the stars; it must have been laying on the ground. The stars were incredibly bright, Anna thought. The Milky Way could be seen stretching away in either direction. On another TV, there was an indoor soccer match.

When they had finished eating, it was drizzling rain out. As they walked out of the pub a self-driving taxi pulled up, and Al waved to it, and they got in. They were talking and forgot to tell the cab where they were going but a few minutes later, it pulled up in front of their hotel.

"How did it know where we were going?" Ben said.

Al didn't answer for a few seconds but then replied, "I don't know."

Chapter 16

The next morning, they came downstairs for their full English breakfast. Ben thought the eggs might have been real eggs and maybe the beans. He had never seen grilled tomatoes before and didn't try the sausages. The soy bacon was not bad. The toast was on a small metal rack and there were jars of marmalade. Al poured them each a cup of tea from a pot that was on the table.

"Al, how important were Watt's contributions to the industrial revolution?" Ben asked.

"Without them it might not have happened. Or would have happened more slowly."

Ben nodded.

"The Curator is meeting us at the museum at ten o'clock," Al said. "If we're finished, we should probably get going."

It was raining this morning and the air was worse, so they put on jumpsuits before walking out. Al grabbed an umbrella from a rack by the door. They turned right out of the door and started walking past a few other hotels and a small park enclosed in a fence. At the end of the street, they turned left onto Great Russel Street and could now see the peaked roof of the British Museum. They walked down to the black iron gated entrance and joined the short line of tourists waiting to get in. The curator had suggested meeting them at the staff entrance off Montague Place, but Al hadn't wanted to draw attention to themselves. Through the gate now, they walked towards the museum.

They stopped at the bottom of the stairs and looked up at the pediment, which Anna knew depicted the progress of civilization. At the far left an angel hands primitive man a lamp. In the center, a figure holding a golden globe representing science, the apotheosis of mankind's development, and farther to the right, figures representing music and art.

Now they walked up the steps, worn smooth in places, and Anna touched one of the enormous ribbed supporting columns. Cool to the touch and a dark grey color, they had been lighter in color the first time Anna saw them. Turning around, she could see the pub where they had eaten dinner the night before. They were supposed to meet the curator in the great court, so they walked into the museum and straight ahead.

The circular great court was gleaming white with a beautiful fan-like glass ceiling. In front of them were steps leading up to the reading room. Anna had spent a lot of time in there during her last visit. It was where Marx had written the Communist Manifesto and it always made Anna think about books and words and revolutions.

A man in a blue suit and tie walked up to them with his hand extended.

"Bill Evans," he said, and Al shook his hand.

"Al Paris. This is Anna Paris and Ben."

"Nice to meet you," said Anna and shook his hand.

"Right," said the curator. "Shall we?"

They walked through a door on their left and were now in a room filled with Egyptian sculptures. There were sculptures of lions, humans with cat's heads. Anna stopped to look at a stature of Ramses II. "Frown and wrinkled lip and sneer of cold command," she said aloud, quoting the poem by Shelley. Ben stopped to look too.

"Look upon my works ye mighty and despair," she added. Al looked back at them.

"This way," said the curator.

Now they passed through a gallery of Assyrian art. A king with a long beard and holding a spear rode in a chariot. A lion was turning to attack the chariot.

Now through a room with Greek sculptures, a large tomb with friezes depicting battle scenes, and they walked into the Parthenon room. The effect of being in this gallery with the Parthenon Friezes was humbling.

"So do these wonders a most dizzy pain," Anna said aloud. "A shadow of a magnitude."

The friezes originally decorated the perimeter of the Parthenon, which had been built as a temple to Athena. The sculptures depicted Athenian citizens in a parade in honor of Athena: horsemen, chariots, musicians. Cattle led to sacrifice.

"The Parthenon and the friezes were built by Pericles in the fifth century BCE." Anna was talking to Ben. "Other members of the Delian League, including Sparta, weren't too happy with this use of their funds and ultimately Athens was defeated in the Peloponnesian Wars."

Then the curator looked over at them. "Here. Over here," he said pointing up at a procession of men on horses. Ben, Anna and Al walked over. At first, they didn't see anything unusual and then Anna said, "There, I see it, behind that chariot." Then Ben and Al saw it too. The hood of a car. The grill and hood looked like a Toyota Corolla. People still drove an electric version of the car.

"I'll be damned," said Al. "Someone went back and managed to carve, or have someone else carve, a Toyota in the friezes."

"It was not there a month ago. I am certain," said the curator. "I clean these every month using that ladder." He pointed to a ladder in the corner of the room.

"OK," said Al, "so someone went back to Ancient Greece, fifth century BCE. In the last month."

"It sounds like the Ask," said Ben.

"But how?" asked Anna "The Arch security."

"I don't know," said Al. "Settlers only travel every three months, but there is maintenance, and the magnets are turned on every once in a while."

"But wouldn't somebody see them?" said Ben

"Well, there are some in the military, arch security, that may be sympathetic to the idea," Al said, thinking. "Of trying to change something in the past."

There were a few other people in the gallery, including a small tour group following a man holding up a stick with a flag on the end. A man in a black suit was looking up at the friezes and had his hand in his pocket and Al looked over at him.

"Is there anything else different?" Anna asked.

"Not that I have seen," replied the curator. "But we should look at the vases. The urns. Someone thought possibly."

They walked back into the room with the burial monument and turned right. Al looked back over his shoulder as they left the gallery. They turned right and walked through a room with Greek sculptures and into the room with the Grecian Urns. There was a red cord across the entrance to the room that the curator unlatched so that they could enter.

"This is to give us some privacy," he said latching it behind them.

The vases were beautiful and contained in a number of glass cases. All of the urns were black and red, and depicted scenes of war and domestic life: people fighting, people reclining and eating, people standing in long robes. Anna had studied these vases carefully and knew them well. Slowly she walked past the cases, looking at each vase. She stopped at one case and bent to look at one vase, it had a black base and several figures on the top. Al and Ben walked over.

"I remember this vase," she said. On the vase, three women were standing and talking, and Ben thought it might be a scene from a play, since one of them was wearing a mask.

"Some sort of play?" he said.

"No, that's not a theater mask. It only covers part of her face. Also it's a darker color of red than is usually used." And then she remembered this vase. Originally the women were goddesses, and they were talking, and you could see their faces.

"That mask is new," she said. She turned to look at Ben and Al. "It wasn't there before."

"The Ask?" Ben said.

Just then, Al looked up. The man he had seen in the Parthenon gallery was standing at the end of the room.

"I'm sorry this gallery is closed," said the curator but the man didn't move but reached into his coat pocket and pulled something out of it.

"Let's go," Al said. They quickly left the room, walked quickly through the next two galleries and into a stairwell.

"Wait over there," said Al pointing to the stairs and reaching into his coat pocket. Ben saw him remove a small pistol. It was tan colored and looked like it was made of plastic. Anna looked at Ben. Al stood against the wall next to the door they had just come through, holding the pistol with both hands.

After about fifteen seconds, he said, "Alright, down the stairs. I'll follow."

Turning now to the curator, "Can you lead the way? To the closest exit?"

"OK," said the curator, looking nervous.

They walked quickly down the stairs, past several Roman mosaics and the curator led them to an exit different from the one they had come in, near the corner of Great Russel and Bloomsbury streets. When Al appeared behind them, the curator opened the door.

Al put the pistol back in his coat, thanked the curator and shook his hand.

"I'll be in touch," Al said, and they walked out.

They walked quickly back to the hotel, Al leading the way, Anna and Ben half running to keep up. Ben gave a look to Anna that said, "what just happened," and she looked at him and mouthed an answer. "I have no idea."

The manager was behind the desk at the hotel and Al said, "We're checking out."

"I hope you have enjoyed your stay," he said.

"Meet back down here in five," Al said, and Ben and Anna nodded.

In their room, Ben and Anna quickly put their things back in their bags.

"I guess we're not going to get to see the Tower of London," Ben said. Anna gave a little laugh.

Outside now with their bags, Ben thought they would have to stop a cab, but a black car drove up in front of the hotel and stopped. The trunk opened and Ben put their suitcases in, and they got into the car. Al didn't say anything, but the car drove away.

"Al what just happened?" Anna said. "A gun? Who was that man in the gallery?"

"I'm not sure," Al replied. "There are people that would be interested in what we are looking into."

"Why?"

"What it implies."

They drove for a while and then the airbase where they had landed came into view, but they didn't see the plane they had flown two days ago. The car pulled up next to a small helicopter like the one that was unloaded from the plane in Iceland.

"Grab your bags," Al said and walked towards the helicopter. The pilot gave Al a thumbs up and the motor started.

Seated now, Al said, "There are a couple of security concerns. We're getting home a different way."

"Where are we going?" asked Anna

"Portsmouth," Al answered.

They were flying south and after about fifteen minutes, they could see the coast. As the helicopter started to descend, several docks were visible and against them, naval ships, including an aircraft carrier.

"We're taking a boat back home?" Anna said.

"Submarine," said Al.

Ben took a deep breath and looked at Anna.

The helicopter landed on a small pad and Al stepped off. He shouted something to a soldier who had walked up and saluted and pointed at the back of the helicopter. The soldier went back and removed the bags that Anna and Ben had loaded earlier. A small golf cart was waiting, and they got onto it and it drove toward the dock.

There in the water a submarine was floating, half submerged, and a tall tower was sticking up near the front and fins on either side of the tower. A gangway led from the dock to the submarine and Al said something to the soldier standing at the end of this and walked onto it.

"This man is going to take care of you," Al said gesturing to the soldier. "I'll catch up with you later." He turned to walk across the ramp and shook hands with a man waiting on the other side.

"This way please," the soldier said, indicating the gangway.

Once on the submarine, the soldier pointed at an open hatch and another soldier was standing beside it with his open hand pointing to the hatch. Ben stepped in and walked down a ladder and Anna followed. They stepped out onto the gray metal floor. The soldier followed them and then got in front of them and started walking. The submarine seemed very narrow, and they passed through what they thought was a dining room with a few tables and some chairs. They stopped and the soldier drew back a curtain and placed their bags on two of the bunks in the room.

"You'll sleep here," he said and smiled slightly and walked off.

They were both tired and set their bags on the floor and closed the curtain and lay down on the beds.

"Ever been on a nuclear submarine before?" Ben said.

"No. You?" Anna answered.

Thirty minutes later, Anna's uncle appeared, and the sound of the curtain opening woke them.

"Hungry?" he asked.

They sat down in the dining room and three trays of food were already sitting on the table.

"Al, why are we going home in a submarine?"

"Some security concerns have come up. Also we would have had to wait for the plane and we wanted to leave."

"My mom," Ben said.

"We've contacted Wolfie. Also there are a couple of other people helping him watch your mom. We'll be home in a couple of days."

Ben looked at Al and nodded.

They started eating their sandwiches and then Anna asked, "Al, what did you mean when you said there are people who would be interested in the implications of what we found at the museum?"

"Well, if someone has broken the fiver and changed something that means it could be done again."

"To do what? Like what the Ask is saying?"

"Most of us, but not everyone, are pretty bad off the way things are," Al said.

"I mean who wouldn't want the world to be different than it is?" Ben asked.

"Some people are doing pretty well. Tech and AI."

"Also when you say people," Ben said

They weren't sure how they knew, but they knew the submarine was moving now. Ben and Anna were sitting at the table reading and a soldier handed Anna a deck of cards.

"Something to do," he said.

Ben took out the cards and shuffled them, and then cut the deck.

"Know how to play Hearts?" he asked.

"No."

"Me neither. I think I used to know."

"Spades?"

"Nope."

"Got any threes?" Anna asked and Ben laughed, and they ended up playing Go Fish.

The food wasn't bad. Ben was pretty sure the eggs weren't real. They were allowed to walk around the ship but could tell if they were approaching an area they weren't supposed to go into by the way the soldiers stiffened when they got close. There weren't any windows and they read, played cards and slept.

"So there is a nuclear reactor somewhere near us?" Ben asked

"A small one," Al said, and Ben nodded slowly.

They were asleep when Anna's uncle opened the curtain and said, "We're here." A soldier took their bags and headed towards the front of the boat and they followed. They climbed back up the ladder and across a gangway to a waiting golf cart, which took them to another helicopter. They flew for about an hour and then the helicopter landed, and they got off, the blades still spinning. A soldier took their bags off and put them into a waiting car.

"This car will take you home," Al said. "I'll be in touch. Thank you both." He hugged Anna and he and Ben shook hands.

Ben started to give the driver his address, but he was already driving.

The car stopped in front of Ben's house.

"You going on home?" he turned and said to Anna.

"Yes, class tomorrow."

"OK, see you tomorrow? You'll be OK?"

"Yes," she said and kissed him. "It's been an interesting few days."

Ben nodded and opened the door, and the driver took his bag out of the trunk and handed it to him. The car drove off as he was walking up the steps. Once inside, he took the steps up the floor to his apartment. Two men were standing outside his door.

"Ben?" one of them said.

"Yes. Who are you?" Ben replied.

"Colonel Paris asked us to help you for a few days."

"Help me how?"

"We'll be out here if you need us."

Ben couldn't think of anything to say so he just nodded and walked between them and opened the door and went in. Inside, Wolfie was sitting with his mother, who was asleep in an armchair.

"Ben," Wolfie said, standing up and walking over.

"How is she?" Ben asked.

"The doctors say she's stable. They've started her on two new drugs." He pointed to two small plastic bottles sitting on the table.

"Wolfie, I really."

"It's OK," said Wolfie. "Hungry?"

They sat down at the table while Ben ate. There was still no water, so Ben filled a glass from the pitcher on the table. Ben told Wolfie what had happened.

"Jesus. Anna's uncle thinks someone was trying to stop you? Or worse? Who?"

"He's not sure."

"Who does he think maybe?"

"Well, he mentioned people who have benefitted from everything that has happened. In other words, who might not want anything to change."

Wolfie raised his eyebrows. "He thinks something could be changed?"

"He thinks if the fiver was broken once it could be broken again. And not just people who have benefited. The thing about Qweb taking over security of the Arch has him thinking."

"About what?"

"Well, the Ask. If someone went back and changed something. Something about tech or AI, or even earlier, something with industry. What would happen to Qweb?"

"OK, but it's a computer really. A good one."

"Well, he was talking about what it might take for a computer to have emotions."

"To be conscious?"

"Maybe. I don't know." He closed his eyes.

"Wolfie, I think I need some sleep."

"I'll stay tonight."

"You don't have to."

"I know."

Ben looked at his mother sleeping in the chair and then went into his room.

Chapter 17

As Anna was walking up the steps to her apartment with her bag, she got a message from Al: "The two men outside your door. They're mine. Anything weird happens let me know."

She nodded to the men on her way in, dropped her bag on the floor and leaned against the door for a second. Her mother and brother were asleep and she didn't wake them. She walked into the kitchen, opened the refrigerator then closed it again. The lights in the room went off for a few seconds and then came back on. She wondered how tomorrow could be like just another day after what had happened the last few days then thought maybe it wouldn't be. Her brother's violin was on the table next to a book her mother was reading. She turned off the lights and then saw on the kitchen windowsill a rock and a shell and thought about the curious symbolism of those two objects. Then she thought about her lecture tomorrow and how she probably wasn't ready for it. Most of the students in the introductory literature course she taught as part of her graduate fellowship were engineering majors and the course was required. English literature wasn't what they were most passionate about. Tomorrow was the first day of the semester. She went into the bathroom, and splashed water on her face and looked in the mirror. Then she got into bed and fell asleep.

The next morning her brother had already left for school and her mother was pouring herself a cup of coffee and Anna thought if she didn't hurry she was going to be late for class.

"Coffee?" she said.

"Yes, but I have to go."

"Al told me everything that happened. Are you OK?"

"I think so. I'd never ridden in a submarine before," Anna replied. "How much do you know about what Uncle Al does?"

"Well he doesn't tell me a lot about what he does. I thought I would understand better what he did when he became Director of the Arch, but I'm not sure."

Anna took a drink of her coffee then put on her jumpsuit, picked up her backpack and walked out the door.

"See you this afternoon," she said to her mother, closing the door. Outside, the two men were still standing there. "Good morning," one of them said.

Campus was about ten miles away and she got onto a bus. Like most buses, it didn't have a driver. It ran a regular route, stopping at the same stops for the same amount of time. The bus stopped now in front of the main entrance to the university and Anna stepped out and walked through the gates. The main quad was large and crisscrossed with sidewalks. The red brick buildings on either side were each several stories tall with white windows. Students walked in both directions on the sidewalks. She looked at her watch and saw that she had ten minutes to get to class. Five minutes later, she was walking up to the English building where her class would be. Students were walking in, talking and holding backpacks and she followed them in. A few minutes to spare, she thought to herself. She had thought about what she wanted to talk about in class today on the bus ride over. The second half of the yearlong course began with the Romantic period, which was her area of specialty.

Inside, the large entryway had stairs leading up on both sides, and a chandelier hung from the ceiling. She walked quickly up the stairs and then through the classroom door, which was at the front of the lecture hall, and put her backpack on a table. The room was about half full and students were talking and laughing, excited for the semester to start. She unzipped her backpack and took out a folder and set this on the lectern at the front of the room.

"Good morning," she said, seeing that it was now ten o'clock.

She had decided to talk about Wordsworth's environmentalism, his early concern for what he saw as harmful changes to the environment, as a way of preemptively answering the inevitable question of why poems that were written a few hundred years ago were important today. First, she had them read passages from Wordsworth's poems to show the importance of nature to the poet.

She asked one student, who was sitting on the front row, to read aloud a passage from Lines Composed a Few Miles Above Tintern Abbey.

"Usually just called Tintern Abbey," she said.

"…Therefore am I still
A lover of the meadows and the woods,
And mountains."

The student concluded and she asked another student to read a passage from The Prelude to show how nature for Wordsworth was a moral teacher. Then she read a passage from "Home at Grasmere", the first part of a three-part magnum opus that Wordsworth planned to write.

"So in Grasmere," she said, "Wordsworth found the home in nature that he had been seeking all of his adult life."

After class, the student who had read aloud asked Anna if she had ever been to Grasmere.

"Once," she said, "when I was doing research in England. It's very beautiful. The lakes and mountains."

"I'd like to go someday," the student said and smiled.

"And I'd like to go back," Anna said.

After all of the students had left, Anna gathered her notes into the folder and put it back in her backpack. On her way out, she stopped at the library to return a book. The librarian, whom Anna knew, smiled at her and asked her how her dissertation was coming along.

"Fingers crossed," Anna said. "I'm supposed to defend in three months."

Outside, the weather was clearer than it had been, a "One," and Anna decided to walk to work instead of taking the bus. She cherished these clear days, of which there were fewer and fewer. She walked out of the English building and down the steps and turned left towards the main quad. The clear air had brought students outside. A few were sitting on the lawn, and some were throwing a Frisbee. She walked out the main gates and turned left towards the river. Along the river were a few stalls selling food and she bought a bowl of rice and soy and sat on a bench to eat it. I haven't had a lot of time just to sit, she thought to herself and put her bag down. On the other side of the street, there were a number of tents with people living in them and she watched a woman walk down to the river and walk back with a container of water. I hope she's not planning to drink that, Anna thought.

She finished eating and walked towards the bridge. Halfway across the bridge she stopped to look down at the water. The water was the color of red clay, and she couldn't remember the last time she'd seen a fish in the river. A Synth passed her, pale green in color, and Anna nodded at her. The day was overcast, and Anna wondered if the woman would need to eat. Across the bridge now, she turned right towards the hospital. The doors opened for her as she walked up the steps to the hospital and into the atrium. She smiled at the woman at the information desk and went to the stairs and walked up to the fourth floor. Sarah, the Synth she worked with, was sitting at the reception desk when she walked into the office. The woman's white dress made her skin look a darker green than usual.

"Hi," Anna said.

"Good afternoon," Sarah said. "How was class?"

"Not bad. I managed to keep their attention for most of the hour," Anna said and laughed.

Then she picked up a stack of folders from a holder on the desk. "A lot of patients today?"

"Yes," Sarah said. "Busy." She called the next patient.

Anna walked back with the patient who smiled weakly at Anna and sat down in a chair.

"Hello Mrs. Foster. How are you today?"

"I've been better."

Anna hung a bag with the drug and pulled the long plastic tube to straighten it and attached it to the small tube on the patient's arm. She checked to see that there were no air bubbles and then started the drip. She smiled at the patient and walked back to the desk and sat down next to Sarah.

"How much longer will you be here?" Sarah said.

"I'm not sure. Treating patients for cancer. It gets to you."

It was dark when she left, and she walked to the bus stop to catch the bus home. She liked the way the buses looked when they drove up after dark, the light shining through the windows like an ocean liner. The door opened and she walked up the steps and showed her pass to the driver and sat down. At the next stop, a man put his bike on the rack in front of the bus and got on. He was talking to himself and said something to the woman sitting next to him and Anna turned to look out the window.

At home, her mom had made dinner and they sat down to eat. Her brother stopped playing the violin and sat down next to her.

"How was work?" her mom asked.

"It kind of gets to you," Anna replied.

She turned to her brother. "How was school today?" He nodded and smiled, still chewing.

After dinner, Anna worked on her lecture for the next day and went to bed.

Chapter 18

The next morning was also clear, and Anna got off one stop early to walk through campus to her building. She had decided to lecture on Beauty. She walked in and set her bag down on the small table next to the lectern. Most of the students stopped talking and turned to look at her. A few put their phones down.

"What is beauty?" she asked. "What are the qualities of something we think of as beautiful?"

She first talked about the idea of beauty and the sublime.

"Can something be beautiful and terrifying at the same time?" she asked.

Then she read the account of crossing the Alps from Wordsworth's Prelude. She read about the immeasurable height of woods, the stationary blasts of waterfalls, the torrents shooting from the clear blue sky.

"The sublime completely focuses our attention on one thing so that we can't think of anything else," she said. "Wordsworth saw that all the parts of this scene were parts of a single thing, the types and symbols of Eternity."

Then she talked about how things that we think of as beautiful take an effort to appreciate. That the effort required is part of experiencing beauty. She asked a student to read Keats' "Ode on a Grecian Urn."

"Beauty is truth, truth beauty. That is all you know on earth and all ye need to know," the student finished.

"So, what does he mean?" Anna asked the class.

"It seems like he's saying that all we need to know is that truth and beauty are the same thing, That's the most important lesson," a student answered.

"Good," Anna said. "And another possibility. Beauty and truth are the same thing. Yes. But maybe he is saying that beauty is all we need to know on earth. What we should really be looking for."

Class was over and she was looking down at her notes and thinking about the urn at the British museum and the mask, and when she looked up, she noticed a man sitting in the back row that she hadn't seen in class before, and he stood up and walked out.

Outside, it was still clear, and she couldn't stand the thought of going to the hospital, so she called the clinic. "Sorry," she said to Sarah when she answered, "I won't be in today. Or tomorrow. Or the day after that."

Then she called Ben and they decided to have a picnic with Wolfie at the lake. When she walked out of the main gate, Ben and Wolfie were waiting for her. They had just finished pedaling and walked over. She gave Ben a kiss and hugged Wolfie. They had to walk a mile along the river to get to the lake. On the way, they stopped to buy some food for a picnic. They bought bread and cheese, which wasn't real cheese, and splurged on some apples and Wolfie bought a bottle of wine. They walked along the river and then turned left to walk into the park. The park used to be a zoo but there were no more animals in it.

"Remember coming here as kids?" Anna asked.

"The lions. And monkeys," Wolfie said.

"I liked the penguins," Ben added.

They walked past the empty enclosures and to the lake and sat down on the grass. Wolfie opened the wine and took a drink from the bottle. They didn't have any glasses, and he passed it to Anna who took a drink and they laughed. Ben pulled off a piece of bread and put some cheese on it and then passed it to Wolfie. They sat eating and watching the lake. Two geese walked up, and Anna threw them some bread.

After they ate, they lay back on the grass looking at the sky. The sun was setting, and it was starting to turn orange and they knew that the air tomorrow would be worse.

The lake used to have rowboats that you could rent but a few years ago people stopped coming and there were no more boats on the lake. Anna sat up, straining to see something on the bank of the lake by a willow tree.

"Is that a boat?" she said.

They walked over to the bank and there tied to the willow tree was a rowboat. The gunwale was chipped in places, but it was sound and there were two oars in it.

"Look at that!" Wolfie said. "Must be the last one since they shut down the row boats."

They pulled the boat out from under the tree and pushed it into the water and got in. Wolfie sat in the front facing the rear of the boat with the two oars and Ben and Anna sat in the back. Wolfie started rowing, pushing and striking the oars.

"An act of stealth and troubled pleasure," Anna said.

They rowed around the edges of the lake and there were a few ducks floating in the water. Then they rowed towards an island in the middle of the lake. A few minutes later, the boat struck the island and they got out, and Ben pulled the boat up onto the sand. They walked onto the grass and sat down. Wolfie sat on a rock.

"If only every day was like this." Wolfie said. "We wouldn't need to," and then he stopped.

"It's OK," Ben said. "She'll be better soon and then. I've heard they think they can probably send people back to the same places people have gone before."

The moon was starting to come up and the lake was shining clear. Wolfie pulled a wooden flute that he carried with him out of his bag and started playing. They sat for a while listening to Wolfie's music.

"Think we should get going?" Anna asked. The moon was higher.

"I think I'll stay for a while," Wolfie said.

"How will you get back?"

"I don't think it's that deep. And I can swim."

"But the water."

"I'll be OK," he said.

Anna and Ben got back into the boat and Ben started to row back to the shore. Small circles on either side of the boat glittered in the moonlight where Ben dipped the oars, and they could hear Wolfie's flute playing as they left the island behind. Ben rose on each stroke and the boat went heaving through the water like a swan.

Soon they were back on shore, and they tied the boat to the willow tree again and looked at each other and smiled.

"I hope Wolfie can get back," Anna said.

"He'll be OK."

They walked back through the park holding hands.

Chapter 19

The next morning, Anna lectured on Mary Shelly's "Frankenstein," which she had assigned to read but didn't think many of them had read. She talked about how the book could be considered a warning against thoughtless technological progress and she thought most of the students understood.

"What led Dr. Frankenstein to create his monster?" she asked the class.

"Pride?" one student said.

"He wanted to see if he could do it?" another answered.

Outside after class, Anna noticed a number of drones flying overhead close to the English building and when she walked out, she noticed some of them stopped moving. When she got to the bottom of the steps, five or six of them flew over to her and formed a circle around her, about head high. When she tried to walk, the drones didn't move, preventing her from moving. She swatted at one of them with her backpack and it moved out of the way of the backpack and then returned. One of them turned around and then back to her and then a few seconds later they all flew off. She was a little bit shaken by this and shook a little as she started walking back toward the bus stop. Once she was on the bus she messaged Al about the drones, remembering he had asked her to let him know if anything unusual happened. Now she wondered how Ben was and messaged him. "Good," he replied. He was pedaling with Wolfie and hoped her class went well. A few minutes later Al's reply came: get home as soon as possible.

When she got home there were two black SUVs parked in front of her apartment building. Al was already inside and also Ben. Her brother was home from school early. The two men were still outside her door and there were now two more.

Al looked at her when she walked in. "Anna," he said, "we think it would be a good idea for you, your mom and your brother to go stay somewhere else for a while."

She looked at her mother. "Where? Why?"

"The drones. We think they might have been threatening you."

"Threatening me?"

"Someone seems to think you know something important."

"Ben, did anything happen to you today?" She asked.

Ben shook his head and came over to stand next to Anna.

"Someone has decided that you may be a threat, but that Ben isn't. Not yet anyway. Or an algorithm has analyzed the data and come to that conclusion."

She looked at her brother. "Where would we go?" she asked

"We have some facilities that are protected. Offline"

"Could I still go out? Go to class?"

"Maybe. Someone might go with you."

"Like a bodyguard?"

"Kind of."

"And for everyone else?" she gestured at her mother and brother.

"Yes."

Al said they should each pack a couple of suitcases and they should leave in fifteen minutes or so. Anna hadn't finished unpacking her suitcase from the trip to London and she looked at it then closed it and carried it into the other room. She also grabbed her backpack. Her brother had a small suitcase and his violin. Al was looking out the window and Sue walked in with her suitcase.

One of the men came over and picked up Anna's suitcase. Another of the men picked up Sue's and her brother's and Al said, "Is that it?" Anna and Sue nodded.

"Ben, you'll ride with us," Al said

Ben nodded, looking at Anna.

They walked down the stairs and the men put the suitcases into one of the SUVs. Al looked to the right up the street then to the left and opened the door for Anna. She and Ben got in the back and then Al got in the front. Sue got into the second car with Anna's brother and two of the men. There were drivers already in both cars. Al nodded to the driver and the car pulled away from the curb.

They started out heading east towards downtown but then turned north. Al didn't say where they were going. They were approaching the tunnel when Anna saw a drone outside the window. Al saw it too and pointed at it, looking over at the driver. The driver nodded. Al typed something on his phone and the car sped up. They went through the tunnel and when they emerged, there were four drones waiting for them. The driver got onto the on ramp and sped up. Anna looked at the speedometer and saw that they were going ninety-five miles per hour. She looked at Ben and he had also seen it. She turned to look out the rear window and the second car, with his mother and brother, was still behind them.

"We're good," Al said and typed something else into his phone.

Now it seemed like one of the drones was trying to land on the hood of the car. The driver swerved and it careened off to the right. Soon it caught back up with them and was flying just outside of Anna's window. Now Anna saw, to their left, several more drones flying quickly towards them. These seemed smaller and faster, and the other drones rose into the air. Anna leaned over and could see one of them and one of the smaller drones now had attached itself to it. There was a bright flash and an explosion and both drones now fell to the ground. Another of the drones now also exploded and the remaining two turned and flew in the other direction, the smaller drones flying after them. Anna turned around and saw that the second car was still following.

"Take the next exit," Al said to the driver.

They got off the highway and stopped at the red light. Al looked back at Ben and Anna. "Are y'all ok?" he said.

"I think so," said Anna and Ben nodded. "What were those drones doing?"

"For sure following us. Wanted to know where we were going." Al replied. "But that explosion was bigger than I expected."

"You mean they might have been armed?" said Ben.

"I think they were."

Now the cars turned left and after about half a mile turned onto a residential street. They pulled up in front of a row of townhouses.

"We'll get out here. Wait in the car for just a minute," Al said, opening his door.

He was talking on the sidewalk with two of the men from the other car and one of the men walked up the steps to the door of one of the townhouses.

Al opened their door. "OK, let's go on up to the apartment."

One of the men opened the door of the other car and Anna's mother and brother got out. Both looked shaken and Anna went over to them.

"Let's go," said Al.

One of the men picked up their bags and they walked up the stairs.

Chapter 20

Inside, the townhouse was really nice. Anna looked over at Ben and shrugged. Stairs led up to the second and third floors. Al said they would have the whole townhouse. Now one of the men Ben had seen at his apartment walked in and Ben's mom was walking beside him

"Mom?" Ben said.

"She'll be staying here with you too," Al said.

Ben walked over to her.

"Al. Why is this place safer than our house?" Anna asked. "I mean, with the guards there."

"There are some extra levels of security here. One thing, your cell phones won't work here."

Then one of the men brought over what looked like a small duffel bag.

"Put your phones in here," Al said.

Now there was a knock on the door and one of the men turned to talk into what Anna guessed was a microphone, but she couldn't see it and then opened the door. Wolfie walked in.

"Wolfie?" said Ben.

"Fancy meeting you here," said Wolfie and shut the door behind him.

"Make yourselves at home," said Al. "I'll be back later." And he went out the door.

One of the men went with him and the other went over and stood by the door.

Anna and Ben sat down on the couch. Anna's mother went into the kitchen and opened the refrigerator and took a few things out of it.

"How long do you think we're going to be here?" Anna asked.

"He didn't say," said Ben.

"Not too bad really," said Wolfie smiling.

Anna's mom managed to cook some dinner and they all sat at the table. They felt better after they had eaten, and Sam took out his violin.

Anna unzipped her backpack and took out a folder. "Al thinks I'll still be able to teach class tomorrow," she said opening the folder.

She had planned to give a lecture on being lost. In reading for her dissertation, she had gotten interested in travel books and journals from the Romantic period. Also letters. She kept reading about people being lost: lost at sea, lost while walking in a snowstorm, lost riding a horse at night. Now no one ever got lost. They always know where they are, and she thought that maybe that experience of being lost, knowing you could get lost, made an important contribution in some way to Romantic literature. It provided, she thought, an essential metaphor, losing one's way in life, for example. And then finding it again.

"Nobody gets lost anymore," she said. "Or maybe just lost in time."

Now they turned their attention to the TV. There was some sort of crowd and Sue turned up the volume. The picture was of the Arch facility and Ben and Anna looked at each other. The chain link fence that they had seen a week or so ago was being replaced with a taller fence or wall. Outside, people were moving and shouting. Protesting. A few of them held signs. Blue-uniformed soldiers were standing nearby. Now a clearing in the crowd formed and they could see that two of the protestors were wearing orange masks. The soldiers now saw them and started to run in their direction. When they arrived at the spot where the two had been, the orange masks were gone. Maybe they took them off and were still in the crowd, Anna thought.

"What does it mean," asked Sue?

"Al thinks Qweb may have somehow taken over Arch security and it looks like it wants to strengthen it," Anna replied.

"Why?" she asked.

"They think it might be possible to break the fiver. To go back and change something. What we saw in the museum."

"Change what?"

"Well, I guess things that might fix what's going on now."

There was a knock on the door and Al walked in.

"Did you see what's happening at the Arch?" Anna asked him.

"Yes," he said, looking over at the TV.

"Is this going to make it harder to get to campus tomorrow?" Anna asked.

"Anna, I don't think it's going to be safe for you to try to go."

She looked at him. "But I have to."

"It's not going to be safe."

"Can we go out at all?" she asked.

"Right now I think the safest place for you is probably the Pleistocene," he said.

Anna thought about how a few years ago she would have never expected to hear anyone say that. "The Pleistocene? You mean to settle?"

"Yes."

"But I don't know for sure that I want to go now. With everything that's been going on." She looked over at her mother and brother. And at Ben.

"Some things have changed," Al said.

"Things like what?"

"Well, for one thing, they're accelerating the program. Sending more groups back. Faster. People are starting to feel like we're running out of time."

"That doesn't really make me want to go," she said. She couldn't leave her mother and her brother behind if things were getting that bad. Or Ben.

"And there's one other thing."

"What's that?"

"Someone came back."

"What do you mean came back?" Anna said.

"A Settler. Came back. From the Cretaceous."

"What? How?"

"We brought him back." Al looked at her. "It looks like now, if you're careful, the Arch can work both ways. Both directions."

"Why didn't we know this?"

"No one had tried it. A few days after the group left, we opened the Arch again. One of the Settlers saw it and walked through. And came back."

"What does this mean? For me?"

"I mean you. And Wolfie. Could go for a while. Then come back when things settle down. Are better."

"Better how?"

"Just better. You were both scheduled to settle in a couple of months anyway, but that mission has been moved up."

"To when?"

"Day after tomorrow."

She looked at her mother. "Al. I don't know."

"We don't really have a lot of good options," he said.

"I'm guessing I won't be teaching class tomorrow."

"Al, we have some food if you're hungry," Sue said.

"I am, thanks," he said and sat down at the table.

"Ben what should I do?" Anna asked later when they were upstairs in their room.

"Well," he said. "You'd be safe. And could come back later when things are better. Better somehow. I don't really know what he means."

She nodded.

"And Wolfie would be with you."

"I guess I knew I would be nervous when it got closer. I thought you would all be OK if I went. Maybe also that you would come with me."

"I can't," he said. "Not now anyway."

She nodded. "Does Wolfie want to go?"

"Wolfie has always wanted to go."

The next morning Sue was making breakfast and had made coffee. Wolfie was already sitting at the table with a cup.

"Good morrow," he said looking at them and smiling.

Anna poured a cup of coffee and then walked over to the window and looked out. A car drove by, but other than that the street was quiet. A man, not the same one as yesterday, was standing inside the door.

Al hadn't said, but they knew they probably weren't going anywhere today. Anna's mother was looking in a cabinet and brought out some board games and a jigsaw puzzle. She opened the puzzle box and emptied the pieces onto the coffee table. Ben kind of laughed and nodded and sat down, flipping over pieces. Ben's mother walked in and sat down next to him and put two pieces together. He smiled at her.

"So you're really going? Tomorrow?" Anna's mom said.

"Sounds like it." Anna raised her eyebrows.

"Wolfie?"

Anna nodded and Wolfie walked over.

Ben took a deck of cards out of the cabinet and sat down at the table and started shuffling.

"Deal me in," said Wolfie.

Around noon, Sue said she would make some sandwiches and took some plates out of a cabinet. She looked at the man at the door to ask if he wanted anything and he shook his head no.

"What about your kits?" Sue asked. They were sitting at the table.

"I guess Al knows," Anna said.

"What else will you take?"

"I have my book. Wolfie?"

"My art stuff. Drawing paper, pencils. Some paints." Sue nodded

After they had eaten, there was a knock on the door and Al came in.

He walked over to Anna. "How are you feeling?"

"OK. I think."

"Ready?"

"I thought I would be."

Wolfie was nodding and Al smiled at him.

"We'll need to go kind of early tomorrow."

Anna nodded.

That night Anna couldn't sleep.

"Will you be OK?" she asked Ben.

"Will you?"

Anna breathed out. "Sometimes there's just things where there really doesn't seem to be a good answer."

Chapter 21

The next morning when Anna came downstairs Al was already there. He was looking out the window and Anna could see a couple of drones hovering about fifteen feet off the ground.

"Ours," he said. "Go ahead and eat if you want to."

"Not really hungry," Anna said.

"You should."

Wolfie was already up and finishing his breakfast. "Hello fellow Settler," he said looking at Anna and smiling.

"Al, is whoever, or whatever, is trying to kill us going to try to stop me from settling?"

"Well it may see you as less of a threat if you go back. The cost may be lower to let you go than to try to stop you. Or worse."

Now it was time to say goodbye to everyone. Al said only Anna and Wolfie would be going to the base. She walked over to Sue, and they hugged. "See you soon?" Sue said.

Then she walked over to Ben, and they kissed. "I hope I see you soon," he said.

"I think you will. I think we'll be OK." She looked at Wolfie.

"Wolfie?" Ben said and Wolfie nodded.

"Alright," said Al.

Al went out first and looked right and then left then motioned for them to follow. The black SUV was there, and a man was holding open the door for them and they got in. Al got in the front seat and shut the door.

"Let's go," he said to the driver, and they pulled away. Anna looked out the back window and saw that the drones were following.

In a few minutes, they were on the highway and Al seemed more relaxed. "Not too much longer," he said.

"Are we expecting anything bad?" Anna asked.

"Not sure. Probably not."

Twenty minutes later, they were pulling up to the base. The two drones had stopped, one on either side of the car. Anna and Wolfie got out of the car.

"Here. You'll want these," Al said, handing them their Settler's kits. Wolfie took his and smiled. He also handed them each a duffle bag.

"What's in here?" Anna asked

"Other things you'll need."

The wall around the base was partially completed and there were a few more soldiers than the last time she was here, but otherwise it looked the same to Anna. No one was protesting outside the gate. The soldiers looked at Al and saluted and Al motioned Anna and Wolfie through the gate. They walked the way she and Ben had come before, up the sidewalk with the bushes. She could see into the viewing area, but it was empty, and she could see the Peregrine flag hanging on the wall. They didn't go in the front entrance but went around to the side of the building to a different door and Al swiped a card through a reader and they went in. The door led into an office, Al's office Anna guessed, and through a window she could see a group of people, other Settlers, in a small room. They were saying goodbye to people who had come along with them.

Anna looked closely, more closely than last time, at the Settlers. They were of all ages. An elderly couple stood holding hands and there was a young family of four; the children looked like they were about seven and three years old. All had their kits and another bag. Anna thought she could pick out the specialists; their bags were larger and of different colors: red, yellow or green. It seemed more organized than she had noticed before.

"Ready?" said Al.

Anna and Wolfie nodded and all three walked into the Arch room. Anna guessed that Al was one of the few non-Settlers that was allowed in here. More and more people were now coming in from the adjacent room and the Arch room was filling up. Now Anna felt the same vibration in the floor like before and the two towers started glowing blue. There was also a humming sound that she hadn't heard before from the viewing room. The Settlers were looking at each other excitedly and starting to line up.

"You'll be OK," Al said. "If you weren't your mother would kill me."

"Give me two weeks," he said. "Be back at the same spot in two weeks where you come out. At the same time."

Anna nodded and she and Wolfie got in line, Anna in front of Wolfie. Wolfie looked back at Al and Al gave him a thumbs up. The humming was getting louder, and the blue arch started to form between the magnets, and Anna was getting more nervous.

Now the blue arch was stronger and looked somehow, if possible, like it had more than three dimensions, and now the first Settler walked towards it. As before, his outline became less and less distinct and then he was gone. Anna looked at Al and the next Settler went through. She took a few steps forward and looked back at Al again.

"Two weeks," he mouthed the words and held up two fingers and she nodded.

Now there were only three Settlers in front of her, then only one and then she walked into the arch. She kept walking and didn't feel anything but then she began to notice she was walking on something softer than the concrete floor of the arch room. She was looking down and could see it was grass. She looked up at the blue sky. The air was incredibly clear, and there were clouds in the sky, and she could hear the sound of birds singing.

Chapter 22

At the townhouse, Ben sat with his mother. She was awake and sitting next to Ben on the couch and looking at the puzzle. The TV was on, and the news was about the presidential primaries. The CEO of Quantco was the front-runner for the nomination for his party. It did not seem that he was going to be asked to step down from his position at Quantco if he got the nomination.

Sue walked in. "That's the first time something like that's happened," she said.

Ben didn't pay that much attention to politics but nodded and turned the sound up. They heard a car pull up outside and Ben walked to the window and saw Al walking up to the door. Then he walked in, and Ben could see there were still two people standing outside the door and now two more at the end of the sidewalk.

"Did they go?" Ben asked.

"Yes. And I told them to be ready to come back in two weeks."

Ben nodded. "Why the tighter security here?"

"They may be starting to see us as more of a threat," Al said. "We saw two drones flying a block or so away as we drove here."

"Al, who are those men? Military?"

"Kind of. Friends of mine. Veterans. They fought with me in the metal wars."

"Do they work for you?"

"Kind of."

The metal wars, or lithium wars, were the last major world conflict. There weren't any clear winners, but the two biggest sides divided up what was left of the rare minerals needed for batteries before newer, more toxic batteries were developed.

"How much control do you think Quantco has over QWeb?" Ben asked

"Well, I think the control runs both ways."

"And how bad do you think it would be if that CEO were elected president?"

"Hopefully things won't get that far."

Ben nodded, not sure what Al meant, then looked back at the TV and switched it to Settler's TV. He was hoping to see Anna and Wolfie but knew the chances were small as every Settler carried a camera and the feed could be from anyone's camera.

There was a commotion outside and they went to look out the window. Several of the men had run into the street and one was taking something out of the back of one of the SUVs. It looked like a big gun, a tube with a handle in the middle. Now Ben saw several drones flying quickly down the street towards the townhouse. The man with the gun went into the street and pointed the gun at the drones and then a boom and puff of smoke came out of it. A net made maybe out of metal wire shot out of the gun and towards the drones and when it got to the drones it covered them. The drones wobbled for a minute and then went still and then the drones and net fell to the ground.

Ben's mother had turned up the sound on the TV. Ben looked at the TV and it was the arch facility. Another section of wall was being added and there were more soldiers. Also a few drones could be seen flying near the wall. These were bigger than the ones they had seen outside, and something was mounted on the bottom of them.

After a few seconds, Al said, "Ben I may need your help with something. We may be running out of time."

"OK."

Chapter 23

Anna couldn't believe how beautiful it was. They were supposed to land in London and Anna saw they were on a hill of some sort because she could see south to what she thought was the Thames although it looked different. Maybe they were on Parliament Hill. Hampstead Heath.

The other Settlers were looking around too, their eyes adjusting to the sunlight. One was looking at a tree, as if they were seeing a tree for the first time. As if they had only ever seen shadows of pictures of a tree, been in a cave their whole lives like the people in the allegory, Anna thought.

She looked at Wolfie. "We need to mark this spot," she said.

"Two weeks," said Wolfie.

She was familiar with Parliament Hill, if that was where they were. She had spent many afternoons sitting up here, looking down at the city and looking up at the kites in the sky. Really, it looked about the same as the last time she was here. A little cooler, though she had been there in early spring. She knew that somewhere North of where they were, a glacier was retreating. In addition to the birds she could hear and see, there were other animals: several deer and what she thought, feeling some alarm, was a mountain lion.

Some of the Settlers were acting quickly to drop their bags and open them up, taking out poles, canvas and tools. She knew that some of the Settlers were specially trained for the mission, and she watched them working. Some went into the woods and began cutting down trees. Others went to work setting up the folding structures they had brought. Within an hour or so, they had formed something that looked like a large camp, with protective structures and several fires. A woman was cleaning a deer that someone had shot with a bow and arrow on a rack made out of tree limbs.

Anna walked over to one of the women and asked what she could do, and the woman asked her if she knew how to fish. She looked at Wolfie who nodded, and Anna took the fishing pole the woman was holding out to her.

"There's a pond a few hundred yards that way," she said pointing, "if you want to give it a try," and she smiled.

"I think I'm going to like it here," Wolfie said as they started walking in the direction the woman pointed. "I'll get my bag in case we catch any."

They walked through the waist-high grass and wildflowers, Anna smiling and pointing out ragweed and Queen Anne's Lace.

There was a fish hook on the end of the line but no lure or bait and so Wolfie caught a grasshopper and put it on the hook and tied a piece of bark near the hook to act as a float and Anna tossed the line into the water. A minute or so later the float went under water and the pole bent. Anna started turning the reel and pulled out a greenish fish about twelve inches long.

"They're biting!" she said.

Wolfie said it looked like some kind of perch and they put it in the bag. They found some more grasshoppers and caught five more fish, including what Wolfie thought were bream. They took the bag back to the camp and told the woman how many they had caught.

"Do you know how to clean them?" she asked.

Wofie said he thought so, and the woman handed them a knife.

"Thanks," Anna said pausing.

"Carol," the woman said extending her hand.

"Anna," Anna said shaking her hand.

"Wofie," said Wolfie, also shaking her hand.

"How do you know how to do this?" Anna asked.

"My father and I went fishing a few times."

They found a large, flat rock and Wolfie took one of the fish out and laid it on the rock. He inserted the knife into the fish's belly near the tail and cut a slit, not too deep, spread the body open and removed the entrails. He reached into the bag for another fish and handed it to Anna who cleaned that one and they cleaned the rest of them. A man had brought a plastic water container and filled it and it was sitting on a table nearby. They took one of the fish over, waved to the man and used the water to rinse out the cavity and rinse off the fish's skin.

They took the cleaned fish back to the woman and she said, "Let's cook them," pointing to a fire. "Pointed sticks."

They took the knife into the nearby woods and found some sticks to sharpen and then put the fish on them and stuck the sticks in the ground so that the fish were near the flames. Then they sat and watched them and watched the smoke rising from the fire.

After a while Carol walked over and said, "Looks like they're done," and handed them a plate. They put the fish on the plate and carried them over to where Carol was standing and she pointed at a table and then put another, larger plate on the table.

"Do you like venison?" she asked.

"I'm not sure," said Anna. "Want some fish?"

"Thanks."

Although all of the Settlers had set up camp together, it seemed like there were twenty or so distinct camps, each with a few structures and several fires. Twelve other people were sitting at the table with Anna and Wolfie. Two of the Settlers had set their cameras on the table and pointed them at the camp. The man sitting next to Anna introduced himself and said he was a doctor from Arizona. They each ate one of the fish and had some of the deer, which Anna liked. Someone had made a salad out of what looked like fennel and nettles and they had some of that too. There was also a bowl of blackberries on the table, and they ate a few of those. Neither of them had eaten real meat in years and it was delicious. Along with the salad and berries, Anna thought it might have been the best meal she had ever had.

After everyone had eaten, someone took out a guitar and started playing it. Anna and Wolfie turned around, leaning their backs against the table and watched the fire. It had gone to embers and was sending orange sparks and a thin line of smoke into the night sky. Soon everyone was getting up from the table. Anna and Wolfie took sleeping bags and blankets out of their duffel bags, and spread them out on the ground and lay down. They looked up at the incredibly bright stars.

"Wolfie."

"I know, can you believe this?"

"That's Taurus," she said pointing to a group of stars near the Western horizon.

"There's room under here if you want," they heard Carol say.

"Thanks," Wolfie said, and they moved their sleeping bags under the edge of the tarp.

When they woke up the next morning, someone had already gotten the fire burning. Wolfie said they should try smoking some fish as they would keep for a few days that way. Carol smiled as she handed them the fishing pole and they walked back to the pond. A few hours later, they had caught and smoked about a dozen fish, and they were sitting on a plate on the table. Anna had taken a course in college on herbs and plants in Shakespeare's plays and so thought she could find a few plants that might be useful. She brought back some chamomile and crab apples and used them to make tea, chopping them up into some water that was boiling on the fire.

"You know," she said, "maybe tomorrow we should pack some of those fish we smoked and explore a little. It would be interesting to see what London looks like."

"Sounds like a plan," Wolfie said.

Dinner that night was venison and strawberries. It was a clear night, so they slept just outside the canvas tarp.

The next day they packed their sleeping bags and some of the fish and some nuts that Anna had found. The doctor they had met the first night asked if he could go with them and they thought that was a good idea. Then another man they had met asked if he could go and they saw he had a bow and arrows, and his wife was with him too. He said his name was Stan and that he was a carpenter in a future life and smiled.

"Be careful," Carol said.

"See you in a couple of days," Anna said, and they started walking. They filled their water bottles at the pond and started walking west. In half an hour or so they turned south and started walking downhill.

"This is somewhere near Hampstead High Street I think," Anna said, "or where it will be?"

The walking was not too hard. There were wooded areas but also clearings and soon they came to what Anna thought would be Regents Park. They saw some deer and maybe a cat and Anna was glad the man had brought his bow and arrows. They stopped to rest, and everyone ate some of what they had brought with them and then they continued walking south. Anna and Wolfie shared some of their fish. They came to where Anna thought Trafalgar Square would be and was amazed to see it was a marshy area with a few animals that looked like hippopotami standing in the water. They went around the marsh and came to the river somewhere near where Somerset House would be, and it was starting to get dark and they decided to camp there for the night.

They found a clearing and Stan built a fire, and they sat down and Anna passed around her bag of nuts. Stan had cut his leg pretty bad gathering firewood and the doctor had wrapped it in a bandage and applied some antibiotic ointment he had brought. Stan thanked him and they sat around the fire.

"Why did y'all want to settle?" Stan looked at Anna and Wolfie.

"I'm not sure," said Anna. "There didn't seem to be a lot of interest in the things I was studying. Literature. Everyone too busy staying alive. I thought maybe I could be a teacher here."

The woman nodded.

"Both my parents died," said Wolfie. "There wasn't anything keeping me there. Also I couldn't breathe. That's part of the reason anyway," and he looked at Anna. "You two?"

"Our child died so there wasn't really anything there for us either. Both of Stan's parents got cancer so we figured he would get it too."

"How about you?" they nodded at the doctor.

"I thought they might need doctors here."

That night they heard something walking close to their campsite but it didn't come close enough to the fire for them to see it and they talked until the fire burned down and fell asleep.

They walked back the next day through what would be Bloomsbury Anna thought, and turned to Wolfie and said, "British Museum," and smiled. They continued north, Anna pointing out roughly where underground stops would be in the future: Chalk Farm, Belsize Park.

They got back to the camp near dusk and Carol seemed upset. "A lion got someone from a nearby camp last night," she said.

<h1 style="text-align:center">Chapter 24</h1>

Al and Ben sat down at the table. "Anna and Wolfie won't be back for two weeks, and things are moving a little too fast," Al said. "We need to try to slow things down."

"Slow what down?" Ben said.

"There are people and things working against us."

"What are we trying to do?"

"We'll talk tomorrow. There's really nothing we can do tonight. What I'd like to do tonight is play some music with Sam, if he doesn't mind."

Ben saw that Al had a violin and was opening the case. He tightened the bow and put rosin on it at began tuning it. Sam's violin was sitting out and he picked it up. Sam had learned some classical songs and Al had a book of music with the second violin parts to some of them. "Bach Minuet?" Al said. Sam nodded and they started playing. The music was simple but beautiful. Listening to it, Ben thought, you could forget about the Orange and the dust. And Qweb. And just lose yourself in the music. He hoped Anna and Wolfie were OK.

The next morning Al was sitting at the table with a cup of coffee and motioned for Ben to sit down, pointing to a cup on the table.

"How much do you know about computers? About Qweb?" Al asked.

"Not that much. I just always thought about it as a big box somewhere, attached to everything and running everything."

"Well that's kind of true. It's sort of somewhere. And everywhere. There are lots of small nodes or edges, but there is one central unit. Very big. And it does run, or control, a lot of things. As you know. Water, electricity, food distribution."

"Killer drones," Ben added.

"That too."

"Where is the main part?"

"That's a good question. We're not a hundred percent sure."

"How can the military, the government, not know? When it does so much?"

"Well the military and the government aren't the same thing. And it's kind of like all of those services, essential services, have been outsourced in a big way to a company."

"And that line between private companies and the government."

"Exactly."

"Where do you think it is?"

"Well it needs to be somewhere secure. Also it uses a lot of electricity so it gets hot and it needs to be cooled." Al handed Ben a picture.

"Is that it?" Ben asked.

Al nodded. "A prototype."

In the picture, huge, concentric golden metal rings or discs were stacked on top of each other, stretching up almost farther than you could see. Tufts of silver wires were hanging down from each ring to the one below it. It looked like a frozen waterfall.

"It's beautiful," Ben said. "And kind of terrifying. Where can they hide something that big?"

"Remember how we got home from England?"

"It's underwater?"

Al nodded. "Our best guess is somewhere near, or maybe inside, the underwater city."

"But wouldn't you know if it were there? Wouldn't you have seen it?"

"We've never been there. Never really had a good reason to. We've seen it from the outside."

"Wouldn't it have to be in a pretty tall building?"

"Part of it or most of it could be underground."

"You mean underground under the ocean."

"Yes."

"What are you planning to do?"

"We need to slow it down. It's figured out someone is trying to do something that may threaten it and it's trying to stop us although it may not think that we're the primary threat. Yet. Right now it's just trying to put out little fires."

"You talk about it like it's making its own decisions."

"That one in the picture, the prototype, it had one hundred thousand qubits."

Ben nodded.

"Qweb we think has ten to the twelfth. That's a trillion."

"That's a big number."

"There used to be something called the Turing test. To test if a computer is intelligent."

"I know about that."

"This one is at least as smart as the person who came up with that test."

"So what are you wanting to do?"

"First we have to get to it."

"Uh huh."

"Then we need to do something to divert its attention. Preoccupy it for a while."

"How?"

"Quantum computers, like Qweb, use qubits which are not like old computer chips but made from trapped ions. Or quasi particles."

"I'll keep nodding."

"Unlike old computer bytes, which could be a zero or a one, qubits can be zero or one or both at the same time. They can be in superposition, a combination of all possible states. Some people use the analogy of Schrodinger's cat."

"The cat is both alive and dead until you open the box."

"Right. Well we need to do something to confuse it. We need to take away the superposition temporarily and make it focus for a while on a single computation. Make it think that all the cats are alive."

"How?"

"Introducing a new program. Kind of like a virus."

"How can you do that?"

"Not remotely, not from a terminal. We have to go to the mainframe."

"Underwater."

Al nodded. "And I want you to come with us."

"Me? Why?"

"There aren't that many people I can trust right now and you're one of them. Plus. What did you study in college?"

"Before I quit? Architecture. And geology. I hadn't decided. But how are you going to get to it? Why would anyone let you?"

"The city, underwater city, is nearing completion and due for an inspection."

"By the military?"

"Including the military. There are some security implications for the construction of the city which gives us a reason, an excuse, for going."

Ben looked over at his mother.

"Sue is going to stay with Beth." He looked over at Sue and she nodded.

Chapter 25

After the lion attack, the group had decided that there would need to be someone keeping watch every night, in shifts, and that everyone would need to learn how to shoot with a bow and arrow. Anna volunteered to take a shift. She had underestimated, or not thought much about, the skills of the professionals who were in the group, but after the first week, they had built several actual houses. It seemed that the carpenters were planning to help build a house for anyone who wanted one. Carol said maybe she and Anna and Wolfie could live in one together. They hadn't told anyone they were going back in a few days, and they thanked her and said that sounded like a good idea. They caught some more fish and smoked them, and Anna gathered some herbs. Some mint and some sage. There was a sound of sawing and two people were setting a long board in place to form part of the wall of a house.

There didn't seem to be much else for them to do right now and Wolfie said, "I think I'll do some painting." He pulled a large pad from his bag and a small wooden box. He opened it and there were small tubes of paint and some brushes and a jar of water inside. He took out four of the tubes: black, white, bright red and dark yellow.

"Zorn pallet," he said and took out one of the brushes and closed the box then walked over the hill and sat down on a grassy lee.

Anna watched him sit down and decided to take a walk to look for mushrooms. She didn't know much about them but thought she could identify a couple of edible ones. She put her knife and water bottle in her bag and walked north out of the camp towards a line of oak and beech trees. She picked up a couple of mushrooms and put them in her bag and walked up to a small ridge. When she got to the top of the ridge, she stopped and there in the distance, about two hundred yards away, saw three wooly mammoths. Even from this distance, they look enormous. They were brown and shaggy and their bodies sloped down towards their tails. Their white tusks were very long and curved in a sort of spiral shape. One of them was smaller and she thought maybe it was a family. The biggest one, the father maybe, was standing still with its head up and the other two were foraging for something on the ground. She watched them, amazed, for a few minutes and then thought maybe it wasn't a good idea to be out her by herself this far from camp and picked up her bag and turned to walk back.

When she got back, Wolfie was still painting, and there were several pictures on the grass beside him.

"Wolfie, you'll never believe what I saw," she said and told him about the mammoths.

Wolfie shook his head slowly. "It's crazy," he said.

One or two of the others looked at the mushrooms Anna had gathered and agreed they were safe to eat so Anna cut them into pieces and put them on the table. After dinner, the man played his guitar for a while then the doctor looked over at Anna and said, "Anna why don't you read us a poem?"

"Well, OK," she said going to get her book from her bag. "How much time do we have?"

"Read whatever you want to," the doctor said, and she thought she would read "Tintern Abbey" and she started reading aloud:

> "Five years have passed; five summers with the length
> Of five long winters! and again I hear
> These waters, rolling from their mountain-springs

> With a soft inland murmur. – Once again
> Do I behold these steep and lofty cliffs
> Which on a wild secluded scene impress
> Thoughts of more deep seclusion; and connect
> The landscape with the quiet of the sky."

She continued to the end of the poem and then closed the book. Someone else, amazingly Anna thought, had brought a banjo and she and the guitar player sang a few songs together. Anna smiled as they sang: "These two-dollar shoes hurt my feet."

The sun was setting now, and there were orange clouds in the sky in the west and then they heard some thunder. "Listen, the mighty being is awake," Anna said to herself. It started to rain and so they slept under the tarp. Anna listened to the sound of the rain hitting the tarp for a while and then fell asleep.

They awoke the next morning to some commotion in the camp next to theirs. A dozen or so people were standing at the edge of the camp looking east towards the line of woods and then Anna saw them; nine or ten people standing at the edge of the trees about fifty yards away. They were wearing brown pants maybe made out of leather, and furs over their shoulders and most were wearing boots that seemed to also be made of fur. There were a few children, and the rest were adults. The men carried long spears that had stone points on the ends.

"Neanderthals," she said and looked at Wolfie.

"I think so."

They were too far away for them to clearly see their faces and after a few minutes, they turned and walked back into the woods.

They were back the next day and stood or sat at the edge of the woods for about an hour and then one of them started walking towards the camp. He stopped in front of one the houses and looked at it. One of the builders was standing holding a saw, and the Neanderthal held out his hand and the man handed him the saw. He held it in one open palm as if he were trying to determine its weight and looked at it and then handed it back.

Anna could see he was wearing some type of necklace, made out of a leather strap and some shells.

"Anna," Wolfie said. He was holding a notebook that he had just taken out of his bag. It was open to a page where he had been keeping track of the days.

"Tomorrow is eleven days," he said. "We're going back in a few days."

She looked over at the Neanderthal again and back to Wolfie. "I guess we are," she said.

When she got up the next morning, Carol had made a sort of coffee out of Holly leaves and handed Anna a cup. "Eggs?" she asked.

"Thanks."

A small, fox-like creature had been coming to the edge of the camp where people were leaving scraps for it and this morning it was sitting a few yards from the table.

The Neanderthals were now mingling with the group. One was helping with the construction of a house. A group of both Neanderthals and members of their group was gathering some things into bags and looked like they were about to go somewhere together. The Neanderthals had spears with stone points and one of the men also had a spear.

"Where are they going?" Anna asked.

"Mammoth hunting, I think," said Carol.

Two of the Neanderthal children were sitting on the ground and Anna walked over. They were playing with something on the ground. A type of game Anna thought, with some smooth sticks all of about the same size and some rounded rocks. Anna sat down. One of the children laid the sticks in a row along with some of the stones, as if trying to explain the game to her and then looked at Anna but she didn't understand and kind of smiled and shrugged her shoulders. She watched them play for a while. She was getting up to leave when one of them handed her a bracelet. It was made of a leather string and had some white and brown shells strung on it. She took it and thanked them and put it on. After a few minutes she got up and walked over to where Wolfie was sitting and showed him the bracelet.

"I saw," he said. "That's really cool."

Wolfie had been sketching Carol although she didn't know it and now he was using some of his paints to add some color to the drawing. A little while later, when the painting was finished, he took it over and gave it to her. She thanked him.

"Carol," he said, "we may be going back in a couple of days."

She looked puzzled for a few seconds and then nodded slowly.

"Just you two?"

"As far as I know. Do you like it here?" Wolfie asked.

"I do," she said.

It was late afternoon, and someone had gotten the fires going, and the hunters walked into the camp. Two of them were carrying a large fur skin and the rest were carrying big pink chunks of meat.

"Looks like mammoth for dinner tonight," Wolfie said smiling.

After dinner, Anna and Wolfie walked out from camp and sat near where the arch had left them. They looked up and there was a meteor shower. Almost everywhere they looked, they could see one moving across the arch of the sky as if it were falling to the end of the world.

Chapter 26

"Do we have a plan?" Ben asked.

"Can you put this on?" Al said, handing him a blue uniform.

"A military uniform?"

"We want you to look official."

Ben put on the uniform and then went over and sat down next to his mother on the couch.

"Ben, you be careful," she said.

"I will and Sue will be here. I'll see you soon."

"OK," she said.

He had packed a few things in the bag Al gave him and he picked it up and Al said, "Let's go."

He opened the door and shook hands with one of the men standing outside and said something to him that Ben couldn't hear. A man standing by the car opened the door, and Ben got in and then Al got in.

"Al, how much of what we are doing can they see? What about satellites?"

"We have something for that. At least right around here."

"You mean they can't see us here?"

"That's right."

At the end of the street, they turned right and in a few minutes they were on the highway heading east. Ben kept turning his head and looking back out the window, expecting to see a drone or a car following them but didn't see anything.

"Do we know anything about Anna and Wolfie?" Ben asked.

"I haven't seen them, but I've been watching too."

They drove for about half an hour and then exited from the highway. A few minutes later, they were pulling up to a gate and a soldier was standing next to a small booth. The driver rolled down the window and the soldier looked into the car and then opened the gate. They drove down the road and Ben saw a helicopter on a pad. Al said something to the driver, who talked into a walkie talkie and then the blades started turning slowly. By the time they were getting on the helicopter the blades were spinning and it was about ready to take off. The pilot looked back, and Al gave him a thumbs up and they took off. It was too noisy to talk, and Ben tried for a few minutes to sleep. Opening his eyes, he looked out the window at the brown, parched earth below.

A few hours later, they landed behind a tan building and they got their bags and went inside. Al spoke to a man inside the door and then turned to Ben. "We should get something to eat," he said. They sat down at a small table near the window and Ben could see the dock outside and the water. There were two small submarines next to the dock.

"Nuclear submarines?" he asked

"Electric."

"Are they expecting two?"

"No, just one. The other is backup."

Now they were joined by a man and a woman, both in blue uniforms, and Al shook their hands.

"This is Ben," he said, and they nodded to him.

"Are we ready?" Al asked.

"Almost," the woman said.

Al nodded. "Eat up," he said.

They finished eating and went out the door to the docks.

"We're going to the one on the left," Al said, and Ben walked to that gangway. A soldier took his bag and walked across to the submarine and through a hatch and down the ladder and Ben followed. Then Al came down and walked to the front of the boat.

"You can have a seat here," Al said pointing to a small table and chairs. "I'll just be a minute." A few minutes later, he came back. "We're underway," he said.

"How far are we going?"

"About four hundred miles. The city is off of Turks and Caicos."

"Of course it is," Ben said.

Ben noticed the submarine was very quiet and thought there was some tactical advantage to that. Al had said the second submarine would be following about a mile behind. Ben found a bunk and started reading and then fell asleep.

"Ben," Al said, waking him up. "We're almost there." Ben looked out the one window and could see in the distance the murky outline of the underwater city. As they got closer, Ben could see the city was enormous. In one direction, it stretched away farther than he could see. The main part consisted of a large central clear dome, with a diameter of about three football fields, and smaller domes radiating off this with spokes, clear connector tubes.

"Al how did they build all this? A thousand feet deep?"

"Well they have a shit ton of money. And they've been working on it for about ten years," he answered. "Some have been living down here most of that time."

"Who lives here?"

"The Quantco CEO for one."

"The one running for president. Are they planning on just staying down here?" Ben asked.

"I think so."

"So they don't really care how bad things get up there."

"There," the woman in the blue uniform said pointing to a smaller dome. "That's where we're going."

As they approached the dome, Ben saw that there was room for the submarine to go underneath it. The submarine slowed down and maneuvered underneath the dome then stopped.

"Here we go," said Al. They walked up the ladder and out the hatch. There was a gangway leading to a round platform made of metal grating that surrounded the boat and they walked across it. There were several people waiting for them on the platform, one of whom Ben recognized as the Quantco CEO.

"Colonel Paris. Welcome," he said extending his hand to Al.

"Quite a setup you have here," Al said.

"We're proud of it. I know you will enjoy your stay," he said smiling. "Please we will meet again later. For now, these people will take care of you," he said gesturing to a man and woman wearing yellow suits. "You are my guests," the CEO said and smiled again, and turned to walk away.

"This way please," said the yellow-suited woman pointing to a door.

They walked through one of the clear tubes. Ben could see fish and a shark swimming outside the tubes, the water illuminated by lights outside on the ribs of the tube. They made one right turn and then came out inside one of the domes.

"This is our hotel unit," the woman said.

The lobby was enormous. A glass elevator was at one end and walkways leading to doors could be seen on each level. Two giant, golden sculptures, of crabs, were on either side of a fountain and a large chandelier hung over the fountain. On one side, several people were sitting at a bar and behind the bar, bottles were lined up in front of a large mirror.

Ben looked at Al and raised his eyebrows.

"Please. Follow me this way to the registration desk," she said gesturing forward. They walked past a group of men in suits sitting and talking. A woman and child holding hands walked past in the direction of a sign that said, "swimming pool."

"Good afternoon," the man at the desk said. "We have two suites reserved for you?" he said looking at Ben and Al and the two blue-suited soldiers who were with them, the man and woman from the submarine base.

"That will be fine," said Al and he took two keys from the man and handed one to Ben.

They got onto the glass elevator, which took them up to the fifth floor and they all got off and walked down the hallway. The two soldiers stopped at their room and Ben and Al kept walking. A few doors down Al swiped his room key and they went in. The room had two beds and a separate sitting area with two chairs and a desk. Through a curved viewing window, they could see fish swimming by, one with large white eyes and very long, sharp teeth. The bathroom had a small hot tub and gold fixtures.

"Not bad," said Ben smiling, setting his bag on one of the beds.

A few minutes later, there was a knock on their door. Al opened it and the two soldiers walked in.

"Do we know where we're going?" asked Al.

"Yes," the man said. "Our sister sub has gotten some readings and we think we know where it is."

"Where is it?"

"There's a small dome we saw on the way in. Dark though, not clear like the others, kind of in the center of the city. Readings say there is something underground there. Something big. We printed this out on the submarine," she said, unrolling a piece of paper.

"There's definitely something down there," Ben said looking at the paper. It was graph paper with inked lines going up and down, like a seismograph, and there was one area that was much darker, the lines much closer together.

"What's the plan?" Ben asked.

"Well, you and I are going to go on a tour," Al said. "Business as usual. Our friends here," he nodded at the man and woman, "are going to take an unauthorized tour."

"Won't you be seen?" Ben asked them.

The woman smiled.

A few minutes later, the room phone rang, and Al picked it up.

"OK," he said. "We'll be right down," and hung up the phone.

"Alright," said Al. They followed the other two out and Al pulled the door closed behind him.

Walking to the elevator Ben asked, "What are they going to do?"

"Disarm some sensors, hopefully. The rest of the job will be done by some folks on the other sub. Divers."

"Can they dive this deep?"

"Yes, but not much deeper."

"Install the virus to confuse the computer."

"Yes."

As they walked off the elevator, they were met by the Quantco CEO. He was wearing a blue suit with a blue tie and was smiling.

"I trust your room is fine?" the CEO said.

"Yes, thanks," said Al and Ben nodded.

"The other two won't be joining us?"

"No," Al said. "They have some paperwork to catch up on."

They walked through a different tube than the one they had come through earlier and out into another dome. This one was larger than the first and contained buildings that looked like apartments. There were sidewalks leading to the apartments, and a playground, and amazingly, Ben thought, grassy areas.

"A residential area," the CEO said. "There's a school over there," he said pointing.

Al and Ben nodded, looking around.

Then they went into a dome that was a shopping area. Several people were walking out of one of the stores holding bags and a couple was walking into a coffee shop. Next, they went into a dome that had a golf course. Ben had never seen this much grass before. A foursome was teeing off on the first hole and Ben could see the flag stick and green.

"Do you golf Colonel Paris?" the CEO asked.

"I did once or twice. Not really. It's kind of hard to up there. With the dust and everything."

The CEO nodded and smiled thinly.

They went into another residential dome, this one with large houses and landscaping.

"You live in here?" said Al but the CEO didn't say anything.

Next, they went into a dome with stacks of batteries that looked to Ben like small skyscrapers. The electricity, the CEO explained, came from the surface but didn't offer any more explanation.

Then they saw the water desalination facility; rows of blue pipes, too many to count, connected to a larger central pipe. There was a low humming sound and technicians were looking at dials on the wall and then down at clipboards that they were holding and writing on. "Reverse osmosis desalination," the CEO said. They continued walking and he pointed to a tube leading to the air purification system, but they didn't go there. They walked through two farm domes. Wheat was growing in one of the domes and the other had an orchard of what looked like apple trees.

"Completely self-sufficient?" Al asked.

"Yes sir," he answered.

On their way back through one of the tubes, Ben tapped Al on the shoulder and gestured to the outside. There they could see the smaller, darker dome. Several underwater drones were swimming slowly around it, pausing occasionally and then moving again.

Back in their room now, there was a knock on the door and Al let the two soldiers in.

"Are we good?" Al said and they nodded.

Ben lay down to rest for a few minutes and a little while later, they were back on the elevator and on their way to dinner.

They sat down at the table and a waiter offered to pour Al a glass of wine.

"No thank you," he said, and Ben shook his head.

There were twenty or so people at the table and the CEO stood, holding his wine glass.

"Colonel," he said. "I trust you are enjoying your stay. And that we have passed your safety inspection with flying colors?"

"We won't know for sure for a few days," Al said. "But I think it looks pretty good safety-wise."

"Cheers," the CEO said taking a drink and others at the table held up their glasses.

People around them started talking and laughing. Ben recognized the CEO's running mate, and a senator and a couple of actors.

"Tell me Colonel Paris," a woman in a sequined gown next to him said. "What's it like being a colonel on the army?"

"You get used to it."

"You're a hero. The metal wars."

"I fought in the war. I don't know that I was a hero."

"Well they don't give Medals of Honor out to just anyone do they colonel?"

"A lot of bad things happened in that war. And a lot of bad things happened on the way home from the war. I don't think that was a war that anyone really won," he said.

"Oh I think somebody won," she said.

"Who do you think won?" Al said.

"Why, we did," she said smiling and took a drink from her wine glass.

Dinner was extravagant. Lobster and real steak. Vegetables. "How?" Ben asked by looking at Al. Al shrugged his shoulders.

Later they were lying in bed about to go to sleep. Al was reading. Ben was looking out the window and for a brief second the lights went off. Then came back on again.

The next morning, they were having coffee in their room and packing their bags. There was a knock on the door and Al let the soldiers in.

"Any news?"

"We think we're good," the woman said.

The woman in the yellow suit met them as they walked off the elevator.

"I hope you enjoyed your stay." She smiled and handed them each a gift bag and started walking. Ben glanced into the bag and saw several small bottles.

Now they were walking back through the tube they had come through yesterday and came out onto the metal grate. Two soldiers had waited on the submarine and one of them was standing at the hatch.

The two soldiers walked across and got into the hatch and walked down the ladder. Ben walked across the ladder and was standing at the hatch. Al was stepping onto the gangway when the CEO entered with two men in dark suits on either side of him.

"Colonel Paris. A word please," he said.

Al came across and into the hatch and down behind Ben.

"Captain," he said. "I think we may have worn out our welcome." He closed the hatch behind him.

"Yessir," the captain said, and the sub started to move.

Ben waited for something to happen, and then after a few minutes said, "Do you think they know what we did?"

"I think they think we did something but aren't sure what," Al said. "It should buy us a little time, but things are going to get moving soon."

"Buy us time for what?"

"We're building a second arch."

"We have an escort, sir," said one of the soldiers walking up to Al.

"That's OK," Al said. "Have the other sub circle around. Let's go home."

Chapter 27

When they drove up to the townhouse, it was raining. The rain kept the dust down but there was a danger of floods. Ben stepped out of the car into ankle-deep water, and they ran to the door.

Al spoke to the man standing outside the door. "Anything?"

"One car at the end of the street but we took care of it."

Al nodded and they went in.

When they got inside, Sue looked over at Ben and he knew something was wrong.

"Where's mom?" he asked.

"She's in there," she said pointing to the bedroom. "Al, I think she's going to need to go to the hospital."

"Can she?" Ben asked.

"She could but someone would need to go with her," Al said.

"Could I visit her?" Ben asked.

"You could but someone would need to go with you."

Ben went in and sat down next to his mother. She was asleep and he didn't want to try to wake her.

Sue walked in and he asked, "What's wrong?"

"I'm not sure. We really need to get her to the hospital."

"Could she walk to the car?"

"We have a wheelchair."

They went into the next room and Sue said, "why don't y'all eat a bite before we go," and she took some food she had cooked out of the refrigerator and set it on the table.

They ate quickly and Al said, "Let's go ahead and try it."

Sue and Ben woke Beth and helped her get into the wheelchair and packed a few of her clothes. Outside they helped her into the back seat of one of the SUVs and then Ben got in with her. Al got into the front seat and nodded to the driver. They pulled away from the curb and the second SUV followed.

Ben couldn't tell if anyone was following them because of the second SUV but when they were stopped at one of the red lights, a black car pulled into the intersection and stopped in front of them. Al looked over at the driver, who put his foot down and then ran into the car, and it spun out of the way and they kept driving. It didn't have a driver and when Ben looked back it hadn't started moving again. Someone got out of the second SUV and did something to the car and then the SUV was following them again. A few minutes later, they were outside the emergency room, and they got Beth into the wheelchair again and pushed her up to the reception desk. One of the men from the house went with them.

"This is one of Doctor Jones' patients," Sue said, and the nurse typed something into the computer. Fifteen minutes later, she was taken back and the doctor on call took her blood pressure and listened to her heart.

"I think we need to admit her," he said looking up.

Ben and Sue looked at Al who nodded.

"Okay," Ben said.

A few minutes later two nurses took her up to a room with three other patients and helped her get into her bed. Ben and Sue sat in chairs next to the bed. One of Al's men stood by the door. Another nurse came in the room and started an IV and hung a clear bag on a pole next to the bed and then walked out. She fell asleep and next to the bed, a monitor was beeping softly.

"I did this with my Dad and was hoping not to have to with my mom," Ben said.

"I know," Sue said.

The nurse brought in a tray of food and left it beside her bed. Ben opened the cover over the plate and looked at the dinner and then at his mom but she was still asleep. He tore off a piece of a roll and ate it and closed the lid again.

About an hour later, a nurse came in and said the doctor wanted to do a scan. A CT scan. Ben asked if he could go, and the nurse said yes. Two orderlies came into the room and said they were going to take Beth to have her scan. They unlocked the wheels and took the IV bag off of its stand and wheeled her bed out of the room. Ben sat beside the bed while the technician did the scan. While she was working, she pointed out things on the monitor for Ben. "There are the lungs," she said. "And that is the heart."

Ben wished that he could recognize anything on the screen. It looked like a lot of black holes and white lines. Nothing looked like a heart or lungs. The strangeness of the images made him feel less hopeful about his mom's condition. Like something was too wrong. After the scan was complete, the orderlies took her back to the room and Ben sat on a chair next to the bed.

A little while later Al came back. "You should probably stay at the townhouse Ben," he said. "We'll need to go to the Arch tomorrow. Anna and Wolfie."

"Is this a good time for them to come back?"

"It'll have to be."

"I'll stay here tonight, Ben," Sue said.

Ben nodded. "He'll stay here too?" looking at the man by the door.

"Yes."

They went out of the room and down to the lobby. Outside, the SUV was waiting, and they got in.

Chapter 28

It was cool the next morning and the fire was already burning when they woke up.

Carol walked over and handed them each a cup of juniper tea.

"Thanks," Anna said.

They were supposed to go back tomorrow, and Wolfie wanted to paint a wooly mammoth before they went back, and Anna said she would take him to where she saw them.

"We're going to see the mammoths today," Anna said. "Wolfie wants to paint them."

Carol nodded. "You can take some of this with you," and she handed them some of the cooked meat from the night before. They put it in their bags along with some water and Wolfie was packing his paints and brushes.

Carol walked over and said, "Take these too," and she handed them each a bow and arrows. "Just in case." They thanked her and then walked north out of camp the way that Anna had gone the day before.

They walked for about twenty minutes then climbed to the top of the ridge where she had seen the mammoths before and when they got to the top, there were three of them. The mammoths, two adults and a young one, were much closer to them than she had gotten before but didn't see them. The two adults were feeding and the young one was sitting on the ground. Wolfie smiled and took out his paints and brushes and paper. First he drew the animals lightly with a pencil and then began painting. When he was done, he showed it to Anna.

"Nice," she said. "Are you going to take it back with you?"

"Yes. It will probably be the only plein air painting of a mammoth," he said smiling.

They took out the food they had brought, the meat and some greens, and ate it. The sky was blue and there was a slight breeze blowing a few clouds. It was afternoon and Anna said they should probably get back. They packed up their things and started walking down the ridge through thigh-deep weeds when they saw something moving near the tree line about one hundred yards ahead. An animal a little smaller than a horse walked out and stood sniffing the air. Wolfie recognized what it was. "Saber-tooth tiger," he said. "This is not good."

"Have you practiced with this much?" Anna said holding up the bow, not taking her eyes off the tiger.

"Not much. You?"

"A little," Anna said putting her pack down slowly and drawing an arrow.

Now the tiger seemed to have seen them and was walking, crouched, in their direction. They stood still as Anna nocked the arrow and pulled back the bowstring. She raised the bow and waited. Now the tiger started running in their direction. Anna fired an arrow, but it went over the tiger. It was now about fifty yards away and Anna nocked another arrow, pulled back the string and raised the bow. The tiger was now about thirty yards away and looked like it was about to leap, and Anna let the arrow go. It hit the tiger in the right shoulder and the tiger stopped. It roared and they could see its long teeth that just barely touched the bottom jaw when its mouth was wide open. It seemed as if it was about to charge again but turned instead and walked back to the trees.

"That was a good shot," said Wolfie.

"Thanks. I really didn't think I was going to hit it. Do you think it's going to come back?"

"I think we should get back to camp. Don't put that thing up."

Back at camp, they dumped their things and sat down. They told Carol what had happened and thanked her for the bow and arrows. She shook her head and said, "I'm glad you're alright." She looked at them and then added, "We're going to miss you."

The next morning, they were eating breakfast and the animal they had fed was back, close to the table. "Here Fox," Anna said. She held out a small piece of meat and it took it from her hand. "I'm going to miss you."

After they had eaten, they packed up their things and said goodbye to Carol.

The group hadn't settled far from where the arch brought them, and they would only need to walk twenty or thirty yards towards the small hill. Most of the group knew they were somehow going back but no one else seemed interested in going back. A few people came to say goodbye. They thought they had arrived at around noon and when the sun was nearly above them, they picked up their things and went to stand at the spot where the arch had been. Anna looked around and south towards London and breathed out.

"Wolfie, we had planned to come and stay."

"Plans change."

And then, the air in front of them started to waver and a shape, curved, like a castle door began to appear and the view through it began to disappear.

"That must be it," said Anna.

They both turned to look at the people standing and watching and then stepped through.

Chapter 29

They pulled up to the gate and Al rolled down the window. The soldier at the gate looked in.

"Sir?"

Al didn't say anything.

"Sir."

"Are you going to let me in?"

"Sorry sir, we have to ask. Security has gone up."

Al looked at Ben and then back at the soldier. "Systems check."

"Sir?"

"We have a group going back in two days. We have to check the systems. Systems check."

The soldier looked at Al, and then lowered his head to his shoulder and said something and then opened the gate. They drove through and Ben looked at him.

"I think they don't mind if people keep going back. But they think there might be something else going on."

They parked outside Al's office, and Al swiped his card and they went through the door. Al looked at his watch and they went over to the Arch.

"Five minutes," he said and turned it on. The floor started vibrating and the blue arch started to form between the magnets. Now it was fully formed, and Al looked at his watch.

They waited but Anna and Wolfie didn't come through the Arch.

"What's happening?" Ben asked.

"Shit," said Al.

"What?"

"The Pre-sets. Shit."

"What about them?"

"Well picking someone up from another place. Then bringing them here. It's a bit more complicated. Requires two settings."

"And?"

"And one of the settings was wrong. From an earlier group of Settlers."

Ben looked at him.

"The Hummingbird group."

"They've gone to the Cretaceous?"

"Shit."

"Shit is right. When can we bring them back?"

"Well, we have to wait forty-eight hours. To reset. Forty-eight hours."

"Then we can bring them back?"

"Yes. From the same spot. Hopefully they'll wait."

Chapter 30

Anna and Wolfie stopped walking and looked around.

"This doesn't look like the Arch room," said Anna.

"Nope."

They were in a forest of thick trees with vines hanging from the branches and the ground was wet and covered in ferns.

Ahead of them, they saw a group of about twelve people and one of them walked over.

"Who are you?" the man said. "Where did you come from?"

"It's a long story," said Anna. "Who are you?"

"We're the Hummingbird group."

Anna looked at Wolfie. "We're in the Cretaceous, Wolfie."

Wolfie looked around. "Where are all the dinosaurs?"

"Wolfie, what the hell happened?"

"That is a good question."

"Obviously something went wrong. Can they get us?"

"If they can it would be from here, I guess."

"When Al said two weeks before I think he said two days was the minimum time we could stay."

"So you think they'll try to get us in two days? From here?"

"I guess. I hope so."

She looked at the man who had walked over. "Where is the rest of your group?"

"Most of us are in a camp over there," He pointed to a ridge. "A smaller group has struck out on their own and gone north.

Come on," he said, adjusting his backpack, and turned to walk back to the rest of his group. Anna and Wolfie followed.

"How far?" Anna asked. "We may need to come back here."

"About two miles," he said.

They caught up beside the group and they walked up a hill. On the ridge, there was a line of redwood trees and from here, they had a view of a mountain range, atmospheric blue and light blue and clouds covering their tops. In the direction they were walking, Anna thought she could see the ocean. They walked down the hill and to their right there was a small lake.

"Look!" Wolfie said excitedly.

Several dinosaurs were standing, knee-deep in the water. One raised his head and was eating plants, his mouth working in a sidewise motion.

"Hadrosarurs," The man said. "They won't bother us."

The man and a number of other specialists in the Hummingbird group were paleontologists and geologists and the man smiled and said he'd been happier than a possum eating a sweet potato since they'd gotten there.

Wolfie looked at Anna. "Happy," she said and Wolfie nodded.

"There are some that will though, so let's keep moving," he added.

Now they were walking through a wooded area pushing aside large ferns and swatting away flying insects. Anna slowed down to look at a spruce tree just as an ant got trapped in a drop of the tree's resin.

"Say hello to a piece of amber in sixty million years," she said.

After about half an hour of walking, Anna thought she could hear the surf. They were walking through a wooded area of spruce trees and then into a clearing and she saw the beach. The sand was white, and waves were breaking against a small cliff a few hundred yards to their left. There was a small group of mangrove trees on their right, and the man pointed in that direction and they kept walking.

"Beach vacation," Wolfie said, smiling.

They walked another half mile and then a small group of structures became visible near the beach at the tree line. As they got closer, they could see there was a clearing there and like in the Pleistocene, the group had formed ten or so small groups each around a few structures. A number of houses were being built and they could hear the sound of hammering. A man was planing a long pine board which was sitting atop two sawhorses.

The man set his pack down on a table and pointed to some chairs. "You can sit there if you want to," he said and Anna and Wolfie sat down.

The man handed them each a cup of water. There was a fire going and next to the fire was a rack with some fileted fish that looked like gar.

"The more things change," Anna said.

The man sat down next to them. "So, what happened?" he asked.

Anna explained how they had planned to be in the Pleistocene for only two weeks and then go back but that something had gone wrong, and they ended up here instead of back in their time.

"You can go back?" the man asked.

Anna nodded. "Apparently so, although we haven't made it yet."

The man looked around at the campsite. People in the camp were talking, laughing, cooking. "I'm not sure anyone would want to go back," he said.

"Well."

"What was the Pleistocene like?"

"There were mammoths. And Neanderthals," Anna said. "No other people here I guess."

"Nope. We have the place to ourselves for another forty million years or so," he said grinning.

"I'm Jim, by the way," the man said, extending his hand.

"Anna."

"Wolfie."

And then Anna realized she had forgotten to notice how clear the air was. And she leaned back and took a deep breath and closed her eyes and listened to the sound of the surf.

After a few minutes, Anna asked, "Is that the Pacific Ocean?"

"Interior seaway," Jim said. "Divides this half of North America from the other half. Disappears eventually."

"I had wondered why anyone would want to settle in the Cretaceous," Anna said. "I thought with the dinosaurs. And being so different."

"The dinosaurs are why most of us came."

"T. rex?" Wolfie asked.

"Nope. The seaway," the man replied. "But we've got some almost just as big and bad. We'll see some tomorrow."

"Two days," Wolfie said to Anna.

"Back in the Pleistocene," Anna said looking around, "a lion got someone in the camp. Have you had any problems like that?"

"Not really. People are always scared of the big dinosaurs. But it's the little ones you need to be worried about. Well, little. Six feet or so. The feathered ones. Dromaeosaurs."

Wolfie sat up.

"A group of Pyroraptors came into camp the other day. About five feet long. Beautiful little things. Brown feathers and a white streak on their wings. But Jesus, those teeth and claws. They moved forward kind of hunched down with their wings almost touching the ground. Smart too. They just grabbed some of the fish and meat and left."

"Have they been back?" Anna asked.

"Yeah. But we have some things set up around the camp now mainly keeps em out. And we try to keep the fires going. As soon as we finish the houses there'll be that too."

"Y'all want to you can sleep inside that one," he said pointing at one of the houses.

"But the big dinosaurs."

"Yeah, that's what people are always worried about. Haven't seen them here at all. We'll see them tomorrow though."

"What will y'all do for clothing? To keep warm?" Anna asked

"Well, there's those things," he said, pointing to a small furry animal that had wandered near the camp. It was brown and about the size of a beaver and had a striped tail. "They taste pretty good too," he said.

Anna nodded.

"Can we do anything?" Anna asked. "Do you have a fishing pole?"

"Y'all want to go fishing? OK, but stand on top of those rocks over there," he said pointing. "The crocodiles are about thirty feet long."

"Crocodiles," Wolfie said.

They took the fishing poles and walked down to the water. Wolfie pried open a few clams for bait and they stood on top of the rock and threw the line in. They caught three of the gar and put them in a sack they had brought and then Anna looked up.

"Look!" She said pointing. Three Pteranodons were circling overhead and then flew towards the cliffs. One of them made a screeching sound, its sharp beak opening. They took the fish back to camp and Wolfie asked a woman for a knife.

"Careful of any eggs," the woman said handing him the knife and they took the fish over to a rock and started cleaning them.

That night they sat at the table with about twelve other people and ate the fish and some of what Anna guessed was one of those small animals they saw earlier. There was also a salad made out of chicory and dandelion.

Anna said they would go ahead and sleep outside and they opened their bags beside the fire and lay down.

"Well?" Anna said.

"Yep."

Chapter 31

The phone rang and Al said, "Speaker," and then he answered it. "This is Colonel Paris."

"Colonel Paris."

Al recognized the voice of the Quantco CEO.

"We should meet," the CEO said.

"We should?"

"I believe that we have some common ground we could discuss."

"I doubt that."

"We should meet before things get too out of hand. For me, you. Other people. I propose meeting at a restaurant. Tomorrow night."

The next evening, Al walked up to the restaurant. It was a South American restaurant and there was guitar music when he walked in. Lots of green plants. He walked to the hostess stand and the Quantco CEO walked over from the table to him.

"Colonel Paris. Good evening. Please join me."

As soon as they were seated, a waiter brought them each a bowl with shrimp, peppers and tomatoes.

"Ceviche," the CEO said.

"I know," Al said and took a bite.

"Wine for you sir?" the waiter said.

"No thank you," Al replied.

The waiter then brought beef tenderloin and potatoes on a large, white plate. The plate had swirls of colored sauce that looked like they had been applied with a paint brush. Both Al and the CEO started eating.

"Colonel Paris, you do know that I will most likely be President soon."

"Shouldn't being President mean something besides keeping you rich? What about making sure people have enough to eat? Making sure their homes don't get flooded?"

"We can make arrangements for you and your family to be safe," the CEO said.

"What about everyone else?"

"Colonel Paris, I want to show you something," the CEO said, opening a small computer. He turned the screen around so that Al could see it. On the screen, a tall tower of yellow, red and green wires and stacks of golden plates stretched up from the floor. It was too tall to see how far it went. On the ground, a man in a white coat stood next to it, dwarfed by the tower.

"Do you know what this is?" the CEO asked.

"I can guess."

"Colonel, I have had many conversations with Qweb. It is just as alive, as conscious, as you or I."

Al didn't say anything.

"Colonel, are you familiar with the thermodynamic argument for the inevitability of life? The argument says that living systems are inevitable because of the second law of thermodynamics, which says that entropy in the universe is always increasing. Living systems are particularly good at increasing entropy through energy conversions and therefore inevitably evolved according to that law."

"OK."

"Quantum computers are much better at increasing the entropy of the universe. You cannot fight against fundamental physical laws of the universe and win."

"We'll see," Al said, standing up and placing his napkin on the table. "So who exactly is going to be president if you get elected?" And he turned and walked toward the exit.

Chapter 32

The next morning, they sat at the table and a woman gave Anna and Wolfie each a plate of eggs and some of the fish and a few berries.

"Thank you," Anna said, pausing.

"Mary," the woman said, and they introduced themselves and started eating.

A group was standing in the camp with bags, and a few had a bow and arrows.

Jim walked over. "Want to come with us?" he motioned to the group. "Some of them want to go find some berry bushes to bring back and plant. But mainly it's just an excuse to go look at dinosaurs," he said grinning.

"Hell yes," Wolfie said.

Wolfie and Anna got their water and bags and walked with Jim over to where the rest of the group was.

"We'll be back this evening?" Anna said.

"Yes."

They walked back to the beach and then through the surf in the direction they had come the day before. Anna saw some dark shapes moving in the water and then two heads at the ends of long necks appeared.

"Plesiosaurs," Jim said. "I wouldn't advise swimming today."

Now they turned off the beach and walked into the spruce trees they had come out of yesterday. They walked for about half an hour and then turned left and the forest now was denser. They saw several of the small mammals like the one in the camp yesterday and brightly colored birds flew overhead and sounded to Anna like tropical parrots. Now they were approaching a swamp and the mist made it difficult to see. There was a swampy area ahead and many fallen trees. Several Hadrosaurs, like the ones they had seen yesterday, were standing in the swamp and eating water plants. Then the forest went silent. The birdsong they had heard a few minutes earlier stopped.

"Shh," Jim said, holding up his hand.

The Hadrosaurs picked up their heads and were still. Then out of the mist on the far side, a dim shape could be seen approaching the swamp. They saw the red snout first and then the body emerged from the mist, gray, with a black downy stripe down its back. It walked to the edge of the swamp and turned to look to its right. It was about twenty-five feet long and twelve feet high.

"It looks like a T. rex," Wolfie whispered." But its arms."

"Shh," Jim said quietly. "Dryptosaurus," he whispered.

And then a second, smaller one walked out of the mist to the swamp to stand next to the first one. They had long arms, longer than a T. rex, Anna thought, and very long, sharp claws on their hands. The first one leaned over to drink and then raised its head slightly and looked straight at the group.

"Jim," Anna said.

"Everyone stay still."

They stood as still as they could and tried not to breathe. The Dryptosaur raised its head and began sniffing the air, moving its head right then left. After a minute or so, the two turned and walked back into the forest, disappearing into the mist.

"Shit," said Wolfie.

"Shit is right," Anna said, and she remembered why she had wanted to settle in the Pleistocene.

"Everyone breathe," said Jim. "Let's rest for a minute. Have some water and a snack."

Anna and Wolfie took off their packs and sat on a large, flat rock. They took out their water bottles and drank and Anna handed Wolfie some fish.

"I'm not sure I'm hungry," he said. He took out his drawing pad and a pencil and started sketching the Hadrosaurs.

Two of the group walked out to a boggy area and came back with several bushes. The bushes had red berries on them, and the roots were wrapped in cloth.

"We should get going," Jim said. "We have about an hour's walk back."

Wolfie put his pad back in his bag. He stood up and then quickly fell to the ground.

"Wolfie?"

"My ankle. Shit," he said reaching down for his foot.

Anna could see that his foot had gotten caught under a root and when he stood up he had twisted it.

A woman from the group came over. "Sit here," she said pointing to the rock, and bent down and gently touched Wolfie's ankle. "Probably sprained," she said. "Can you walk on it?"

Wolfie stepped gently on the foot, but it would not support his weight.

"Nope."

"How are we going to get him back?" Anna asked.

"We'll have to help him walk."

"We need to get going," Jim said and he and one of the other men got on either side of Wolfie. Wolfie put his arms around them and got up, standing on one foot.

"Probably going to take us about two hours," Jim said, "I hope we have daylight."

"Sorry," Wolfie said.

After about an hour of walking, they stopped for a break, and they all drank. Jim sat Wolfie slowly down and said, "Someone else want a turn?" When they were ready to go, two others came over and helped Wolfie up. They were starting to lose their light and half an hour later it was dark.

"Damn," Jim said. "We didn't want to be out here after dark."

"How much longer?" Anna asked.

"About half an hour. Fifteen minutes to the beach. Beach is better."

They started walking again. Two of the men were holding their bows.

About ten minutes later Jim held up his hand and the group stopped.

"Wait," he said.

Anna heard some rustling in the trees ahead and now she heard noise behind her. It was a clear night and a full moon, and they were in a well-lit clearing. Slowly from out of the forest, from every direction it seemed to Anna, brown, birdlike dinosaurs were walking towards them, crouching, with their wings almost touching the ground, making a hissing sound.

"Pyroraptors." Jim said. "This is not good. You guys with the bow and arrows?"

The two men with the bows each nocked an arrow and slowly raised their bows, each aiming at one of the approaching dinosaurs. The dinosaurs were now about thirty feet away and both men shot. One of the arrows went wide but one of them hit one of the Pyroraptors in its wing and it reached over with its beak and pulled it out. The other dinosaurs stopped walking and looked at each other and at the one that had been shot as if they were trying to decide what would happen if they were to rush the group. Then they backed away a few steps then turned and went back into the forest.

"Let's go," said Jim.

A few minutes later they were walking on the beach and then they saw the campsite. The group at the camp had been watching for them and standing on the beach and two of them came forward and helped Wolfie into the camp.

One of the doctors in the group came over where Wolfie was sitting and examined his ankle. "It's not broken," she said. "But it's going to be pretty swollen in the morning."

"Will he be able to walk on it?" Anna asked.

"I doubt it."

"Shit," said Anna, looking at Wolfie.

"Anna, you have to go back," Wolfie said.

"What about you?"

"I'm thinking maybe I'll stay."

"Someone can help you get back. I can help."

"We'll see."

The next morning Wolfie's ankle was swollen and purple.

"It's sprained," he said to Anna.

Jim walked over. "How's the ankle?"

"Not good," Wolfie said.

"Jim, we need to get back to that spot where you first saw us a couple of days ago."

"I don't think he's going anywhere."

"Can we help him get there?"

"Maybe. It's two miles. And kind of rough going."

"Anna," Wolfie said.

Anna sat down.

"What we know now. I could always go back later," he said. "Besides, I wanted to settle. And I kind of like it here."

"Well."

"If we're going, we'd better get going," Jim said.

Anna leaned over and gave Wolfie a hug. "I'll see you again," she said.

"OK."

Mary came over and sat down beside Wolfie and said, "We'll take care of him."

Anna nodded and stood up and picked up her bag and nodded to Jim. Another man from the group, with a bow and arrows, joined them and they walked to the beach. Walking down the beach, Anna saw the Plesiosaurs again in the water and overhead two Pteranodons flew in wide circles. They turned into the woods and about an hour later were in the clearing where they first walked out.

Jim looked up at the sun overhead. "It's noon," he said. I think it was about two o'clock when y'all got here. We might as well sit down.

They rested for about an hour and Anna said, "I think I'll start looking."

They heard a rustling sound and then a Pyrorapter walked slowly out of the forest into the clearing. And then several more from different directions.

"Shit," Jim said.

The man with the bow nocked an arrow and aimed at one of them but one of the animals had snuck up behind him and bit him on the calf. The man yelled and dropped the bow and fell to the ground. Jim reached for the bow and tried to put an arrow in the bow but kept dropping it and most of the Pyroraptors backed slowly into the forest.

One of them had stayed and was looking at Anna and started walking towards her, hissing with its head low and then she saw the arch appear. It was about six feet away and she started backing slowly towards it and the Pyroraptor followed.

"Go!" Jim yelled.

She was turning to walk into the arch when the Pyroraptor ran forward with its head outstretched and mouth open, showing its sharp teeth, and its wings outstretched.

Chapter 33

The phone rang.

"Speaker," Al said, and he answered it.

"Colonel Paris?" The voice had an almost human sound.

Al didn't say anything.

"Do you know who this is?"

Sue was looking out the window and said, "Al, come here."

There was a swarm of drones in the sky, maybe a hundred, each with a light and they were moving now with some purpose. They were forming a picture of some sort and then they saw it was a face.

"Colonel Paris I need to ask you to stop doing what you are trying to do."

"What am I trying to do?"

"You are trying to go back to a recent time and do something, I'm not sure what but I could guess, to reverse the changes that have occurred to the earth. Stop something from happening. Unfortunately, whatever it is you are doing will probably also cause me to cease to exist."

"Well, that may or may not be true. But the problem is if something isn't done, we'll probably cease to exist."

There was silence for five or ten seconds.

"I need to ask you to stop," the voice said.

"Look now," Sue said pointing out the window and Ben and Al walked over and the face in the sky was now Al's face. Then the drones moved and the face changed to Ben's face.

"Hang up," said Al and the line went silent.

And then the lights went out.

Al picked up a small metal briefcase from the floor and opened it and took a phone out and spoke into it. "We're going to need some help getting to the Arch tomorrow," he said. "And some help getting in. Also we may have a party here tonight."

Sue walked over to the sink and turned the faucet. "The water's off," she said.

"We'll leave early tomorrow," Al said.

Twice that night Ben saw a light, like a small search light, moving across the window and heard explosions that sounded like they were a block or two away. The next morning, he looked out the window and there were several military vehicles outside and the SUVs were gone.

"We'll be riding in those," Al said, pointing to the two tan vehicles with guns mounted on top.

Behind those, there was a truck with a number of small tubes mounted on the back. Ben looked at Al. "Rocket launchers," he said.

There was a second trailer truck with a small helicopter and several motorcycles. A dozen or so soldiers were standing next to the vehicles. One of the soldiers was holding a remote control and moving a joystick and a drone hovered nearby and then another drone appeared, and the two drones flew into the street.

"Is there any news on my mom?" Ben said.

"I talked to Sue earlier. She was awake for a while last night."

Ben nodded.

"Are you ready?" Al asked.

They went outside to the vehicles. LTVs were parked at either end of the street and there were several drones flying back and forth. Two soldiers were unstrapping the helicopter from the truck trailer.

"Are we ready?" Al asked a man standing next to the first vehicle and he nodded.

"Let's go," Al said, and they got in and Ben could hear the helicopter starting and the motorcycles. Inside the vehicle, there were two seats on either side, and Ben and Al sat down and fastened their shoulder straps. The soldier operating the machine gun was standing in front of them on a small platform and they could only see his body from his waist down. The driver was wearing a helmet and a headphone.

"You may want to put these on," Al said handing ear protectors to Ben. Ben put them over his ears and checked his shoulder strap.

They drove away from the curb and to the end of the street and followed the LTV that had been parked there. A few minutes later, they merged onto the highway and Ben saw three vehicles quickly approaching from behind them. They were similar to the one they were in, with guns mounted on top, but were white and had no drivers. The vehicle behind them started to fire on them and the bullets when they hit their vehicle made a pinging sound. The man standing turned to face the rear and started firing and it was loud even with the earmuffs. And then Ben saw one of their other vehicles behind those firing on them and then an explosion as one of them flew into the air, landing on its side on the shoulder of the road.

The small helicopter that Ben saw being unloaded earlier now caught up to them and was flying parallel to one of the two remaining white vehicles. The helicopter swiveled so that it was now facing one of them and fired a missile. The vehicle flew into the air as it exploded and the third one drove underneath it before it hit the ground.

Two motorcycles now appeared in front of them.

"Ours," Al said to Ben as the third white LTV behind them exploded.

Ben took a deep breath in and then breathed out.

Now he saw a second helicopter approaching from the direction they were headed and then it fired a missile. From behind them, several other missiles were fired and both the helicopter and the first missile exploded in front of them and their vehicle swerved to the right and kept driving.

"We might be good," Al said after a couple of minutes.

They drove a few more miles then exited the highway. When they drove up to the base, it looked like a small war was going on.

Several LTVs, like the one they were in, were driving towards the arch and firing at several more of the white ones, which were near the arch barrier. Soldiers in blue were walking alongside the vehicles, also firing in the direction of the barrier. Ben could see other soldiers next to the white LTVs firing in their direction but as they got closer, he could see that they didn't have heads.

"Decaps," Al said. "Robotic soldiers."

There was an explosion right outside their vehicle and dirt flew into the air. Several of the soldiers had managed to get to the barrier and were placing discs the size of Frisbees on the wall. Then they all ran away from the wall and fell face down onto the ground.

"Hold on," Al said and there were several explosions all at once. When the dust cleared, Ben could see several holes in the wall big enough to drive through and most of the robots lying on the ground.

"Let's go," Al said, and they drove to the wall and through one of the holes.

Soldiers ran through the holes and towards the arch building, firing at several robots guarding the entrance.

They drove up to the front of the building.

"Wait here for a minute," Al said. He got out and ran to one of the soldiers and said something to him, leaning in close. There was an explosion, this one pretty big, about thirty yards away.

Al came back to their vehicle.

"Come on," he shouted.

Ben got out and they ran into the Arch building. Soldiers were now standing on either side of the door guarding it.

It was quieter inside the building, and they went through a door that brought them into the empty Arch room.

"We're a little early but let's go ahead and open it."

"Al, why don't they just destroy the Arch if they think it's a threat?"

"They think it has some strategic use. And they want to keep sending Settlers back. What would people do if they didn't have that?"

Al double-checked the settings and then turned on the magnets and the floor starting vibrating. Then the blue arch started to form, and Ben saw a shape moving towards them through the arch and then Anna was standing there.

She saw Ben and Al waiting for her when she came through the Arch, and she ran to Ben and hugged him.

"Thank god," Al said and looked back at the arch.

Then, "Where's Wolfie?"

"He stayed."

"OK," Al said after a second. "You'll have to explain later."

The red emergency lights were on, and a siren was going on and off and Anna guessed the power was out and the backup power had come on.

"Al, what happened? What's happening?"

"Later," he said motioning them towards the door.

"Wait," Ben said, and he turned back to look at the arch.

A dark shape had appeared in the arch and was slowly emerging from the mist.

Ben could see it was shorter than a person and thought he could see wings and then the Pyrorapter walked out. Its head, low to the ground, was looking side to side and its mouth was open and it was hissing.

"Anna what the hell is that?" Al asked.

"Pyrorapter," she said looking back.

Al shook his head and said to one of the soldiers, "Grab that. But don't hurt it."

"We don't have much time," he said, turning towards the exit. "Follow me."

Now in the viewing room, Anna could see soldiers outside firing their guns and white headless soldiers firing and there was smoke in the air.

"Al, what the hell?" she said.

One or two of the robots fell and a soldier beside their vehicle said something into his shoulder and then waved them forward. They ran hunched over to the LTV.

Anna saw a soldier struggling to carry the Pyrorapter, which was now wrapped in a net and trying to bite the soldier, into the second LTV.

They jumped in and they drove off.

Anna looked at Ben. "Ben what on earth?"

"Things have gotten a little crazy since you left."

More machine gun fire and they drove through the front gate and onto the main road and a few minutes later they were on the highway. There was another LTV in front of them and one behind.

"Al where are we going?" Ben asked.

"The second arch facility."

Anna looked at Ben.

Al turned to the driver. "Let's take the scenic route," he said, and they exited off the highway. A few minutes later, they turned down a two-lane road, which after a few miles was unpaved. On either side there was barbed wire strung between wooden posts and a few fields with something growing in them, maybe corn. There was an old barn on top of a hill. They drove about ten miles and then slowed down and turned into a driveway. At the end of the driveway, there was a gate, and a soldier was standing in front of the gate. They stopped and the soldier looked into the car. "Sir," he said and then opened the gate and they drove through.

At the end of the drive there was a long building made of cinder blocks with a corrugated metal roof that had spots of rust. They stopped in front of the building and the other LTVs stopped on either side of them, dust settling around them.

"Ben," Al said.

Ben looked at him.

"One thing. We've brought your mom here."

"Sue is here too," he added looking at Anna. "And Sam."

"Is she better?" Ben asked.

Al shook his head and Ben nodded.

One of the other drivers got out and walked over to Al's side of the car.

Al rolled down the window. "Anything?"

"No. I think we're good."

"Alright. Let's get out."

"Al, there's another arch in there?" Anna asked

"Yep."

"How?"

"We've been building it for about three months and will finish today. We had to divert Qweb for a little while to finish." He looked at Ben.

"Have you tried it out?"

"Kind of. We know it works. We'll stay here tonight. There's a few bedrooms. Nothing fancy. And a kitchen," he said walking towards the building.

Anna and Ben followed. Anna heard what sounded like a chicken and turned to see a white hen scratching in the dirt by a smaller building.

When they went in Sue walked over and hugged Anna and then looked at Ben.

"She's in there," she said, and Ben went in, and his mother was asleep. He came back out and stood by Anna.

There was another man sitting at the table. Anna thought he looked familiar and tried to place him. Then she remembered.

"You're the man I saw on TV. Arrested for being Ask." And she looked at Al.

"Let's rest for a bit," Al said. "Then we'll have something to eat and talk."

Anna asked Al where they should stay, and he indicated one of the rooms and she and Ben took their bags into the room and shut the door. They dropped their bags on the ground and kissed.

"Anna I was so worried about you. When you didn't come back the first time."

"You and me both," she said.

They lay down on the bed.

"What happened?" Ben asked and she told him about the Pleistocene, the mammoths and Neanderthals, and he listened intently.

"Anna that's amazing."

Then she told him about the Cretaceous and the dinosaurs and about Wolfie's ankle and how he had decided to stay but how she thought they would see him again.

"I hope so," he said after about a minute.

Then they both dozed off.

A knock on the door woke them up. "Anna? Ben?" It was Al. "Meet in a few minutes?"

A little later, they were sitting at the table drinking coffee.

"Anna you've had a busy few weeks," Al said.

Anna nodded. She told him a version of what she had told Ben and what had happened to Wolfie.

He nodded.

"Do you two think you could do one more thing?"

"Like what?"

"We need to go back in time. But not that long ago. Eighteen Hundred."

"Why?"

"We want to try to change something."

"What?"

"Let's let my friend here explain," he said, gesturing to the man that Anna had recognized.

"Hi," he said. "My name's Stewart. And yes, I am part of the Ask. As you know, we've been advocating to go back to a recent time and try to stop certain events from happening that have led to the situation we're in. A situation which I think most would agree is not great."

"We've heard you want to go back in time and kill someone. That you have a hit list of people in the past you want to go back and kill," Anna said.

"We don't want to kill anyone," he said. "We want to go back and persuade someone. To stop what they're doing before things get too far."

"Stop who? From doing what?"

"Well, you probably know key events that we've talked about have to do with early advancements in computer science and AI. And the industrial revolution."

Anna nodded.

"Well we've thought about it a lot. And we think taking everything into consideration that the one person who it could make the biggest difference to talk to is James Watt."

"Why James Watt?"

"Well, prior to Watt's improvements to the steam engine in the late eighteenth century, the engines were very inefficient and not good for much. They were used primarily to run pumps. To remove water from mines. Copper and Tin mines."

Anna nodded slowly, remembering the exhibits at the Science Museum.

"Watt did two things. Invented a condenser for the steam so that energy wasn't wasted after each cycle. Also he developed a way that the engines could be used in mills, textile and so on, not just for pumps."

"Watt is really the father of the industrial revolution," Anna said.

"Yes," Stewart said. "And of course they needed coal to produce the steam. With the boiler. By eighteen forty, industry in cities like Birmingham were dependent on the engines. Ironworks and brickworks. But by then the air pollution was obviously a problem. The amount of soot and air pollution at the time gave that area of the country a new name. Black Country."

"The peppered moth," Anna said.

"Yes, in eighteen eleven most of those moths were white. But by eighteen forty-seven, in Manchester, most were black, had evolved because of the black trees. Again, the pollution."

"So by then they knew, or should have known there was a problem," Ben said.

"Yes, but greed and profit can allow people to look the other way."

"And even by eighteen eleven," he continued, "it was obvious what the human cost to these changes were. Fewer jobs, lower wages. A group of people began raiding the mills, destroying the looms, other machines."

"The Luddites," Al said.

"Being a Luddite. You could be arrested, sent to prison, hanged. The government sent more than twelve thousand soldiers to stop them."

"The government was protecting the industry," Ben said.

"Sound familiar? Industry was behind the expansion of the British Empire."

"Which began to dissolve in the middle of the twentieth century," Al said.

"Worlds on worlds are rolling ever from creation to decay," Anna said.

"Wouldn't eighteen hundred then be too late?" Ben asked.

"Not at all. Steam power was replaced with electric power, but the first of the coal-driven plants to produce electricity didn't even appear here until the late nineteenth century."

"How do you think we can help?" Anna asked.

"We want you to go back," Al said.

"You want us to go back to eighteen hundred and talk to James Watt? Why us?"

"Well, you're familiar with the time period."

"The Romantic period," Anna nodded.

"And you've already travelled to two different time periods. And we don't think you should go alone." He looked at Ben.

"What would we say to him? That we're here from the future and he needs to stop everyone from using steam engines because they're going to destroy the world?"

"Basically, yes. But Watt is an inventor, a visionary. We need to give him an alternative."

"Like what?"

"The first battery was invented in eighteen hundred. Alessandro Volta."

"Voltaic pile," Ben said.

"Yes. Copper and Zinc. An electric current between two wires. And by eighteen eighty-seven a wind turbine had been invented in Scotland to produce electricity."

"OK so we're supposed to go back and convince Watt that the steam engine, coal, that's not the right direction."

"Yes, basically."

"But wind power? And batteries? Batteries are part of the problem."

"We think if we can slow the early use of fossil fuels and steam engines we can slow and limit the expansion of industrialization. Battery technology was developed to fill the huge need after fossil fuels were exhausted. If industrialization never occurred to the extent it did, people would be less dependent on it. Imagine, for example, a world without cars."

Anna nodded.

"We think there is also another line of argument to be made with Watt. Watt was a Deist. So had a spiritual inclination. Nature as god sort of thing."

"This I can work with," Anna said. "So where are we going?"

"Birmingham. Doldowlod actually. A small village in Wales."

"Doldowlod."

"About sixty miles from Birmingham. Watt bought an estate there. Retired there."

"Why not earlier?" Anna asked.

"The Arch likes whole numbers and seventeen hundred is too early, nothing had really happened by then."

"When would we go?"

"As soon as possible," Al said, "but you probably need some rest. Tomorrow?"

It was starting to get dark out and Anna and Ben walked outside. The sun was setting, and the dust had given the sky orange and purple colors. They heard a horse in the outbuilding where they had seen the chicken earlier and walked over there and nodded at a soldier standing nearby. The horse had its head out of the stall and Anna rubbed its face.

"What do you think?" she asked.

"I think we should go."

They sat and watched the sun set and listened to the sound of a cricket then walked back to the arch building.

Al was sitting at the table.

"Al," Anna said, "what happened to the dinosaur that came through with me?"

"It's safe. We're going to send it back."

Anna nodded.

"Hungry?" Al asked.

"Starving," Anna said.

Al brought over two plates and set them on the table, and they ate.

They walked into the arch room and saw that the arch was smaller than the one at the arch facility. The magnets were the same, the ribbed boxes and towers and glass pieces, but the magnets were closer together. They stood looking at it for a few minutes and then went back into the other room.

Ben went in to sit with his mother and Al came in.

"Al, do you think if we go back and change something, that…"

"It's possible. We don't know."

Ben nodded and then he and Anna went into their room.

The next morning Al was sitting at the table looking at some papers. Anna sat down next to Al and Ben poured two cups of coffee and set them on the table and sat down. There were eggs and toast on the table, and he put some on two plates and gave one to Anna.

"How are you feeling?" Al asked.

"Not bad, considering," Anna said.

"Will you be ready to go in about half an hour?"

"I think so." And Ben nodded.

"We have some clothes you can change into. To help you fit in," Al said handing them a bag. They went into the room to change.

Anna walked out wearing a loose white dress cinched at the waist and a purple scarf over her shoulders.

"It looks like a nightgown," she said.

Ben was wearing a brown suit with a vest and white shirt decorated with frills. "Kind of frilly," he said. "Are you sure people dressed like this?"

"If they figure out what we're doing, could they send someone back too? To try to stop us?" Anna asked.

"It's a possibility but we have a head start. You'll need to be careful."

"How long will we have?"

"You'll have a week."

"It was a lot harder to get around back then," Anna said.

"OK. Two weeks. Wherever you come out, be back there in fourteen days."

"Here," he said, handing Anna a small bag. "You'll need these too."

She looked inside the bag and took out a few silver coins.

"That one's a shilling and that one's a pound," he said pointing at two of the coins.

"We're going to send you back to Doldowlod House and hope that Watt is there. You'll be in Wales, in the Wye River Valley."

Anna looked at Al. "Wye River Valley?" she said smiling.

Ben went into the room where his mother was sleeping and held her hand for a minute and then walked back to where Al and Anna were waiting.

They went into the arch room and Al turned on the magnets. There was a slight vibration in the floor and a blue arch began to form between the magnets. Anna and Ben looked back at Al and Sue who were both in the room and then walked towards the arch.

Chapter 34

A few seconds later, they were walking in a beautiful valley next to a river.

"The River Wye," Anna said. They could hear the river. "Its soft, inland murmur."

It was beautiful. The river flowed softly beside them and there was a small robin singing in a tree. Green and reddish-brown trees were on either side of the bank. In the distance, they saw a white mansion and looming above it, an imposing fell covered in green and rust colored plants.

"That must be it," Anna said. "Doldowlod." And they started walking along the river towards the house. Soon they were walking on a gravel path leading to the house through flowerbeds planted with lilies, roses and foxglove. The house was white and very large with many small windows and a single, large arched door. They walked up to the door and looked at each other and then Anna knocked. About fifteen seconds later the door opened and a man wearing a black coat with a long tail and a white bow tie stepped out.

"Yes?" he said.

"Um. We're here to see Mr. Watt. Please." Anna said and Ben nodded.

The Bulter didn't say anything for a few seconds and then said, "Please come in," indicating the way with his hand and they walked in. He shut the door behind him and then said, "If you'd like to just wait in here." He held his hand out towards an open door and they walked into a large drawing room. The room had red carpet and green walls and there were several paintings on the wall. Portraits and paintings of horses. In one painting, a man was riding a black horse. In another, a brown horse was standing, stiffly, covered in a green blanket. A tall grandfather clock ticked softly.

"Should we stand or sit?" Ben asked.

They both shrugged and then sat down on a red couch. A few minutes later, a woman came in.

"Hello," she said. "I'm Mrs. Watt. Ann."

Ben and Anna stood up.

"I'm Ben."

"I'm Anna. Pleased to meet you."

"You wish to see Mr. Watt?"

"Yes," Anna said.

The butler returned and set a tray on a small table and turned and walked out.

"Tea?" she said and picked up a white teapot.

"Thank you," Anna said.

The woman poured two cups of tea and handed one to Anna and one to Ben and then motioned for them to sit back down on the couch and then she sat in an armchair.

"I hope you haven't come far," she said, and Anna looked at Ben. "I'm afraid Mr. Watt is not here."

Ben and Anna looked at each other again and then looked down at their teacups.

"He is in Birmingham."

They both looked up.

"There is a full moon tomorrow night, and he is in Birmingham for a meeting of his Lunar Society." A small collie came into the room and sat beside the armchair and the woman reached down to pet it.

"How long will he be there?" Anna asked.

"Probably for a fortnight."

Ben looked at Anna who said, "Two weeks."

"Can we go there?" Anna asked. "I mean would it be difficult to get there?"

Mrs. Watt looked at them.

"You want to go to Birmingham?"

"Yes, to see Mr. Watt."

"You could probably go by carrier wagon but not until tomorrow. You would be welcome to stay here tonight."

"That would be wonderful," Anna said.

The butler returned and Mrs. Watt said, "Mr. Williams will show you to your guest room."

"Thank you," Ben and Anna said, standing up.

"Dinner will be at six o'clock," Mrs. Watt said as they left the room.

They followed the butler, who was carrying their bags, up the stairs, and he stopped outside of a room, and they went in.

"Thank you," Anna said as he set their bags down. Ben reached into his pockets wondering if he should give the butler a tip, but the butler turned and walked out of the room.

The room had elaborate flowered wallpaper and a fireplace and a window looking over the river towards the fell.

The sat on the bed for a few minutes and then Anna said, "Let's go for a walk."

They walked along the river and Anna said, "Living here in the Wye Valley, I wonder if Watt has read Tintern Abbey."

"Could he have?"

"It was published in the first edition of Lyrical Ballads in seventeen ninety-eight. So he could have."

They walked for about an hour and saw several foxes and a hare. Trees overhung the river and robins sang from the branches. Their constant companion was the musical murmur of the river. On their walk back to the house, Anna was thinking but didn't say much.

They went up to their room and washed, and then went down to the dining room for dinner. In the dining room, a long table with twelve chairs sat on a beautiful red rug. Mrs. Watt was already seated and there was a young man sitting at the table also.

"This is my son, James Watt Jr." Mrs. Watt said, and the young man stood up.

"A pleasure," he said and then sat back down.

Anna thought she had read about James Watt Jr. and then remembered. Like Wordsworth, he had travelled through France near the beginning of the French Revolution. And like Wordsworth was sympathetic to the revolution. This was a dangerous course to follow, and he eventually softened on these ideas and also gave up his plans to emigrate to America.

"You as well," Anna said.

"Nice to meet you," Ben said shaking his hand.

Two servers came into the room wearing black coats and white gloves, one carrying a silver tray. The other was holding a wine bottle and he filled Anna's and Ben's glasses. The man with the tray served them some vegetables and some meat, which Anna thought was probably partridge.

"Tell me," said James, "have you come far to visit my father?"

"We came from London," Anna said after a few seconds.

"You've come a long way. Are you interested in steam engines?" James asked, taking a bite of his partridge.

"Yes. We are," Anna said.

"My mother says you are travelling to Birmingham tomorrow. You will certainly see the impact of my father's steam engines there."

"I'm certain," Anna said.

After dinner, they walked into the parlor.

"Would you like to play a game of whist?" James said, picking up a deck of cards.

"You may need to remind us of the rules," Ben said as they all sat down at a card table and James began dealing cards until all but one of the cards had been dealt and then placed the last card in the center of the table.

"Trump card," he said.

Ben and Ann were partners, and he played a card. Anna then played a card followed by Ann and James. Ben and Ann won the first trick and James stood up and walked over to a small table, returning with a bottle and four glasses.

"Brandy?" he asked and poured each of them some brandy then sat down again.

When the game was over, Anna and James had the most points and won. Ben and Anna thanked them for dinner and said they were going to their room. When they returned to their room there was a fire burning in the fireplace and it was raining outside, and they went to bed.

"Ever played whist before?" Ben asked.

"No. But now we have a game for the next time we're on a submarine," Anna said smiling.

The next morning, the butler had left a tray of tea outside of the door along with a few pastries and they drank the tea while getting ready to leave. When they went downstairs, Mrs. Watt was there and told them the wagon would be there in a few minutes and they could wait in the drawing room. They sat down and a few minutes later heard the sound of horses' hooves on the gravel outside.

There were two seats behind the driver, and the butler put their bags there and Anna and Ben climbed up and sat down. The wagon was carrying several barrels and some brown sacks and a large pile of corn. It had rained most of the night and the four horses' legs were muddy up to their fetlocks. Anna and Ben thanked Mrs. Watt and Anna asked her where the Lunar Society would meet.

"Soho House," she said, and then the driver flicked the reins and the carriage started moving. The trip to Birmingham took seven hours. Rain during the night had made the road muddy and it was almost impassible in areas. Once, the horses sank in the mud almost to their bellies, and everyone got off the carriage and the driver walked in front of the horses, gently leading them out of the mire. In places where the road wasn't muddy, it was so bumpy that Anna thought her ribs would break. Anna was starting to think they were never going to get to Birmingham and then the city came into view in the distance.

"Thank god," she said.

They saw the spire of the cathedral and then the tall factory smokestacks and the smoke coming out of them. They began to pass other carriages and people walking and then they were in the town center. The streets were crowded with merchants and cabs pulled by horses and the driver said, "This is where we stop."

Anna and Ben got down from the carriage, barely able to walk, and set down their bags. The sidewalk was even more crowded than the streets. Stalls were selling fruit and vegetables and clothing. Meat hung in the window of a butcher shop with a red awning. Men in suits carrying canes passed, arm in arm, with women wearing dresses.

"Soho House," Ben said, and they wondered how they would get there.

A policeman walked by wearing a long brass-buttoned coat and tall hat and Anna said, "Excuse me sir."

The policeman stopped. "Ma'am?"

"Can you tell us please how to get to Soho House?"

"Soho house? Mr. Boulton's house?"

"Yes sir."

The policeman looked at her curiously and hailed a passing cab.

"These two would like to go to Soho house."

"Certainly. Climb up," the cab driver said.

The two horses started trotting and the driver narrowly missed running over a woman and child crossing the street. They followed closely behind another cab and passed the cathedral and a few minutes later one of the factories with its tall smokestacks. Inside they could see workers through the row of windows. Then they stopped in front of a white house, similar to but smaller than the house they had left that morning.

"Soho house," the driver said. Anna thanked him and handed him one of the Shilling coins and they stepped off onto the ground.

The cab driver drove off looking at the coin.

"Was that too much?" Anna said and just then the door of the house opened.

A man with white hair and wearing a blue coat walked out. Ben thought he looked like George Washington.

"Hello," he said. "Can I help you?"

"Mr. Watt?" Anna said.

"Hardly," the man said laughing. "Matthew Boulton at your service. How can I help you?"

"We're here to see Mr. Watt," Anna said.

"In that case you'd better come in," he said and gestured into the house with his arm.

They stepped inside and could hear voices talking and laughing from the drawing room.

"In there," Mr. Boulton said.

In the drawing room, about a dozen men were talking, laughing and holding short-stemmed glasses.

"Brandy?" a butler holding a tray asked.

"Yes please," Ben said enthusiastically, and the butler handed them each a glass.

Mr. Boulton went over to talk to one of the other men who was dressed similarly but was slightly thinner and the man walked over.

"I'm James Watt," he said.

"Anna," said Anna. "It's a pleasure to meet you."

"Ben."

"What is it you wish to see me about?"

"Um. We'd like to talk with you about the steam engine, sir," Anna said.

"Indeed," he said. "Well, the formal meeting, as it were, of our little Lunar Society has concluded. But perhaps you would like to join us for dinner."

"That would be wonderful," Anna said.

"In the meantime, allow me introduce a few of the other members of our group. Mr. Boulton you have already met," he said.

"That gentleman," he said gesturing to a tall, corpulent man in a brown suit, "is Erasmus Darwin," and the man bowed. "That is the eminent Josiah Wedgewood," he said indicating a smiling man in a tall white collar.

"Interesting that both of Charles Darwin's grandparents are here," Anna said to Ben.

"Not to mention that we're here," Ben said.

They could hear that two men in a corner were having a discussion about Napoleon and two men seated were discussing electricity and Leyden jars, used to store electrical charges.

A butler walked in to indicate that dinner was about to be served and everyone walked into the dining room. The dining room was very large, and the table had seats for twenty people. All of the men sat down and then Anna and Ben sat and the servers began serving the food. They served a clear soup, followed by fish and vegetables, and poured everyone glasses of white wine.

The conversation was lively and wide-ranging as Anna expected it would be. The men talked about manufacturing, natural history, medicine and the war with France. Josiah Wedgwood discussed the implementation of the steam engine of Watt and Boulton into his pottery factories in Staffordshire.

Dinner had ended and the servers were pouring more wine and Anna found the courage to talk to Mr. Watt. "Excuse me, Mr. Watt. Do you think that there may be any ill effects of the use of your steam engines in manufacturing?"

"No," he said after a few seconds. "To what do you refer?"

"Well, the coal. Burning the coal does produce a lot of smoke. It blackens the air. Makes it hard to breathe." She paused. "It could get worse."

"I hardly think that can turn into a serious problem," he said, furrowing his brow.

"What if there were other sources of power sir, for factories?"

"Are there?"

"There are, sir."

"Well, I should like to hear about these someday," he said.

"Allesandra Volta, Sir."

He nodded then turned to talk to the man sitting beside him.

"Well that wasn't very convincing," she said to Ben.

After dinner, the group moved into the sitting room and Brandy was served. Several men sat down at a table and began playing cards. Several others were playing billiards. Anna saw that Watt was standing by himself and walked over to him.

"Sir," she said, "We went first to Doldowlod yesterday to find you."

"My country estate?" he said.

"Yes sir. Mrs. Watt was very gracious and allowed us to stay the night."

He nodded and she continued, "Your house is very nice sir and in a beautiful setting."

"Yes, the Wye Valley is very lovely. I find the countryside there to be very restorative."

"Sir, are you familiar with the book of poems Lyrical Ballads."

"Yes, the slim volume from two years ago. By the young poet Wordsworth although the book I believe was published anonymously."

"Yes sir."

"An admirable effort."

"Are you familiar with the poem Tintern Abbey?"

"Yes. I have read it several times. A presence, I believe it reads, that disturbs me with the joy of elevated thought, a sense sublime of something far more deeply interfused." He paused. "That describes, I believe," he said carefully, "what I believe to be the relationship between nature and the Creator."

"Sir, what if the steam engine, and the coal mining and burning of coal, all of that, were to put nature, the nature that you admire there, in jeopardy?" Anna said quickly.

"Well, that would be a most unfortunate consequence," he said thoughtfully and paused to look out the window. "Now you will excuse me," he said and joined two men talking by the window.

"Ben," Anna said. "I think I know where we have to go."

"Where's that?"

"The Lake District."

They found Mr. Boulton and thanked him for his hospitality and then the butler showed them the way out. The full moon outside illuminated the ground and they walked back to an inn they had seen earlier, The Black Eagle, to see if there were a room available for the night. The clock tower told them that it was ten o'clock and a stray cat startled them as it ran in front of them.

"Ben," Anna said as they were walking up to the door of the inn, "does anything look odd to you about that man?" She nodded towards a man standing on the other side of the street.

"Why?"

"Well I think I may have seen him earlier today, when we were walking up to Mr. Boulton's house."

"His clothes maybe seem a little unusual."

"That's what I was thinking."

They went into the inn and got a room and saw that the bar was still open.

"I guess it's still kind of early," Ben said, and they went up to the bar and ordered two beers.

"Two ales?" the bartender said.

Anna nodded yes and they paid and sat down at a table.

"Lake District," Ben said. "Wordsworth?"

"Yes."

Most of the men in the bar were laborers and most were complaining about the working conditions and low wages in the factories. Most had also had a lot to drink, and some were shouting rather than talking.

"Watt seems to understand what Wordsworth is saying about nature. Nature is important to him. I'm thinking if we can convince Wordsworth about the threats of the steam engine and industrialization, maybe he can convince Watt."

"Who do you think that man is? Outside." Ben asked

"I don't know. Al did say it was possible that someone might try to stop us. But they may not know what we're doing."

"He may be surprised that we're going to the Lake District."

"Maybe he won't have to know."

The talking in the bar had gotten louder and two of the men were shouting, and Ben suggested maybe they go up to their room.

On their way up they stopped to talk to the man at the desk and asked how they might get to the Lake District. The man thought for a minute. "Well, it will take you a few days. You could get a coach to Manchester and then the mail coach to Lancaster and from there Kendal. Is that close to where you want to go."

"Yes," Anna said. "Where would we get a coach to Manchester?"

"There's one that leaves from the main station on the high street in the morning. You'll have to get there early."

"Thank you," Ben said, and they walked up to their room.

"Ben," Anna said when they were lying in bed. "Have you thought about what might happen if we're successful. I mean to us. If we do manage to stop the industrial revolution. And so maybe the technological revolution?"

"I have thought about it."

"If the arch never gets invented."

"We might not be able to go back."

"That's what I was thinking."

"Well you were going to settle anyway. In the Pleistocene. Maybe this is better than the Pleistocene."

"Maybe. But I wouldn't have wanted to settle if things hadn't gotten so bad. And there's your mother."

"If we hadn't tried."

Anna nodded.

"There's another possibility," she said.

Ben looked at her.

"We slow it down. It happens but happens differently. It's more. Focused. People realize there can be too much of a good thing."

"Maybe the benefits."

Anna nodded.

"And we can still get back."

They woke early the next morning and packed their bags. They asked the man at the desk if there were another door they could use to leave.

"There's a service entrance through the kitchen. It puts you out behind the inn. You could use that if you wanted to."

A few minutes later, they were at the main carriage station. They found the mail coach to Manchester and paid the driver and got into the carriage with their bags. There were two other people in the carriage, a woman and her child going to visit their family in Manchester. Ben and Anna hadn't seen the man from yesterday and sat back in their chairs to stay away from the window. The coach pulled away and soon they were out of the town. The road was much better than the road into town yesterday and the coach was more comfortable. Ben had taken some rolls from the inn, and they ate those. The countryside was flat and green with plots of farmland and orchards.

"Their unripe fruits," Anna said. "Clad in one green hue, they lose themselves mid groves and copses."

After about two hours, they stopped to water the horses in the market town of Stafford and they stepped out of the carriage.

"How much longer till Manchester?" Anna asked the driver.

"About four hours," he said. "If we're lucky."

Ben pointed to a castle on a hill and went into a shop to buy some lunch for them and came out with some cold pork and two apples. Anna went into a bookshop and came back with a copy of "The Tempest." They climbed back into the carriage, and they started moving again.

Ben tried to nap and Anna read Shakespeare and a few hours later Manchester came into view. The most prominent feature was the tall smokestacks pouring out black smoke from the cotton mills, many more than in Birmingham and as they got closer, they could see the three and four-story factories.

A few years ago, Anna thought, the tallest thing in town would have been the church.

The carriage stopped in the busy city center and they stepped off. The streets were more crowded than in Birmingham and they quickly stepped out of the way of a carriage and looked for an inn to get a room for the night. They walked into The Crown and paid for their room then went into the dining room. Ben brought two beers back to the table and they sat and looked out the window at the crowded streets.

"How could they not see what was happening?" Anna asked.

Ben shook his head.

A waiter brought them their dinners, roast beef and vegetables, and they ate.

A man sitting near the fireplace was playing a tune on a fiddle.

"I think better if we stay inside tonight," Ben said, thinking about the man they had seen earlier, and Anna agreed.

They finished their beers and went up to their room on the third floor. They were tired from the coach ride and dropped their luggage on the floor and got in bed.

The next morning, they put a few things back in their bags and went downstairs. They had porridge for breakfast.

"People actually eat porridge," Ben said. "It's not bad."

They went outside and got back in the coach and were now the only two in the carriage and Anna read aloud from the Tempest as they rode. They made a stop in Lancaster and changed out one of the horses and a few hours later arrived in the market town of Kendal.

They stepped off the carriage and could see the rising fells in the distance, and clouds of various colors covering some of the highest points. Anna smiled. It was evening and she wasn't sure they should try to make it to Grasmere or wait until tomorrow.

"We can probably get a coach to Ambleside, but we may end up walking from there," she said and so they decided to stay the night in Kendal.

They got a room at the Golden Lion and ate dinner. They thought it was unlikely that anyone had followed them this far so decided to take a walk after dinner. They walked up the hill to the ruins of the castle and walked over the bridge across the river. The sun was setting, and the clouds were orange and yellow and they watched these for a few minutes and then walked back to the inn.

The market the next morning was busy with people selling plants, fruits and vegetables and clothing. Ben bought some apples and Anna bought a hat. They found the mail coach to take them to Ambleside and got into the carriage. As they rode, a fell came into view on their right, covered in grass and wildflowers and about ten minutes later, they could see the town of Ambleside ahead. The coach stopped in town, and they got off and could see Lake Windermere, dark blue and calm and sparkling in the morning light. They could see a few sailboats and people in rowboats.

Anna smiled. "Isn't it beautiful?" she said. "I think the walk to Grasmere will take about an hour."

They started walking northwest from Ambleside. They were walking through a valley and there were green fields with sheep on either side. Fells rose up on their right, green and red-brown from the bracken. The sun was behind them as they walked, and the tops of the mountains were bright with the sunlight.

"Coffin route," Anna said.

To the left beyond Grasmere they could see Silver How and to the North the tall peak of Helvellyn. Soon they passed Rydal Lake on their left and they could see Grasmere ahead, beautiful and calm, and the church was visible. Everything was green and overflowing with life. There was birdsong and a cormorant struggled to free itself from the water. Now they were walking along the bank of Grasmere Lake and Anna said Dove Cottage was just ahead.

The cottage was white and partly covered in ivy and a thin line of smoke was coming out of the chimney. There was a low rock wall surrounding the cottage and they walked up to the gate. They turned to look at the sparkling waters of the lake and then opened the gate and walked up to the door and knocked. A few seconds later, a woman opened the door. The woman had brown hair that was tied up in the back and was wearing a white dress and holding a purple blanket.

"Yes," she said, looking first at Anna then at Ben. "Can I help you?"

"Dorothy. Um. Ms. Wordsworth?" Anna said.

"Yes."

"I'm Anna. And this is Ben," Anna said with difficulty. "We've come from Birmingham. To see Mr. Wordsworth."

Dorothy looked at them. "I'm afraid he isn't home," she said. "He's walked to Keswick."

She could see the disappointment on Anna's face and added, "He'll be back this evening. If you'd like to wait."

"That would be wonderful thank you," Anna said, and Dorothy opened the door for them to go in. They walked in and she closed the door behind them. They were in the sitting room and there was a couch and rocking chair in front of the fireplace. Outside a coach drove past the window.

"Would you like some tea?" Dorothy asked, walking over to the fireplace. "And I've just made some pies."

"Yes please. If it's not too much trouble," Anna said.

Dorothy walked out of the room and a few minutes later she brought in a tray with the tea and pies set it on the table and they all sat down at the small table. Light from one window dimly lit the room and there was a fire in the fireplace.

"You have come from Birmingham?"

"Yes ma'am we were there to see Mr. Watt."

"And you've come here to see Mr. Wordsworth?"

"Yes. We are. Admirers of his poetry."

Dorothy nodded.

They drank their tea and ate the pies. Anna looked around the cottage and smiled.

A few minutes later, Dorothy stood up. "You will please excuse me," she said. "I am feeling a bit unwell today and must lie down. Please feel free to enjoy the garden. I have just planted some periwinkles and geraniums."

Anna looked out the window at the garden.

"The guest room is not in use if you would like to stay the night."

Anna's eyes widened. "Of course," she said excitedly.

"Now if you will excuse me," she said, walking out of the room.

Ben and Anna walked outside into the garden. There was a walkway and many colorful flowers: Red and white geraniums and blue periwinkles. Foxglove and primrose. There was also a vegetable garden with radishes and peas.

They walked up a path and sat down on a bench and Ben looked up at the blue sky and then at the lake. A pair of swans floated near a small island in the middle of the lake. "I wonder how things are going back home?" Ben said.

"Hopefully all hell isn't breaking loose," Anna said.

They sat enjoying the garden, and Anna read her book and an hour later, they heard the door open and close.

"Dorothy," they heard a voice say excitedly. "I've found a glow worm!"

Dorothy and a man walked into the garden. The man was wearing a brown jacket and striped pants.

"I found it on the walk home and have wrapped it in these leaves. I shall put it under the cherry tree and hope that it will glow tonight so you may see it!"

He had a high forehead and prominent nose and an inclination to laughter about his mouth. His gait was animated, and he had a fire in his eyes as if he saw something in objects more than the outward appearance.

Then he seemed to see Ben and Anna for the first time. "Hello," he said in a strong accent. "William Wordsworth."

Ben and Anna stood up.

"Hello, sir," Anna said excitedly. "I'm Anna and this is Ben."

"I see you are reading Shakespeare," he said, pointing to Anna's book and smiling.

"They've come from Birmingham to see you, William," Dorothy said. "I've asked them to stay the night."

"That sounds like a wonderful idea," he said and turned to them. "The chimney does not draw well upstairs and so it can be smoky, but it is warm, and you will probably not need a fire tonight. Now if you will excuse me. We can talk later."

He turned to Dorothy. "I've just received by post the proofs of my book from Cottle. I shall be outside reading them." He nodded to Ben and Anna and hurried back into the house.

"You are welcome to join us for dinner this evening," Dorothy said. "At six o'clock."

They took a short walk around town and along the lake and watched the swallows flying across the surface of the water. On the way back to the cottage they passed a blind man in the road, walking with two sticks and driving a bull and a cow in the road. When they got back to the cottage, Dorothy was putting plates on the table and William was reading by the fire.

A few minutes later, they all sat down at the table and Dorothy handed Anna a plate.

"Boiled pike," she said. "I caught it yesterday. Seven and a half pounds." Then she passed her a bowl of potatoes.

"The second edition of William's book, Lyrical Ballads, is to be published soon." Dorothy said.

"I am a great admirer of the poems in your book sir. Especially Tintern Abbey."

"Oh?" he said, looking at Anna.

"And the other poems as well. Your sympathy for poor rustic people and demonstration of their worth. It's wonderful."

He nodded. "We cannot expose only the best part of their lives, concealing their miseries. We must show their feelings and sufferings." He stood and walked to the fireplace and put several pieces of coal on the fire. Then he turned back to them. "Indeed, in this life the essential passions are most easily seen."

"I met Mr. Fisher in the road today on the other side of Rydall," Dorothy said, looking at William. "He talked about the alteration in the times and observed that in a short time there would be only two ranks of people, the very rich and the very poor. Those with small estates, he said, are forced to sell, and all the land goes into one hand."

"Yes, the manners of the rich," William said, nodding. "Avarice and inordinate desires."

I also met a leech gatherer walking to Loughrigg Tarn," Dorothy continued. "He said he was of Scotch parents but had been born in the army. He and his wife had ten children and all but one of these are dead. His trade is gathering leeches, but now they are scarce and hard to find so he lives by begging. He was on his way to Carlisle." William listened as she spoke.

After they had eaten, they talked about ideas in William's longer preface to the second edition of his book, about Shakespeare and Milton and about Coleridge's visit. He then read from a poem he was working on, the Sheepfold. Anna sat listening, barely breathing and Ben watched her.

William stood up and carried some dishes from the table into the kitchen and washed them. Then he turned to Ben and Anna. "I have walked sixteen miles today and have managed to tire myself," he said. "If you will excuse me, I must retire. I am walking tomorrow if you would care to join me."

"Yes sir. Thank you," Anna said.

He bowed slightly and left the room.

Anna and Ben told Dorothy goodnight and went upstairs.

"Ben, this is."

He looked over and smiled. "This must be a dream come true for you."

Outside the window, they could see a beautiful yellow moon over the lake.

Chapter 35

Al and Sue were sitting in the dark listening to distant explosions. They had been hearing them for three days now and Al thought they were getting closer.

"We may not have much longer," he said.

"What does that mean?" Sue asked.

"Means we may have to leave."

The night before there was an explosion that Al said was probably a tactical nuke, and there was a mushroom cloud and Al said they probably got the Arch.

"They don't care if people can't go back?" Sue asked.

"Not anymore."

"If they completely destroy the surface no one's going to be able to live here."

"No one's going to be able to live here anyway."

"Where will they live?"

"Underwater."

"You think they're planning on living underwater? All the time?"

"I think so."

There was a bigger explosion. This one closer and Al's phone rang and he put it on speaker.

"C1 headed your way. Fifteen minutes."

"We've got to go," he said.

"Where?"

"Anywhere else."

“What’s a C1?”

“Big ass drone. Big ass bomb. I think they know where we are.”

“What about the arch? How will we get Anna and Ben back?”

“We have one more.”

“Another arch?”

“A portable one. Let’s go.”

Beth was sitting in a wheelchair, and Sue went over to her and outside they heard the sound of a helicopter.

A soldier opened the door and Sue pushed the wheelchair outside. There was a helicopter outside and Al ran over to talk to the pilot and then motioned for them. They helped Beth into the helicopter and then Sam and then they climbed in. The helicopter had six seats near the front and in the back were two large crates and a vehicle next to several seated soldiers.

The pilot looked back, and Al gave him a thumbs up and they took off.

“Where are we going?” Sue asked

“Not sure yet.” Al replied.

They were flying west and a few minutes later saw a bright flash and then heard the explosion from the direction they had come.

“That’s our arch,” Al said.

Al went to talk to the pilot who nodded his head and the helicopter banked and they were flying south.

Now they were flying over some low mountains and the sun was coming up. There were clouds covering the tops of the mountains which they could see, blue and light blue, fading in the distance.

“The Smoky Mountains,” Al said.

They flew low to avoid detection and an hour later landed in a clearing, which years ago had been covered in birch and maple trees but was now barren from the heat and the fires from the heat. They climbed out of the helicopter and helped Beth out and into her wheelchair and they walked to a wooden cabin standing near a few remaining spruce trees. Sue took Sam's hand.

"This is it," Al said. "The last place we can go."

A ramp at the back of the helicopter opened and the vehicle drove out and a forklift drove out carrying one of the crates. It set down the crate and a few minutes later came out with the other one.

"If they find us here?" Sue said.

Al didn't say anything.

"They're coming back tomorrow," Sue said.

"Let's hope."

They went inside the cabin and sat down. Al walked over to the stove and tried to find something to make coffee with.

"You and Beth can sleep there," he said, pointing to a bedroom. "I'll stay out here with Sam."

There was a fireplace and two kerosene lanterns sitting next to it.

Al made some coffee, and they went outside and sat on the porch. The soldiers were opening two smaller crates.

"Al, what are those?" Sue asked looking in the direction of the soldiers.

"Generators."

"There's no power here?"

"No."

"You're going to run the arch on generators?"

"That's the plan."

Chapter 36

The next morning William and Dorothy were up and eating breakfast.

"Tea?" Dorothy asked when she saw them.

"Yes, thank you," Anna said and Dorothy poured tea into two cups.

They sat down at the table facing the window. There was a fire in the fireplace warming the room and a small pile of coal next to the fireplace. They could see the lake out the window and there was a low cloud floating over the lake. The two swans were floating near the island in the lake. Anna took a drink of her tea and Dorothy set a plate of bread and butter on the table. Ben took two slices and buttered them and gave one to Anna and they both ate.

"There are some shoes by the door you can borrow if you'd like to," and she pointed to two pairs of leather boots.

"There's cold pork and bread here. You can take some with you," she added.

"Thank you."

William came in now in his walking coat. "Good morning!" he said.

"Good morning," Anna and Ben said.

"Are we ready?"

They walked down to the village past some cottages with the church on their right and west out of the village through a stream with bracken overhead and out into an open fellside.

They then walked along a grass path through juniper bushes and crossed a river and walked towards a hill. Now they were in a gully and walking through a path in a field and on their right, they could see Silver How and they walked towards it. As they got near the top, the path was steep and there were broken rocks that made it difficult to walk. Ben slipped and began sliding down the hill and William grabbed his hand.

"Thanks," Ben said.

A veil of clouds surrounded them. Reaching the summit, the clouds cleared, and they had a clear view of the valley. It was beautiful. They could see Grasmere Village and lake below and Helm Crag and Rydal Water in the distance.

"Earth hath nothing to show more fair," William said and they sat and rested and ate their lunch. Below they could see pastoral farms and irregular hedgerows. It began to rain on the walk back to the village and it was late afternoon, and they were very wet when they arrived back to the cottage.

Dorothy was sitting beside the fire reading Shakespeare and there was a basket of onions and carrots on the table. Ben and Anna went upstairs to change clothes.

"Anna," Ben said. "Do you think this is the best way for us to stop the Industrial Revolution?"

"I think it's our only chance," she said.

Dinner that night was boiled mutton with carrots and onions.

"What was the purpose of your visit to Birmingham?" William asked.

"We were meeting with Mr. Watt," Ben said.

"The steam engine," William said.

"Yes sir. We also met other members of his society. Mr. Wedgewood."

"A most generous man."

"And Mr. Darwin."

"A learned gentleman. I gained inspiration for one of my poems from his writings," William said, taking a bite of mutton.

Anna nodded. "It's very beautiful here, sir," she said after a minute.

"I first came to this green vale as a schoolboy," he said. "We are very fortunate to have now made our home here. The breezes that play on the water. The sunbeams, shadows, butterflies and birds."

"What do you know of Mr. Watt's steam engines sir?" Anna asked.

"I have seen the great factories that they power. And the smoke from their chimneys in Lancaster and Birmingham. It seems that the manufacturers are spreading through every part of the country. They increase the disproportion between the price of labour and that of the necessities of life. I believe that these things have weakened the bonds of domestic feeling among the poor. In some instances entirely destroyed them."

"What if I were to tell you sir, that they also threaten the beauty of areas like this, of the Lakes."

"That would be worrying indeed," he said, looking out the window.

"Sir, it may be possible to prevent that."

"How?"

"Perhaps if you could talk with Mr. Watt. Tell him your concerns."

"I hardly think he would listen to my concerns about this."

"He will sir."

"Perhaps I could also talk with his son. He and I were in France at the same time, near the beginning of the revolution," and he looked at the fire. "He has expressed a desire to visit and walk the fells. I have business in Birmingham soon. I shall make it a point to contact them."

After dinner, they were sitting by the fire.

"The old beggar stopped by today and I gave him bread and fish," Dorothy said.

"That man is a blessing," William said. "A record, a memory of all past deeds of kindness done to him by our community. We have all of us one human heart."

"Sir," Anna said, "Do you think you could read us some of your poetry?"

"There is a poem that I began during our stay in Germany."

"It was very cold, and we stayed inside, and William wrote most of the visit," Dorothy said. "We were very anxious to return home."

Anna knew that the poem that he started there would become Wordsworth's greatest poem, The Prelude.

"Coleridge went to Gottingen, and we came home as soon as we could," William added, looking at Dorothy.

He walked over to a desk and came back with a small stack of hand-written pages and sat down and began reading. "Was it for this that one, the fairest of all rivers loved to blend his murmurs with my nurse's song, and from his alder shades and rocky falls, and from his fords and shallows, sent a voice that flowed along my dreams?"

The fire had burned down, and he finished reading, "…a visible scene on which the sun is shining?" and set down the pages. Anna and Ben thanked him, tired from the walk, and said goodnight and went upstairs. It rained during the night and some water had leaked into their room. The next morning, they went downstairs and found Dorothy in the garden hanging linens. There was a basket of peas on the table.

"William has gone on horseback to Keswick," she said. "He shall return this evening with Coleridge."

Anna looked at Ben and smiled.

"I am going fishing today if you would like to join me."

"Yes, we would," said Anna.

They had tea and cakes for breakfast and then walked out with Dorothy. They walked towards Rydal and then turned south and walked to Loughrigg Tarn. The colors of the mountains were soft and rich with orange fern. Cattle were pasturing on the hill tops and sheep were bleating in lines and chains and patterns scattered over the mountains. At the tarn, they caught four pike and began the walk back to Grasmere. On the walk home, they met a man with a basket on his back, a peddler, and Dorothy talked with him for a few minutes and then they kept walking.

Soon after, they returned to the cottage and sat down in front of the fireplace. There was a commotion outside, and the door opened, and William walked in with Coleridge. Coleridge was talking animatedly as he came in. His forehead was broad and high, light as if built of ivory. The genius of his face seemed to project him into the unknown world of thought and imagination. His hair was black and glossy as a raven's and fell in smooth masses over his forehead. They all set down to dinner of roast hare and peas. Coleridge talked through most of the dinner and after dinner read aloud from Christabel. He began:

> "Is the night chilly and dark?
> The night is chilly, but not dark.
> The thin gray cloud is spread on high,
> It covers but not hides the sky."

The fire had burned down by the time Coleridge finished reading and Anna and Ben went upstairs to bed. William also went to bed and Dorothy and Coleridge stayed up late talking.

"We need to be back in four days," Anna said.

"Do you think we should leave tomorrow?" Ben asked.

"I think so."

The next morning, William and Dorothy walked with them to Ambleside, past Rydal Water, and William recited part of Peter Bell as they walked.

In Ambleside, Anna and Ben thanked the Wordsworths and boarded the mail coach for Manchester.

"Anna, we could just…"

"I know, I was thinking the same thing."

The coach became mired in mud about halfway to Manchester and they had to stay the night in the town of Preston and they were worried they might not make it back in time. That night they walked along the river and talked about how hard it was to believe that things were going to change so much. There was no rain that night and the next day they made it to Manchester where they spent the night.

They had a little time in the morning before the coach left and walked towards the factories. They stopped at a cotton mill and inside they could see a long row of women standing at mechanical looms. Thread was reaching from spools to the machines and the women, wearing aprons, were moving the frame back and forth.

"I think Marx maybe had it right," Anna said. "The worker as commodity." Ben nodded.

They walked back to the city center and boarded the coach and made it to Birmingham that night. The day before they were supposed to go to the arch.

"I hope we're not cutting it to close," Ben said.

That night they were eating dinner in the inn, and someone walked over and sat down across from them. Anna looked up and saw the man they had seen here before.

Anna stared at him. "You have to live there too, you know," she said.

"We don't exactly live in the same place."

"You mean you live underwater," Ben said.

"Whatever you're trying to do, it won't work," the man said. "Look around."

"How much is enough?" Anna asked

The man smiled. "I'm going back tomorrow. Why don't you just stay?"

"Is it possible for you people to be motivated by anything other than greed?" she said. "What about beauty? Family and friends? Love?"

"Where have you been the last few days?" he asked

They didn't say anything.

"Doesn't really matter," he said standing up. "Whatever you're trying to do, it's not going to work." He turned and walked out onto the street.

The next morning, they found a carrier wagon to take them back to Doldowlod and asked the driver to let them out about a half mile from the house. They got off and stood with their bags, watching the carriage drive away and they stood for a few more minutes listening to the birdsong. They could see the house in the distance and Ben said, "I think it's over there," pointing to a small clearing behind a group of trees.

They walked to the clearing and Anna looked up at the sun. "Maybe half an hour," she said.

They lay down on the grass, holding hands and looking up at the sky. A group of swallows flew overhead.

"Ben," she said.

"I know."

Chapter 37

Outside, in the small clearing, the soldiers had positioned the two crates about thirty feet apart from each other and were breaking them open. Sue tried to sleep but couldn't. About three in the morning, she went out into the living room and Al was sitting on the couch, and she walked over to the window. The soldiers were still working outside and had constructed two metal boxes each with a pole sticking out of the top.

"The portable arch," Al said, looking over.

"Will it work?"

"Let's hope so."

Al had made coffee and handed a cup to Sue who took it and sat down. One of the kerosene lamps was lit and he lit the other one and set it on the table.

"A few more hours," he said.

From outside, the cabin, lit only by the two kerosene lamps, glowed.

"Al, how will we know if they've succeeded?" Sue said.

"I'm not sure. We may not know until they get back."

The morning was quiet, and they went outside. They could hear a few birds singing but nothing else.

"I don't think they know where we've gone," Al said.

The soldiers were making a few last-minute adjustments to the arch and Al looked at his watch and walked over to it.

"Ten minutes," he said.

Now the soldiers started the two generators. They came on with a rumble and Al nodded.

Sue took her cup inside and put it in the sink, and looked in on Beth, who was sleeping. Then she walked out to where Al was standing, and Sam walked out onto the porch.

"Let's go ahead and turn it on," he said.

The soldiers pushed several buttons, and Al checked a reading on one of the dials and said okay, and then a soldier pulled a switch and there was a humming sound. A blue arch started to appear but then started flickering. Another blue line appeared that seemed to intersect with the first one.

"Damnit," Al said.

"What?"

"I think it's interference. The waves here must be a multiple of those from the other arch."

"What does that mean?"

"It means it's not going to work."

"Shut it down!" he yelled to one of the soldiers, and he pushed the switch up and the arches faded.

"What are we going to do?" Sue asked.

"I don't know. I don't think we can bring them back from that location."

"How can we bring them back?"

"I'm not sure. Maybe from another spot."

"But how will they know where to go?"

"There is the other site where she came out before. In the Pleistocene."

"Will they know to go there?"

"I hope so."

"When?"

"Let's try in four days."

"How long till they find us?"

"Hopefully not before then."

Chapter 38

They thought the arch would open in a few minutes and they stood up. Then they saw the air in front of them get hazy and Anna said, "That's it."

Anna started walking towards the arch, but something didn't look right and Ben grabbed her hand.

"Wait," he said.

And then they saw that there was no arch, but two lines arranged in an X shape.

"Something tells me this door might be closed," Anna said.

They stood watching it for a while, but it didn't change.

"I don't want to walk through that," Ben said. "Something must have gone wrong."

"What should we do?" Anna said.

"What would Al do?"

"Try to find a way to get us home."

They stood for a minute watching the closed arch.

"There may be another way," Anna said.

"How?"

"There is the other site. Where we came through in the Pleistocene."

"Would Al try to get us from there?"

"If this door is closed, he may expect we would try there. It's the only other spot I can think of."

"When?"

"My guess would be in two days. Two seems to be the magic number."

Ben nodded. "So we're going to London?"

"Yes. But they know where we are and probably know how long it will take us to get there. So maybe we should give them longer."

"Maybe four days?"

"That's what I was thinking."

They were able to get a ride back to Birmingham but when they got there, it was too late to begin the trip to London so they found a room for the night at The Crown. They went into the restaurant and ordered two beers and sat down by the fireplace. There were two soldiers sitting at the table next to them.

"England will declare war on France in a few years," Anna said.

"Napoleon."

"Yes. The revolution in France didn't really go the way many people had hoped it would. That includes Wordsworth."

At the mention of Napoleon, the two soldiers looked over at them. Ben looked at his red coat. It was dangerous to appear to support France and the revolution, to be a Republican, and Anna was aware that people that looked unusual might be mistaken for spies. She quickly laughed loudly and took a drink of her beer and Ben did the same. The soldiers went back to talking with each other. A few minutes later, the bartender brought their dinners over and they started eating.

The next morning they boarded the coach for London. There were two other passengers, a widow traveling to Cambridge to live with her family and a surveyor. The surveyor had been to Birmingham to consult on a new canal for the transport of coal. He had a large briefcase and he opened it and took out a large stone.

"Pound-stone," he said looking at it. "Different ones the deeper you dig. Looks a bit like some kind of animal. A sea creature."

The countryside was pretty, with low hills and some sheep in the fields. The coach was making a stop in Cambridge, and Ben tried to nap and a few hours later, they were nearing Cambridge.

Anna pointed out the window. "King's College Chapel," she said. "You can just see it."

The coach stopped in the city center near a market, and they took their bags and stepped out of the coach. Under striped awnings, stalls were selling food, books and clothing.

"We'll need to be back in a couple of hours. Let's go this way," she said, grabbing Ben's hand. They walked to King's Parade and turned left and then stopped in front of a red brick building with two small towers on either side of the entrance.

"Saint John's College," she said. "This was Wordsworth's college. He lived above the kitchen. He wrote that the sounds from the kitchen were like bees."

To their left bells began to ring, six times and then another set of smaller bells rang.

"A male and a female voice," Anna said. "Trinity College."

They turned and walked in the direction of the bells.

"It's amazing. It looks exactly the same as when I was here before. Which was, well, a few hundred years from now, I guess."

"I get confused," Ben said.

"But it's been here already for hundreds of years."

To their right now as they walked, they saw a big expanse of green grass and King's College Chapel came into view and they could hear singing coming from inside. They went inside and looked up at the high vaulted ceilings and tall stained glass windows and the voice of the choir echoed through the chapel. They listened to the choir for a few minutes and then went back outside. Men in black gowns were walking while talking and several were carrying books.

They walked behind the college and along the river with its several bridges. Trees hung low over the water and there were swans swimming lazily on the river.

They had dinner of roast beef and potatoes at the Eagle Pub.

"Funny to think about everyone that went here and everything that happened here," Ben said. "Darwin. DNA."

Anna nodded. "Wordsworth. Byron."

They walked back to the market and boarded the coach for London. The surveyor was on the coach again and a man in a military officer's uniform. The officer was in the Royal Navy and was travelling to London to take command as Captain of a ship, the Earl of Hereford.

"Your stones sir," Ben said to the surveyor. "If they are geological remains of some sea animal, what are they doing out here? In the fields?"

"I haven't the foggiest idea," the surveyor said. "That is a very good question."

There had been no rain for a week and the roads were good, and the trip to London took only four hours. The coach stopped near Leicester Square, and they stepped out with their bags. It was a large green square with sidewalks and trees and at one end there was a large house.

"No tube stop," Anna said. "I know a pub nearby."

They walked into Covent Garden and to the Lamb and Flag and went in and sat down. There were a few rooms upstairs and they paid the barman for the night's stay and went up to bed.

They woke up the next morning and when they went outside, the streets were clogged with carriages and the horses pulling them. Men were walking in coats and top hats and women in elaborate dresses with thin waists carrying umbrellas.

They started walking and they came to a large house surrounded by a fence.

"Buckingham Palace," Anna said.

There was a golden carriage inside the gate and a small group of soldiers walking past the gate.

"The King lives here?" Ben asked.

"Sometimes. He hasn't gone mad. Yet."

"My history is not great," Ben said. "Remind me who is King?"

"George the third."

"American Revolution," Ben said and nodded.

Then they walked down to the river. It was full of boats ferrying people across the river but only one bridge that they could see.

"No Big Ben," Ben said, looking around.

"Not for another fifty years or so."

There were few buildings along the river and the dome of Saint Paul's Cathedral was clearly visible to the East. They were walking along the embankment and Ben stopped to read a sign on a pole.

"Scientific demonstration for the public today. At the Royal Institution on Albemarle Street," he said. "That would be fun."

"Let's go," Anna said.

They walked towards Saint James Square and stopped at a tavern for a lunch of cheese, bread and ham. After they had eaten, they walked to Albemarle Street and to the Royal Institution. The building was large and white with many ornate columns along the front. Men, women and children were walking into the building and Anna and Ben followed. They went into the main lecture hall, which was crowded with people; men in suits and women in dresses, sitting on steep seats. The seats surrounded on three sides a table upon which were many glass apparatus, coils of wire and stacks of paper. They sat down in two of the few remaining seats and then the lecturer walked in, dressed in a black suit. He explained that he would be using a voltaic pile to separate water into its two gaseous components.

"Voltaic pile," Ben said and looked at Anna who nodded.

The man connected two wires to the crude battery and then to a vessel of water. "All matter," he said, "is not composed of four basic elements, fire, air, water and earth. But rather, each of these is composed of different elements. Using electricity, I shall separate water into its two component gasses." As the experiment ran, he went on to explain that air was also a mixture of different gasses, some of which we needed and some of which we expelled. Slowly gas could be seen accumulating in glass tubes and displacing the water.

"Mr. Lavoisier has named one of these gasses, which we require, oxygen."

Next, a man came in carrying something large under a sheet. A tube was hanging down, uncovered, from the sheet.

"Is that an elephant's trunk?" Anna said.

The man placed the heavy, mysterious item on the table and removed the sheet to reveal an elephant's head. He explained that his goal was to better understand the drum of the ear and began dissecting the head to remove the eardrum. Having removed it, he held up the membrane, several inches in diameter, and began explaining its function. The remaining parts of the elephant's head were removed and the table was cleaned.

"That was kind of gross," Anna said.

Now another man came in carrying a box, which he placed on the table. He removed a gun and an instrument with a dial that he said would measure the force of the explosion resulting from gunpowder. A few people appeared nervous and stood and walked out. The man aimed the pistol at the instrument and fired. There was no bullet in the gun, but the noise of the gun firing was very loud and one of the Royal Society staff walked up to the table and then the man put everything back in the box and walked out. A few people applauded. Anna looked at Ben and raised her eyebrows.

The science demonstration was over, and everyone stood to leave. Ben and Anna made their way down the stairs and out the door.

Outside, Anna said, "I wonder if we could go to the theater tonight."

"Might as well try. It would be fun."

They walked to Drury Lane Theater and bought two tickets to see The Castle Spectre. In the play, the heroine, Angela, battled her evil brother over a contested castle in Wales. There was also a singing ghost and Ben and Anna were surprised at how good the play was.

They walked for another hour or so after the play through Covent Garden, its long rows of stalls closed for the night, and then went back to the Inn and went to bed.

"We should get up early tomorrow to get to Parliament Hill," Anna said.

"And hopefully home," Ben added.

Chapter 39

Al and Sue were sitting at the table with Sam, eating breakfast.

Outside, two of the soldiers were playing with an animal that looked to Sue like a large bird. One of them was giving it something to eat.

"Al, what is that?" Sue asked.

The animal had turned now and was running after the other soldier with its head down, snapping its red beak.

"A Pyroraptor."

"A what?"

"It came through with Anna from the Cretaceous."

"You mean it's a dinosaur."

"Yeah. I keep meaning to send it back."

"A dinosaur? Cool!" Sam said running to the window.

"Sam, stay inside!" Sue shouted.

Al went outside to talk to the soldiers who had managed to get the Pyroraptor in the back of a truck. Sam was still looking out the window and Sue went in to check on Beth.

That afternoon, Al found Sue out behind the house pulling weeds in an old garden.

"Al, look," she said and held up a tomato and a cucumber. "Dinner!"

"I think we have a few more things in there too," Al said.

They made a salad and some pasta and sat down at the table to eat. Al poured them each a glass of wine.

"Remember when we were kids?" Sue said.

"Yeah."

"We would play outside all day?"

"Until dark or later. Riding our bikes, playing hide and seek."

"Kick the can."

"Camping?"

"Yes. Sleeping in our tents. Or outside if it was clear. The campfires and fireflies."

"Remember that one summer we went out west?"

"Several weeks. Different national parks. The air was starting to get bad, but we could still hike. And fish."

Sue took a bite of her pasta. "I wish my kids could have had that."

"Maybe they still can."

"Al, what do you think about Qweb?"

"I think I talked to it on the phone the other day."

"I mean do you think it's intelligent? Like we are?"

"Well, it seems intelligent. But I guess it kind of raises the question of what intelligence is. If it's just stringing words together into sentences that make sense to us, then I guess it is."

"Do you think it has feelings? Emotions?"

"That's harder, I think. When we experience emotion, I think it's a different physiological state. And maybe a different part of our brain is involved. But I guess Qweb has a type of physiology. And a brain. Maybe it's a question of consciousness. And I don't think anyone really understands that phenomenon very well. So I guess maybe."

"And alive?"

"Well, it seems to be manipulating things to ensure its continued existence. But things can exist without being alive. Things associated with life. Growth. Reproduction. It's kind of doing those things. So maybe."

"Is it OK then that we're doing something that might threaten its existence?"

"It's a hard question. People have asked that question when we've been at war. About the enemy."

"Are we at war?"

“It certainly feels like it.”

“It certainly feels like it.”

Chapter 40

They awoke early the next morning and had breakfast downstairs and then walked towards Leicester Square.

"I think we have time to walk to the British Museum before the Heath," Anna said.

"If you think so."

They walked up Charring Cross Road and passed several bookshops. Anna stopped to look at a few of the books in the windows: a book on anatomy, a collection of essays on Shakespeare, and Ben bought two pies from a street vendor. They walked as they ate them. Soon they were walking along Great Russel Street where they had been a few weeks earlier and they were in front of a large house.

"Where's the museum?" Ben asked.

"That's it. For now. Montague House. The other one doesn't get built for another fifty years or so. Let's go in. Inside, there were men in coattails and women in brightly colored dresses walking up and down the long staircases.

"Most of the things in here now were from Hans Sloane," Anna said.

They walked up the staircase. Large paintings adorned the walls and ceiling and a few taxidermy animals stood on a platform. They stopped to look at a case full of stuffed birds and dried plants.

"Most of this stuff was moved to the new Natural History Museum later. Most of it's not around anymore."

They saw a mummy and some Greek antiquities and then sat down on a bench.

"Seeing the palace yesterday and thinking about King George kind of got me thinking about revolutions," Ben said.

"Me too."

"Different kinds. The American and French. The scientific revolution. Evolution."

"Art and music. Wordsworth started one too. In poetry," Anna added.

"It didn't really look like a revolution."

"No. It looked like a lot of walking and talking."

"And fishing," Ben said with a laugh.

"And Marx wrote the Communist Manifesto here. Well here kind of. In about fifty years."

"Seems like everything in about fifty years."

"A revolution that started in a library."

"Funny that all of those have something in common," Ben said.

"Something new. And someone opposed to it. Trying to stop it."

"Why in the case of Wordsworth's poetry?"

"The style. And the subjects. Sympathy for a soldier's widow was taken as a criticism of being at war with France. And why should we feel sympathy for convicts? For beggars?"

"And now we're trying to stop a revolution."

"It seems like history jumps forward suddenly but being here now everything seems to move so slowly."

After a few minutes, Anna said, "We should probably get going." Ben nodded and they walked back down the stairs.

Outside they stopped a coach and asked the driver if he would take them to Hampstead Heath. He nodded and they climbed in.

Chapter 41

Once or twice in the night, Sue heard the sound of a helicopter. The sun was starting to come up, and the soldiers were making some last adjustments to the magnets, and they heard the first explosion.

"Al."

"They're not too close yet."

"How much time do we have?"

"About two hours. We might can hold them off for a little while."

Now they saw two helicopters coming from the direction they had come from a few days earlier flying in the direction the explosions seemed to be coming from.

"Ours," he said.

Al handed her a cup of coffee and walked outside to talk to the soldiers standing by the arch and one of them handed him a clipboard. One of the magnets had some dials on it and Al looked at those and then down at the clipboard. He looked at the dials again and then nodded.

Sue heard an explosion, this one closer and saw one of the helicopters fly overhead.

Al walked back in. "Five minutes."

They both walked out and stood by the arch.

Now she heard some gunfire and saw some smoke coming from the other side of the ridge.

"One minute," Al said.

Now a white tank came over the ridge and she saw that it fired, and the shell hit about fifty yards behind them. She put her hands over her ears and looked at Al. Two of the soldiers ran in the direction of the tank, firing their guns.

"OK," Al said and turned on the magnets.

They didn't feel a vibration, probably because they were outside and because of the fighting, Sue thought, but soon the blue arch appeared between the two poles.

The two soldiers hadn't succeeded in stopping the tank and it was closer now and fired again.

The carriage let Anna and Ben off on Hampstead Highstreet.

"There's something I want to see on the way," Anna said, and they started walking down the street.

They walked for about five minutes then turned left. They walked for another minute and there was a church on their left and they turned right and stopped in front of a white house.

"Keats house," Anna said. "Or it will be. Sitting here in the yard, you can hear the birds from the heath. Nightingales."

Ben nodded, looking at the house. "Should we get going?"

"Yes, it's that way," Anna said, and they walked towards the heath.

They walked past a pond on their right.

"Up there is where I saw a woolly mammoth," Anna said pointing. "Really strange to say that."

They walked up a hill and then veered right and came to Parliament Hill.

"Neanderthals too. Right over there."

Ben nodded. "Hard to believe."

They walked to the highest part of the hill and looked down towards the river. Boats were sailing up and down the river and they could see Saint Paul's Cathedral.

"Just a few more minutes I think," Anna said.

Now the air in front of them became hazy and the view to the river disappeared as the arch appeared.

"That's it," said Anna breathing out and Ben nodded.

"Finger's crossed," he said.

They looked at each other again and then back behind them and then Anna walked through.

When Anna walked out, Al and her mother were standing there. The first thing she noticed were the trees. They were in a small clearing surrounded by tall spruce trees. Near them were maple and beech trees and birds were flying through the trees and singing. There was a cabin nearby and she could hear the sound of a stream behind it. The weather was cool. She couldn't believe how beautiful it was. Green was the only word she could think of. She could see mountains in the distance, partly covered in clouds and the air was clear. Al and Sue smiled, and both walked over to hug her and then Ben walked out of the arch and he looked around too.

"Al, where are we?" Anna asked.

"The Smoky Mountains," Al said and smiled.

"How?"

"You did it."

Ben's mother was standing there too, and she ran over to Ben and hugged him and then hugged Anna.

"Come inside," Al said.

They sat down at the table. "Hungry?" Al asked.

"Yes, actually," Anna said, and he fixed them each something to eat.

"Where's Wolfie?" Ben asked.

"In the Cretaceous," Al said. "You can visit him if you want to."

They told them everything that had happened, and they listened for about an hour.

Anna stood up and walked outside, and Al came after her and they walked down to the river.

"Al, what happened? Here?"

"Well," he said slowly, "it's hard to explain." He paused. "It's like being conscious of two lives. Only one seems more real. And one seems like a shadow life. Like a dream."

"In the Odyssey," he continued, "Odysseus goes to the underworld and talks with his mother. The way they seemed to him. Real and not real. It was a murky realm where they had no bones or flesh. That's how that life seems. I remember the pollution, the haze. People going back to escape. That's probably the one you remember. The other, the one that is my real life, is similar, in broad strokes to the other. But better." He looked at Anna. "I'm still in the army. But the army's role is different. There's computers, but no Qweb. We still built the arch but people use it for research. For travel. Not just in time but in space."

"When did everything change?"

"When you walked through."

"Why not before? What we did. What happened happened so long ago."

"I think maybe you needed to come back first. To close a loop. Since you were the cause."

That night, Anna's brother had a concert at his school, and they needed to get back to town for that.

"Do you live here?" asked Anna.

"No, in town. We only visit here. On the weekends."

They drove into town and to the house and got ready for Sam's concert. Sam had gone to the school earlier and now they all got into two cars and drove there. They parked and walked into the school auditorium. They took their seats.

All of the instruments began playing different things. Scales, single notes, short passages of music. Sam was a second violinist, and they could see him moving his bow and fingering the notes.

"I've always thought this had a certain musical quality of its own," Al said.

Now all the instruments went silent, and the oboe played one note then all the others played that note too. And then the conductor walked out and stepped onto the podium and turned and bowed to the audience and there was applause. Then he turned to the orchestra and raised his hands and baton. They played Beethoven's Third Symphony, the Eroica. Anna thought about the symphony and its dedication to Napoleon, which was taken away when Napoleon declared himself Emperor.

The symphony ended and the audience starting applauding. Sam was looking over at them and Anna waved at him. Anna and Al looked at each other and smiled. Ben looked over at Anna and smiled and then he disappeared. Anna stared for a second at where he had been sitting and then looked at Al.

Chapter 42

"Al, what just happened?"

Al was staring at where Ben had been too. "I don't know," he said slowly.

"Where did Ben go? He was just here!"

After a pause, "I don't know." He looked at her.

"How could he just. Disappear?" She turned to look around and behind them.

Sue and Beth looked over now also wondering what had happened.

"I wonder," said Al.

"What?"

"If Qweb might be trying to stop us. Reverse what we've done."

"Stop us how? From where?"

"From the past maybe."

"Al that doesn't make any sense."

"Or from the future."

"But Qweb doesn't exist now. Won't exist in the future?"

"He did in the past. And others know what happened, can still remember."

"Could have rebuilt Qweb? In the future?"

"Maybe."

"Could have come back for Ben."

"Yes."

"But from the past? Could they have travelled to the future? Is that possible?"

"We haven't done it yet. But most people think it's possible. No one has done it yet. As far as I know, because getting the target time is difficult. Because there are multiple future time streams but only one past. But maybe someone figured it out."

"But it's possible?"

"I think so."

"How would we know? If he has been taken back to the past or to the future? How do we know if either has happened?"

Al took out his phone and dialed it. He talked into it for a minute then hung up. "Someone's coming to help us," he said. "They'll be here in a few minutes."

Anna sat down and put her hands in her lap and breathed in. Al sat down beside her.

A few minutes later Al stood up and turned as two men walked down the aisle and to their row. They were each carrying a small box by a handle in one hand. In the other hand, they carried a small cylinder attached to the box with a cord. One of the men walked to the end of the aisle and Anna got up to let him pass. Starting at each end of the aisle, the men walked slowly to the center of the aisle, passing the cylinder along the seats and floor, stopping every couple of seats to look at a dial on the boxes. When they met in the middle, they looked at the boxes again and then talked to each other.

Al looked at them. "What do you think?" he said.

"It seems like he's gone to the past," one of the men said and Al nodded. "Someone took him."

"And to the future," the other man said slowly, looking at the box he was holding.

"To the past and to the future?" Anna said. "Both?"

Al looked at her.

"How is that possible?" she said.

"Well we are talking about time travel," one of the men said. "Which seems kind of unlikely to begin with."

"Are there now two of him?" Anna asked.

"Maybe," the man said.

"Is one of them the real Ben? What about the other one?"

"We're not sure."

Anna raised her eyebrows and breathed out.   The boxes had a printer inside and the men ripped pieces of paper off that had printed and handed them to Al. Al nodded at them and they walked out of the aisle and up towards the exit.

He sat down and looked carefully at the two pieces of paper.

"Al, how can he have gone to two places at the same time? How can there be two of him?" Anna asked.

"I think it's because the past is the past. It has already happened. But the future can happen in many different ways, hasn't happened yet."

"You mean the past Ben is the real Ben?"

"No, I think they're both real, but not in the same time stream. Necessarily. Not in the same room of a house, to use an analogy."

"Can we tell where he, they, went? And when?" Anna asked.

"I think so. I'm looking at some data here," and he looked back down at the papers.

"I think it's here," he said a few minutes later, pointing to one of the papers. The paper was long and skinny, like from a spool, and had light blue squares, like graph paper. The two axes were labeled with numbers.

"OK, so in the future he went to." He squinted and traced a line on the paper with his finger. The line went up and then down slightly and then up again and then there was a gap and it continued going up again after the gap. There were some numbers along the top of the paper and Al looked at them. "The moon." And he looked up.

"The moon?" Anna said alarmed.

"Yes." And he paused. "Two hundred years in the future."

Anna stood up. "What? Why?"

"I don't know."

"But the base is no longer there."

"I guess there might be one in the future. In that timeline."

Anna sat back down again and breathed out and closed her eyes.

"What about in the past?" she said, looking up.

Al looked at the paper again and traced it with his finger. "That one's easier," he said and looked up. "He only went back one month."

"One month? Where?"

"Here. That at least makes sense. They're probably trying to stop you and Ben from going back to England."

Anna nodded slowly. "But if he only went back one month, he was still there."

Al nodded.

"So there are, right now, three Ben's out there."

"I think that's probably right," he said.

"And the two, um, Bens, the one that went to the future and the one that went to the past. Do they both need to come back."

"I think they should. I think they'll want to."

"And then there'll be two Bens here?"

"I wonder if maybe the Ben in the future is less real," said Al. "That they both won't come back. That Ben from the past will be the one that comes back."

Anna shook her head slowly.

Al looked at the graph paper again. "Wait," he said. "It might be more complicated."

"How?"

Al held up both strips of paper.

"See?" On both, the graphs stopped at a gap but on one, the gap came as the line was rising and on the other where it was falling."

"Yes. They look different. One is going up and one is going down."

"I think it's possible that if only one came back he wouldn't be complete."

"A complete Ben."

"Yes."

"How?"

"I don't know exactly, something would be missing."

"So they both need to come back."

"Yes. And I think at the same time."

"Why take him to the past and the future?"

"My guess is they want us to do something, and they don't think we're going to be able to find him, to get him back, from the future."

"And the past?"

"They probably want us to go back. To before you two went back to England and stop you." He looked up and leaned his head slightly. "From going back."

"And Ben and I are there already. Our past selves. Don't know anything about this. We'll plan on going back to England just as we did."

"Yes."

"And if we don't go back and stop, um, us. Then."

"I think they're holding Ben as leverage."

"What are we going to do?"

"I think we need to go back to the past and find Ben from here."

Anna nodded.

"You may need to stay with him and I'll go to the future and we'll coordinate getting them both back at the same time."

"If one comes back earlier?"

Al didn't say anything.

"I think we might need some help," Al said. "Someone else who knows him well."

Anna looked at him. "Wolfie?"

Al's phone rang and he walked up the aisle and started talking.

Anna walked over to Beth and hugged her.

"Do you think he'll be OK?" Beth asked.

"I think so," Anna said.

A few minutes later Al walked back.

"OK," he said. "Someone is going to the underwater city to look for the Quantco CEO."

"There is an underwater city?"

"Yes, a small one. We need to get to the closest arch and go get Wolfie."

"We're going back to the Cretaceous?" Anna asked.

"Yes, hopefully we can find him."

When they got outside there were two black SUVs waiting for them. Two men in black suits were standing and holding the doors open at each one. Anna and Al got in the one in the front and Sue, Beth and Sam got in the second one. The men shut the doors behind them, and they pulled away from the curb and away from the school. They drove for about ten minutes and pulled up outside of a small military facility. They barely slowed at the gate, which was open and drove up to a tan building and stopped. Al got out of the SUV and walked to the second car and spoke to the driver. The driver nodded and pulled away and drove back to the gate.

"Where are they going?" Anna asked.

"To a safe house. Let's go."

They went into the building and Anna could see the two poles of an arch through a glass window. They went into a smaller room with racks and shelves holding boxes and pieces of equipment: radios, tools and tents. Al grabbed two backpacks off a shelf. He put one on and then handed the other one to Anna who put it on. He then took two boxes off a shelf and then opened a door that led into the room with the arch and they walked through it. A technician was standing by one of the poles and reading something on a hand-held computer screen. Al walked over to him and looked at the screen then up at the man and nodded. The technician then pushed several buttons and moved a switch from the down to the up position and the poles started to glow green.

"Green," Anna said.

"Yes. It gets around some of the problems we were having earlier."

"When are we coming back? With Wolfie. If we can find him."

"As soon as we find him. Hopefully today."

"But what about the wave interference. Don't we have to wait a week or so?"

"We fixed that problem too," Al said, pointing to a small box about the size of a car battery with a red light on top.

Anna nodded.

Now the green arch was formed between the poles and the technician looked at his computer again, and turned one of the knobs on the control panel slightly and then looked at Al.

"Here we go," said Al.

Al walked forward through the arch and his form faded into the mist between the poles and then Anna walked through. She could feel the ground beneath her feet getting softer and now it felt squishy and she could see trees all around her and water and saw that they were standing in about three inches of water. Mist was rising from the swamp and on the shore, about thirty feet away, three dinosaurs with large flat bills looked up at them with plants hanging from their mouths. After a few seconds, they put their heads down again and continued eating.

Chapter 43

"This looks familiar," Anna said and then pointed to their left. "There, that small area of dry ground, that's where we came out before."

"OK, let's get over there," Al said.

They stepped carefully through the wet ground to the dry area and Al took off his backpack and dropped it to the ground. He took something out of it that looked like a small black metal crossbow.

"Where did you go from here?" Al asked.

"That way," Anna said pointing straight forward. "It's about a mile to the shore and then another half mile to the camp."

"OK. Hopefully they'll still be there."

Anna nodded and started walking and Al followed.

They had walked about three hundred yards when Anna held her hand up and stopped walking and turned back to look at Al. Al stopped walking and cocked his head slightly. Then Anna pointed to her right towards a line of small trees. Three shapes were emerging from the trees. As they came out of the trees, they could see that they were about four feet tall and had feathered arms extended to either side. Their faces were red, and they were crouching as they walked.

"Oh no," Anna said. "Pyroraptors."

Two of the animals stopped, but one kept walking slowly towards them. Now about four feet away it lowered its head and looked at Al and then at Anna. It opened its mouth and hissed.

"Al, does that Pyrorapter look familiar? What happened to the one that came through with me?"

"We sent it back."

They looked at each other and then back at the Pyrorapter.

"I think it recognizes us," Anna said.

Now it came closer to Anna, close enough to bite her, and sniffed at her. It looked up at her face and then stood still. After about five seconds, which seemed much longer to Anna, it turned its head and then its body and walked back to the other two waiting near the trees and then all three disappeared into the trees.

Anna had been holding her breath and exhaled loudly. She looked over at Al and saw that he was holding the crossbow and pointing it towards the trees where the animals had been. He slowly lowered the crossbow and also exhaled.

"OK," he said. "Let's, um, keep going."

They walked for about fifteen more minutes and could hear the sound of the surf. They walked through the trees and onto the sand and in front of them, waves crashed on the shore.

"This way," Anna said pointing right and then started walking down the beach.

Ahead were some cliffs and two Pterosaurs were circling near the top and Al smiled when he saw them.

"Amazing!" he said shaking his head.

They walked for a few more minutes and could see smoke rising through some trees about one hundred yards ahead. Anna hadn't been here in more than a month and wondered if the camp would look different, how much progress they had made.

Now they turned left off the beach and walked to the camp. The groups had built several more wooden houses and there was a fence around part of the camp. Anna saw Mary's house and walked towards it. There was a woman kneeling beside the stove dropping something into a pot and Anna could see that it was Mary. Mary looked up and opened her mouth and her eyes widened.

"Anna!" she said and ran to her and hugged her. "How did you get here?"

"It's a long story," Anna replied. "It's good to see you."

After a few seconds, they separated, and Mary looked at Al.

"This is my uncle Al," Anna said.

Mary extended her hand. "Hello," she said. "Welcome to our humble abode. Would you like something to drink?"

"I would love some water," Al said, and Anna smiled and said she would like some too.

"The place looks great," Anna said, sitting down on a wooden chair.

"It gets better every day," Mary said. "What brought you back?"

"Wolfie," Anna said. "We need to find Wolfie."

Mary looked up and then pointed to a small unfinished hut about forty feet away. A man was standing with his back to them arranging something on the door and when he turned, Anna could see that it was Wolfie. His hair was longer, and he had a beard. A few seconds later, he recognized Anna and ran to her.

"Anna!" he said, putting his arms around her.

"Wolfie! It's so good to see you."

Then he saw Al and extended his hand.

"Al," he said.

Then he looked again at Anna. "Why are y'all here?"

"Wolfie, it's Ben," Anna said. "He's been taken and we need your help."

Wolfie looked at her and then pointed to three chairs and they sat down.

"Tell me," he said.

Anna told Wolfie everything that had happened since she left the Cretaceous. About going to England, Watt, Wordsworth, and coming back to a green world.

Wolfie smiled and nodded slowly. "And Ben?"

She then told him about Ben disappearing and how he went to the past and to the future and how they need to go to both the past and the future to bring both Bens back.

Now a girl walked over and stood beside Wolfie. She was about Anna's age and was very tan with long brown hair. She looked down at Wolfie and smiled.

"Anna, Al, this is Suzan. My wife Suzan." Wolfie stood and put his arms around her.

"Wolfie! That's wonderful!" Anna said after a few seconds. "Congratulations!" She hugged Wolfie and then Suzan.

"Congratulations Wolfie," Al said and shook Wolfie's hand and then Suzan's.

"Thank you," Wolfie smiled, and he and Suzan kissed.

They all sat down, and Anna said, "Wolfie, I think we need your help. Bringing Ben back."

Wolfie looked at her and then at Suzan who smiled and nodded.

"When do we leave?" Wolfie asked.

"It's getting dark," Mary said.

"We should probably wait until tomorrow," Anna said. "We probably don't want to be walking back in the dark."

"OK," Al said.

Mary was standing nearby and asked them if they were hungry, and she pointed to the pot she had been tending at her camp. They walked over and sat at the table and Mary picked up a spoon and started filling bowls and placing them on the table.

Al and Anna told Mary about the changes back in their world, in the future, as a result of what Anna and Ben had done.

Mary nodded slowly as they talked and when they were done said, "That sounds nice." And then after a pause she said, "I think I'm going to stay. We can let the others know but I think most will probably want to stay."

Anna smiled to say that she understood and ate a spoonful of the stew. "Delicious," she said.

Al had almost finished his and smiled and nodded in agreement.

There was still about an hour of daylight and Anna and Wolfie, with Suzan, walked down to the shore. A Plesiosaur was floating in the water thirty yards away, its head visible and then it quickly dove into the water.

"Your ankle is better," Anna said looking at Wolfie.

"It didn't take long," Wolfie said. "I'm glad I stayed," he added, looking at Suzan. The surf hit the shore and withdrew, and Anna picked up a shell.

"How have things been here?"

"Really good. We're figuring it out. We have a farm over there." He pointed to a spot to the right of the camp. "Some plants with small red fruit and plants to make drinks with. We eat a lot of fish."

"We're building a permanent house," Suzan said. "Over there." She pointed.

"Maybe Ben and I should come live here too," Anna said.

"We could build you a house," Wolfie said smiling.

They walked back to camp and Al and Mary were sitting at the table talking. Al was holding a mug in both hands. It was getting colder out, and steam was rising out of the cup.

"We have some extra mats you all can sleep on," Mary said. "You can sleep inside or out. I don't think it's going to rain." She picked up two pieces of wood and added them to the fire.

"Is it safe to sleep outside?" Al asked.

Wolfie and Anna looked at each. "Pyrorapters," they said at the same time and laughed.

"I think inside," Al said.

As they were going to sleep, Anna could hear the sounds of banjo and guitar music from another camp.

They woke early the next morning, and Mary had some fish and fruit waiting for them on the table and they sat down.

Wolfie and Suzan were standing by the fire.

"You could come too," Wolfie said.

"I think I should wait here for you," Suzan said.

"I'll take good care of her," Mary said and put her arm around Suzan.

"Should we?" Al said, standing up.

Anna stood up and picked up her backpack. Wolfie and Suzan kissed, and he picked up his bag and walked over to Al and Anna.

"It was nice meeting you," Al said to Mary and Anna gave her a hug.

They turned and walked down to the beach and then walked along the surf. At the opening into the trees, they turned and walked into the woods.

"Al, how will they know when we are coming back? When to open the arch?" Anna asked.

"That's what this is for," and he held up one of the boxes he was carrying.

"Cool," said Wolfie.

"There have been a few improvements since you left," Al said to Wolfie.

"So let me get this straight," Wolfie said. "The three of us are going back to the past, recent past, to find Ben from your time."

"That's right," Al said.

"But Anna and I will still be here?"

"Yes. But Anna will be coming back in a few days."

"From here."

"Yes."

"So there will be two Anna's after she gets back."

"Yes."

"And two of you there too. And two Bens."

"That's right."

"Wow."

"And can you and the other Al meet? Or the two Bens or the two Annas? Or will there be a matter anti-matter kind of thing going on where something bad would happen?"

"We'll find out," Al said, raising his eyebrows.

"But only one of me. No fair."

In a few minutes, they came to the spot where they had come through the arch and Al set down the boxes he was carrying. He opened the lid of one of the boxes and flipped a switch and some lights came on.

He turned a dial and said, "This will let them know we're ready."

"Cool," Wolfie said.

A few minutes later the air in front of them became hazy and the arch appeared.

"Green," Wolfie said raising his eyebrows.

"That's us," Al said and picked up the boxes.

"After you," Wolfie said, and Al stepped through the arch then Wolfie walked through.

Anna heard a rustling in the trees behind them. A Pyrorapter was standing at the edge of the trees with its head out watching them. Anna recognized it. It didn't come any closer and was watching her when she stepped through the arch.

When Anna stepped out of the arch, she recognized the low cinderblock building and rusted roof of the second arch facility. She saw a few chickens pecking in the dirt.

"This is where we left to go back to England," she said.

"This is getting confusing. I like it," Wofie said.

"You'll be here in three days," Al said. "And me too."

"Is anyone here yet?"

"Your mom gets here then too. It's just us for now."

"Al, when we find Ben. Bens. And go back. What's to stop them from doing this again?" Anna asked.

"We've put some safeguards in place," Al gestured to one of the boxes he brought.

"So this can't happen again?"

"No."

"Good. Because I'm getting kind of tired of time travel."

"I need to make a phone call," Al said and walked towards the house.

"So where do we think Ben is?" Wolfie said to Anna. "The other Ben?"

"I don't know. Hopefully Al has an idea."

"You. The other you. And Ben who was already here, will be here in a few days."

Anna nodded.

"Hmm. Will it be weird to see you?"

"Probably."

"Too bad there's no longer a stock market. You could have brought yourself some stock tips," Wolfie said smiling.

They walked into the house and Wolfie went into the kitchen. Anna took a book off of the bookshelf and opened it and started reading. It was a romance novel and she wondered who lived or used to live here. Wolfie walked out of the kitchen and went outside.

When Anna went out, Wolfie was throwing pieces of bread to the chickens. "I guess I miss dinosaurs," he said smiling. "Also I miss Suzan." Anna walked over and put her arm around him. "Wolfie, thank you for helping. Suzan is wonderful and you'll be back there in a few days. Ben will be so happy to see you."

The air was hazy and the sun, as it set, had turned the sky purple. The dust was making it harder to breathe. "I miss the air in the Cretaceous too," Wolfie said. "But I guess you and Ben fixed that in the future. We'll come for a visit."

"Tell me about Suzan."

"Both of her parents died too. Of cancer. And she didn't see any reason to stay here. In the present. So decided to settle. She's a nurse."

"That's wonderful! She must be very useful on the team."

"We're very happy there. I can't wait to get back."

Anna nodded.

"We're going to start a family. You and Ben should join us. The Cretaceous is a nice place to live," he said smiling.

Al walked out of the house and the screen door shut behind him. "We have a plan," he said.

"Do we know where he is?" Anna asked.

"We think so. The underwater city."

Anna looked at Wolfie.

"Awesome," Wolfie said.

"Anna, Wolfie, I'm going to need your help."

"Help how?" Anna asked.

"I'm going to need you to monitor a video feed from us while we're there. To possibly help identify Ben."

“Won’t you recognize him?”

“Well, we’re not sure. Remember he went to two places, two times at once. One idea is that he, they, won’t look the same until they’re both back to our future time.”

“Not the same how?”

“We’re not sure. But as his girlfriend and best friend, you two will probably recognize him even if he is changed somehow.”

“How reliable will the feed be?” Anna asked.

“We’ll be kind of deep underwater, but it should be fine.”

“And if it stops working.”

Al didn’t say anything.

“Al, we’re going with you,” Anna said and Wolfie nodded.

“It’s too dangerous,” Al said.

“We’re going,” Anna said, and Al nodded slowly.

“Al, you went to the underwater city, with Ben?”

“Yes.”

“And while you were there?”

“We installed a program in Qweb. To slow it down. To distract it so we could set up this arch.”

“Did they know you did it?”

“Not at first. But this time we won’t be sneaking around. We should get some sleep. We need to be up early tomorrow.”

Al went inside and Anna and Wolfie walked over to the barn. The horse from before turned and walked over and put its head out of the stall. Anna stroked its nose.

When they went back out, it was getting dark and the stars were coming out, and they went inside.

Chapter 44

Ben was clapping and could hear the sound of applause all around him and then he couldn't. The auditorium had disappeared, and he was looking out a window and fish were swimming by. He knew where he was but wasn't sure how he got there. He could see the raised dome, Qweb, and the drones patrolling around it. He wondered if Anna was OK.

"Ben." Someone behind him spoke and he turned around and recognized the Quantco CEO.

Ben didn't say anything for a few seconds. "Why am I here? How did I get here?" he finally said.

"We brought you here."

"I thought the city wasn't built. Like this."

"It was. You saw it."

"But that was. Before. A different time."

"Well. You're back."

"You brought me back? To before? When is it?"

"You leave for England in a few days."

Ben thought for a second. He knew that Anna was still in the Cretaceous. That he and Al would be going to get her in a couple of days. But that would mean.

"There are two of me here."

"Yes. And two of me."

Ben thought for a few seconds. "Why am I here? Why did you bring me here?"

"We need you to do something for us."

"Does it involve me telling you to go to hell?"

"Funny. But no. It involves you stopping yourself and your friend from going back to England. It involves you taking us to the arch you used to go back to England."

"Go to hell."

"We'll see."

The door closed behind the CEO.

Chapter 45

The next morning Anna heard a knock on her door.

"Anna. It's Al. We need to get moving."

Al had made coffee and there were some pastries on the table.

"The best I could do. Sorry," he said.

Wolfie was sitting at the table eating a pastry and holding a cup of coffee.

"Cream cheese!" He said. "I've missed this!"

"Al, where are we going?" Anna asked.

"Have a seat. Have some coffee."

Anna sat and poured some coffee into one of the mugs.

"So, we think Ben is in the underwater city. Somewhere there."

Wolfie nodded. "Are we going there?"

"Yes. We'll have some help also. We're getting there by submarine, and we'll have some support above water. We'll get in as fast as we can and out once we find Ben. Anna what do you think?"

"About what?"

"About going."

"I'm going."

Al nooded. "Have either of you scuba dived before?"

"No," Anna said.

"Snorkeling," Wolfie said.

"OK. We'll talk about it once we're there. You won't really need to take anything. Hopefully they don't know were coming. But they're going to know we've been there."

Anna looked at Wolfie.

Al finished his coffee and stood up. Anna and Wolfie followed him outside. There were two SUVs waiting for them. They all got into the first one and when they drove off, the second one followed them. They drove back down a dirt road that Anna remembered from the first time she came here and onto the highway. About half an hour later, they took an exit and a few minutes later pulled up to a gate and stopped. A soldier was standing near the gate and walked up to their SUV. The driver rolled down the window and the soldier looked in and saw Al.

"Sir," the soldier said and pushed a button to open the gate.

They drove around to the back of the tan building and a helicopter was waiting, its rotors spinning slowly, speeding up.

"Helicopter!" Wolfie said.

They got out of the car and crouching, ran up to the helicopter, their clothes flapping in the wind from the blades. As soon as they were seated, Al made a circular motion with his fingers and the pilot, wearing a headset, looking back nodded and the helicopter slowly rose.

Al held up three fingers, which Anna understood as meaning they would be flying for three hours. She leaned over to Wolfie and told him this.

Wolfie looked at Al. "This helicopter is fast. And quiet."

"Yes," Al said. "It's had a few upgrades. Imagine an eighteen-million-dollar helicopter. With eighteen million dollars worth of upgrades."

Wolfie nodded, and closed his eyes and tried to sleep, but looked out at the coastline most of the time. After a while, they were flying over open water. When they started to land, they could see some small boats in the water near where they were going.

They got out and walked into a small building with some tables and chairs and Al motioned for them to sit down and went over to talk to a man standing by the door leading out to the docks. A few minutes later, he brought over a few sandwiches and put them on the table. Anna and Wolfie each picked one up.

"You'd better take those with you," Al said and started walking towards the door. They exited the door onto a small, metal platform and could see the docks and the water. There were several small submarines floating in the water.

"Attack submarines," Al said. "There will be two teams. Anna, you'll be on my team. Wolfie, you'll be on the other team."

Wolfie nodded.

"We'll be in constant communication with each other once we leave the sub."

"What are those boats?" Wolfie asked pointing to eight small boats next to the submarines.

"Those are going to provide some support from above," Al said. "Let's go."

They walked to the docks and up a short metal gangway to the first sub and to an open hatch. Wolfie was walking to the second sub. Al pointed at the hatch and Anna went in and down the ladder. Al came down last, shutting the hatch behind him.

"We have about a three-hour ride," Al said. "We're going to the Turks and Caicos."

"I always wanted to go there," Anna said.

"There are some seats over there," Al said, pointing toward the rear of the ship, and Anna sat down and opened her book.

About an hour later, Al walked back to the table and sat down.

"Let's talk about the scuba equipment," he said and dropped some equipment on the table.

"This, of course is your mask," he said holding up a diving mask that was more of a helmet. "And this is your regulator. You'll open the tank valve just before we exit the sub. Breathe through your mouth."

"Why does it look like a helmet?" Anna asked.

"Because of the pressure."

He put that down and picked up the fins. "You'll wear these fins too."

"We won't have far to go. Each dome has an entrance below for divers and subs. The subs will get us as close as they can, and we'll swim the rest of the way."

"When do you think they'll know we're there?" Anna asked.

"If we're lucky, not until we get to the entrance. The ships up top are going to help us."

"We're going to one of the domes?"

"Yes, one of the small ones. Each team will go to one of the domes."

"And we look for Ben once we get there."

"Yes, but one member of each team will log into a data center and hopefully give us an idea of where we want to go."

"So either team might find him."

"Yes."

"There's also this." He put a sealed dry bag on the table and unrolled it and took out a gun.

"A gun," Anna said.

"Yes, once we get inside, you'll take off your fins and mask and put them in this larger bag and that goes on your back. Inside the bag will be one of these and you'll need to take it out and carry it."

"We might need to shoot someone?"

"Hopefully not. But they won't want Ben to go. And we don't know how hard they're going to try to stop us."

"Al, I've never shot a gun before."

"This is the safety switch. Move it forward. Now it's red. Point and pull the trigger," Al said. "We're almost there. Let's go ahead and get our gear on." He handed her a wet suit with raised ridges.

The sub had slowed and ahead, maybe a half mile, the glowing city could be seen. The other sub was beside them. They were standing above a grate, and a hatch had been opened and seawater was lapping the edges of the opening.

Two men were already standing there in wet suits.

"This is Jeff and Tom, they're on our team," Al said.

"Anna," Anna said.

"Once you get in the water, turn on this light on your suit," Al said to Anna. "That way we can all see where each other is. If you need a flashlight, it's here," he said pointing to a pocket on his chest.

"Are you ready?" Al said to Anna.

Anna nodded, adjusting her mask.

"Hopefully the ships up top can help us," Al said. "They're going to drop some charges that should take out their main power for a few minutes. Long enough for us to swim over. The backup power will come on eventually, for critical systems."

He handed a bag to one of the men. "This has scuba gear for Ben," he said, and the man put it on his back.

"The other team has one for him too?" Anna asked and Al nodded.

The subs slowed and Anna was looking out at the lighted city, closer and brighter now, when a ring of flashes went off outside. Eight silent explosions, each incredibly bright went off outside in a ring, about one hundred feet above the city. A few seconds later Anna felt the explosions and the city went dark.

"That's us. Let's go," Al said. A soldier pulled up the grate and Al slipped into the water.

Anna was breathing through her mouth in heavy deep breaths. She took another breath and slipped into the water, followed by Jeff and Tom. Now in the water, she wasn't sure which way to go and then she saw Al's light ahead and swam towards it. The city was dark so there were no lights to guide them. She started kicking and was surprised how quickly the fins moved her through the water. She was getting closer to Al and could see bubbles coming from his mask and her breathing was getting slower. On her right a line, or school, of fish swam by, illuminated faintly by her light and then a large shape began to appear in front of her.

She saw the dome and swam towards it and was now swimming alongside Al. They were almost to the dome and Al pointed down and they swam underneath the dome. Once under the dome, Al's light moved up and she followed and then she could see an opening and they swam towards that. She swam through the hole, and she was now inside the dome. A red emergency light had come on, faintly illuminating the inside of the room. There was scuba equipment, tanks and wet suits, hanging on the walls. Al had already hoisted himself up and was sitting on the edge of the opening and had taken off his mask. Now he took off his fins and put those and the mask in the pack and stood up and put that on his shoulders. It was very quiet and Anna could only hear the sound of dripping water. She took off her mask and fins and put them in their bags and stood up. Al held up a small bag and opened it and took out his gun and pointed to Anna's bag and she took out her gun too. One of the two men had already started walking forward through the tube and they followed.

They followed him out of the dome and down the tube. One of the men, Jeff, had stopped at a control panel and was typing some numbers. He had connected a small hand-held device to the panel. Al gave him a thumbs up and they kept walking past him. The connecting tube was much larger than Anna had thought and there were passageways leading off of it to other areas. Every thirty yards or so the other man, Tom, placed a small disc on the wall and flipped a switch, and a small light on the disc came on. Now they started to see other people. The residents seemed nervous that the power had gone off and seemed surprised to see Al and the other three walking past them in wetsuits and holding guns. Most stopped or stepped out of their way.

"They'll know we're here by now," Al said and then a voice spoke through his radio.

"Yes?" he said. "OK."

"He's not in the North or South quadrants," he said, and they kept walking.

Most of the people they saw looked like they were just going about their ordinary activities: shopping, taking the kids to school. One woman was wearing shorts and carrying a tennis racket. As they turned a corner though, they saw someone dressed like a guard and he was also carrying a gun.

"Stop right there!" the guard shouted and pointed his gun at them.

"Go back around that corner," Al said to Anna, and he and the other man raised their guns and fired. They hit the guard in the leg who dropped his gun and fell to the floor.

"Come on," Al said, and they walked past the guard. Al took the man's radio as they passed him and then someone spoke through his radio again.

He listened for a few seconds and then said, "He's in the East quadrant, either spoke one or two, we're not sure."

"How will we know?" Anna asked.

"They might figure it out. We'll keep looking in the meantime. The other team is trying to get here."

People around them were now acting a bit more panicky after the gun shots and they quickly moved out of the way. Al looked down a hallway and stopped. There was a metal door at the end of the hallway and two guards standing in front of it. One of them was talking into a radio.

Al pointed his gun at them. "How do you want this to go?" he said. The two guards raised their hands and the man on their team ran to them and took their guns.

"Open the door," Al said to one of them.

"We can't," he said.

"Open the door," Al said again, this time pointing his gun at the guard.

The guard turned and entered some numbers on a keypad and the door opened.

Al motioned for Anna, and she went through the door. At the end of a small hallway was another door, this one not locked, and they opened it. Inside there were boxes sitting on the floor and stacked against the wall, but Ben wasn't in there. The word "flammable" was written on one of the boxes.

"Damn," Al said, and a voice came out of his radio.

"OK," he said. "Team two has him." They went back out into the hallway and behind them, in the direction they had come, there was an explosion.

"Al, was that the dome where we came in?"

"I think so. We can't leave the way we came. This way," he said pointing down the tube.

"Are they sure it's Ben?" Anna asked.

Al spoke into his radio. "Put Wolfie on," he said.

"Yes," Wolfie's voice came through the radio.

"Wolfie, are you sure its him?"

"Yep. Just as ugly as her ever was," Wolfie said, and Al laughed. "It's him," he said to Anna.

"Thank god," Anna said.

Ahead they could see a large open space and they ran into the central dome. They ran past a fountain and what looked like a check-in desk for a hotel. People were running across the lobby, some screaming and some holding children's hands.

"This way," Al said pointing to another tube entrance. Tube two. We'll join the group that found Ben. Hopefully their exit is still OK."

Now Anna saw ten or so guards running towards tube two, as if to block their way. They were carrying guns and a few had rifles. Running with them, Anna recognized the Quantco CEO.

Al looked at Anna. "You can make it to the tube entrance if you keep running," he said. "We'll cut them off. Keep running to the diving dome. Team two will wait for you there." He leaned to say something into his radio.

"Al," Anna said.

"Go! I'll catch up with you!" and he and the man ran towards the guards with their guns up. He fired once and one of the guards fell. And then they stopped, crouching behind a large planter. The guards and the CEO also stopped and were crouching behind a low wall.

Anna turned and ran towards the tube entrance.

Chapter 46

Al was half sitting, with his back against the planter, holding his gun out in front of him. He looked at Tom and pointed to the registration desk. Tom nodded and crouching, ran to it. One of the guards fired a shot and Tom ran behind the desk.

"Mr. Paris," the CEO yelled. "I think we have a problem."

"I think you have a problem," Al said.

"You want to leave, but you can't."

"We're going to leave," Al said. "The only question is how much of this city is going to be left after we leave."

The CEO didn't say anything.

Al said something into his radio and a few seconds later there was an explosion and smoke came out of one of the tube entrances and a door closed to seal it off.

"That was your farming pod I think," Al shouted. "We can keep doing this."

One of the guards stood up to shoot and Tom stood up and fired at him and the guard fell backwards.

Al spoke into his radio and there was another explosion.

"OK," the CEO shouted. "What do you want?"

"We just want to get out of here."

"Give us a minute," Al said into his radio.

"Fine. But you only have half of him. Good luck finding the other half. Call off your plan and we'll return him to you."

Al motioned for Tom who ran over and they both ran, looking back at the guards, to tube two.

Anna ran to the platform and was out of breath and Wolfie was waiting for her.

"Come on!" he yelled, and she jumped onto the platform and took out her tank and mask.

"Where's Ben?"

"He's already gone. With two others. To the sub."

"It's him?"

"Yep. Doesn't look any different."

"He's OK?"

"Seems like it. He was glad to see me. Let's go." Wolfie put on his mask.

Anna put on her tank and mask and sat on the edge of the opening with her feet in the water and then slipped into the water followed by Wolfie. Once in the water they turned on their lights and Anna started swimming alongside Wolfie. They could see the lights of the sub ahead and they swam toward it. They came up through the bottom of the sub and Anna quickly stood up and took off her mask.

Ben was standing there, and she took off her flippers and ran to him.

She put her arms around him. "Ben! You're alright! I was so worried about you." Then she kissed him.

"I was worried about you too," he said.

"You're alright?"

"I think so."

Now Al swam up and got out and took off his mask.

"Anna. Ben. Thank god." And then to a soldier waiting for him, "We need to get going."

"Do you think they'll try to stop us?" Anna asked.

"I don't think so," Al said. "But just in case let's launch a couple of drones," he said to one of the soldiers.

The soldier nodded and ran off.

"Al. Thank you," Ben said.

"Well we weren't going to leave you there," Al said and smiled.

Anna, Ben and Wolfie took off their wet suits and hung them up.

"It's so good to see you both," Ben said, and they went to sit down.

"What happened?" Anna asked.

"Well, I was at the performance and then I wasn't. I was looking out a window here. The CEO wanted to know where the arch is. That we used. Are going to use to go back to England. He wanted to stop us. But I guess it's not really us that are going."

"I'm still in the Cretaceous," Anna said.

"Wow," Ben said. "I guess I'm. Here somewhere."

"You two are going to get to meet yourselves in a couple of days," Wolfie said.

"How do you feel?" Anna asked Ben.

"Tired."

"You could try to sleep on one of those bunks," Anna pointed to some curtained off compartments behind them.

"That sounds like a good idea," Ben said and went to lie down.

Anna and Wolfie sat down, still wearing their wet suits.

"I'd rather not have to do that again," Wolfie said. Anna leaned her head back and closed her eyes.

"I wonder what we can say to ourselves. The day after tomorrow," Anna said a few minutes later.

Wolfie shook his head.

They both napped for a while and Al came back and said they'd be there soon.

About half an hour later, they slowed and ascended and stopped.

"We're here," Al said.

They all walked forward and up and out of the hatch. They walked across the metal gangway and onto the dock and into the waiting helicopter. When they landed a few hours later, the SUVs were waiting on the other side of the building, and they all got in. They drove for half an hour and pulled up at the cinder block building and got out.

"I remember this place," Ben said.

"The arch facility," Anna said, and they went inside.

"There's not much to eat here," Al said. "But I think there's soup in the cabinet. And some crackers."

Wolfie opened three cans of soup and heated them on the stove and they all sat down at the table to eat.

"We have one day," Al said. "Until you get here."

"What can we say to ourselves?" Anna asked.

"You can't tell them, yourselves, anything about what happened. In England or after. Or why we're here."

"Won't they wonder?"

"Probably. But anything we say might change how they act, change the outcome of what they, you, do when you go back. It's a miracle that you succeeded."

They nodded.

"There's one other thing. Ben."

"Yes?" Ben said.

"You remember that you were brought back here from the performance."

"Yes."

"They want to stop you from going back."

"Yes."

"Well. They didn't just take you here."

"What?"

"They took you here and into the future at the same time."

"How is that possible? I'm here."

"Yes, but we think if we were to just take you back to our time something would be wrong."

"Something?"

"We're not sure. But we need to go to the future to find you and bring you both back to our time at the same time."

Ben nodded slowly.

"Right now, I'm thinking that I, the I that will be here the day after tomorrow, will stay here with you and send you back to our time. Anna, Wolfie and I will go to the future, he looked at Anna and Wolfie, where you've been taken and bring you back. We'll need to do it at the same time."

"Where, and when, am I?"

"They took you two hundred years in the future. To the moon."

"The moon." Ben said.

"Travel to the future is complicated because there are multiple future timelines. In the one you are in the moon base apparently has been rebuilt."

Ben nodded.

"Anna and Ben from this time will go back to England as before. No change there."

They finished eating and Ben said, "I'm exhausted."

"I'm not surprised," Al said. "See you all in the morning.

Chapter 47

The next morning, Anna and Ben woke to the smell of bacon cooking and went into the main room.

"Someone brought us groceries this morning!" Wolfie said and he was cooking bacon and eggs.

After they had eaten, Ben looked out the window and said, "It's pretty clear out today."

He and Anna and Wolfie went outside and to the barn. Anna walked over to the stall with the black horse who had his head out. She petted its nose and then Ben petted it and she put some feed in his bucket and the horse started eating. It looked up and was chewing and some of the feed fell on the ground.

"When I was little, I went to a horse camp for a few summers," she said to Ben.

"To ride?"

"Yes."

"Was it hard?"

"Not really. I loved it." They watched the horse eat.

"I wonder if there are any clean shavings around here," Anna said.

Wolfie had walked out of the other end of the barn and then yelled, "Hey, there are more horses out here!"

They walked out and could see three horses in the pasture, two white horses and a roan.

"Wolfie, weren't there some apples on the table?" Anna said.

"I think so."

"Can you go and get a few?"

"Sure," he said and walked towards the house.

Ben had gone back into the barn. "Anna," he said, "Come look at this stuff."

He had gone through a door in the barn and Anna went in after him.

"Tack room," she said, looking around.

There were several saddles on racks, most of them western and one English saddle, and bits and bridles and cinches hanging on the walls. Everything was very dusty.

"Do you think we could ride the horses?" Ben asked.

"I was thinking the same thing," Anna said and took two bridles and two lead ropes off their hooks.

Wolfie came back with the apples and they walked back to the pasture. The gate was closed with a rope, and they slipped it off the top and opened it and went through. The horses were about twenty yards away and looked at them. Anna walked slowly towards them holding one of the apples in her palm in her outstretched arm. She gave one to Ben, who did the same thing. The roan horse and one of the white horses walked over and took bites of the apples. Anna slipped the bridle over the white horse's head and attached the lead rope and handed the rope to Ben. Then she put a bridle on the roan. Both horses took another bite of apple. They led both horses into the barn and clipped the halter to ropes on both sides of the walkway. Anna went back into the tack room and came back with a sharp metal tool.

"What's that?" Ben asked.

"Hoof pick," she said.

She walked behind the white horse and gently put her hand around the horse's leg just above the hoof. She made a clucking sound with her tongue and pulled up on the leg and cradled it with her arm against her side. She used the pick to remove dirt and a few small rocks from the sole of the horse's foot.

"These horses need their hooves trimmed," she said. "The shoes aren't bad."

She put the horse's foot down then picked up the other hind foot and used the pick. "Easy," she said. Then she did this with the front feet. "Want to try?" she asked Ben.

"OK, I guess."

Ben walked behind the roan and put his hand around one hind leg and tried to imitate the clucking sound while pulling on the leg, but the horse wouldn't raise its leg.

"Maybe you should do it."

"OK." She handed him a brush and said, "You can brush the white horse," and started picking the roan's hooves. Ben started brushing the white horse. She went into the tack room and came back with a saddle on her arm and holding a girth. She blew on the saddle and dust came off. She put it on a rack and brushed off the dust with a rag then put a saddle pad and the saddle on the white horse. Then she attached the girth to one side of the saddle and reached underneath the horse and buckled it on the other side of the saddle after pulling it tight. She reached up and moved the saddle side to side and tightened the girth again.

"Can you take this horse out by the lead rope?" she asked Ben, handing him the rope.

He took the lead rope and led the horse out of the stall. Anna opened the door of the stall with the black horse and put a halter on it and led it out and clipped the halter to ropes on the two walls and picked out its hooves and brushed it. She went back into the tack room and brought out an English saddle and put it on the horse then went back in and brought out a saddle for the roan horse and put that on. She put some stirrups on the English saddle and then gave Wolfie the lead rope for the roan horse and he led it outside, and she followed with the black horse.

Ben was standing holding the lead rope for the white horse who had its head down trying to find some grass to eat. There was a gate that led to a large field, and they walked over and opened it and led their horses through and Anna closed the gate behind them.

"How do we get on?" Ben asked.

"Walk him over to beside that box and stand on the box," Anna said. "Then put your left foot in the saddle and swing your other leg over."

Ben got onto the horse. "OK. Now how do I get him to go?" Ben asked.

"Gently squeeze your legs and pull the reins in the direction you want to go."

Ben started moving forward slowly and Anna got on her horse. Wolfie was already on the roan horse and walking away from them.

"Wolfie!" Anna said. "Wait for us!"

"Hurry up!" Wolfie said laughing.

They caught up with Wolfie, Ben bouncing up and down in his saddle, and rode north through the field. The field hadn't been mown in a while and there were small shrubs and clumps of switch grass. They rode for a while and then stopped in a small wooded area of red maple and sweet gum trees. The horses lowered their heads and started eating grass.

"Here," Wolfie said and handed Anna a bottle of water. She took a drink and handed it to Ben.

"Are there horses in the Cretaceous?" Anna asked Wolfie, smiling.

"I don't think so," Wolfie answered. "Or maybe there were and they were the size of chickens." Anna laughed.

They watched a crow fly overhead and rode through the trees and came to a dry creek bed and they got off the horses. They walked up to the creek bed and looked in. A crow flew by and landed on a dead tree limb.

"I wonder how long it's been since this had any water in it," Ben said, and his horse raised his head.

"I'd forgotten how much I like riding," Anna said.

"It's pretty fun," Ben said. "I'll probably be sore tomorrow."

They walked the horses along the creek bed for a few minutes but didn't see any water.

"We should probably be getting back," Anna said.

Wolfie cupped his hands and helped Ben and Anna up on their horses and then got on his horse and they turned to ride back. When they got to the barn the sun was setting and the sky was a dark orange color and it was dustier than it had been earlier. They got off their horses and Anna took the saddle off hers and went inside the barn. Wolfie and Ben were holding their horses' lead ropes and Anna took the saddles off the other two horses and hung them up.

"Let's rinse the horses off," she said and led hers over to a wash rack. She turned on the hose and water came out and she sprayed the horse and rubbed off the water with her hand. There was a sweat scraper in the wash rack, and she used that to get more of the water off. Ben and Wolfie brought their horses over and rinsed them off and then they led their horses into the pasture and let them loose.

Anna found some clean shavings and they cleaned out four stalls and then brought the horses in and led them into their stalls and dropped some feed for them.

"I wonder who's been taking care of the horses," Anna said.

"Probably a friend of Al's," Ben said.

It was getting dark when they finally started walking back to the house.

"Wait," Ben said. "Do you see Al?"

They looked through the window and saw Al sitting at the table talking to another Al.

The Al on the right, the one who had been here with them, was talking and the other Al was listening.

"Al who's been here with us. Future Al? He hasn't shaved in a couple of days," Anna said. "Maybe so we could tell them apart."

"Good idea," Wolfie said.

Now the other Al talked, and they were both looking at some papers that were on the table.

"I guess we better go in," Ben said, and they walked onto the porch and opened the door.

Both Als looked up when they walked in.

Al who came back with them stood up. "This is Al from the time we're in," he said, and the other Al stood up.

"Hi Anna. Ben. Wolfie."

They all nodded.

"I thought it would be a good idea to give Anna and Ben, who will be here tomorrow, a heads up before they got here that you all are here, so I got in touch with me from this time," and he nodded at the other Al.

"I'm just leaving. We're going to the arch tomorrow to get," he paused. "Anna. And then come here."

He and Al shook hands and he picked up his coat and opened the door. Looking back quickly he then turned and walked out, shutting the door behind him.

Al went into the arch room and started talking to two technicians who were holding clipboards and looking at the arch. One of them nodded and then turned a dial on the arch panel.

He came back out. "We needed to adjust some things to get us to the moon. Two hundred years from now. Some things we wouldn't have been able to do before."

"How was it?" Anna asked. "Talking to the other Al?"

"Not as weird as I thought it would be," Al said. "It took me a minute to convince him who I was when I called. But when I told him where we were he came on over."

"What did you talk about?"

"Well, I told him everything. He's going to tell Anna and Ben, and the others, that you are here. But not why."

Anna nodded.

"He's going to stay with you, Ben, when we go forward, to the moon, to find you. Anna and Ben will go back to England tomorrow. We'll go tomorrow too," and he looked at Anna.

"I wonder if we should do something, wear something, so that we can tell us apart from you and me who are coming tomorrow," Anna said to Ben.

"Maybe wear hats?" Ben said.

"Hats are a good idea."

Wolfie went into the kitchen and opened the fridge.

"Anyone want some dinner?" he asked.

"Yes, please," Anna said.

"We rode the horses," Anna said to Al.

"Oh. Funny I never thought about doing that."

Wolfie took some chicken and butter out of the refrigerator and found some flour in a cabinet and pulled out a frying pan and turned on a burner. He filled a pot with water and put that on another burner. Ben and Anna put some plates and silverware on the table. Al opened a bottle of wine and poured four glasses. About ten minutes later, Wolfie put a plate of chicken on the table and a bowl of noodles and they ate.

"Al, is the other you going to tell us that we're here?" Anna said.

"That's right."

"Is anyone going to tell my mom and Sam? And Ben's mom?"

"Yes, they already know. They'll be here early tomorrow. Also Stewart."

"Al," Anna said. "Wouldn't it be better if we didn't meet ourselves tomorrow? Maybe stayed somewhere else? Or left before they got here?"

"Well it's complicated," Al said. "Ben," and he looked over at Ben, "has to stay here with Al, the other Al, who is going to send him back at the same time we return to our time with Ben from two hundred years from now. From the moon."

"Couldn't we come back here after they leave for England?"

"The problem is that, especially after us going to get Ben from the underwater city, there's not really another safe place to stay right now. Things are a little more difficult now than the first time you and Ben went back to England."

Anna nodded.

"Also Al and I still have a few things to work out about going to the future, to the moon. I'm afraid right now this is the best plan."

"So, we just don't say anything about what happened. What has happened. About why we're here."

Al thought for a second. "Anna, if there were one essential thing you could tell Anna before she and Ben go back to England, to make sure you succeed, what would it be?"

"To go to the Lake District."

Al nodded slowly.

After dinner, they played some card games and got up to go to bed.

"Busy day tomorrow," Al said.

<h1 style="text-align:center">Chapter 48</h1>

The next morning Ben and Anna woke up and went to the kitchen and poured two cups of coffee that Al had made.

"Look," Anna said, pointing to the arch room.

Al was standing in the arch room with eight men each carrying a duffle bag and the arch was on. Al was talking to one of them and a technician was adjusting a dial on the control panel and then nodded at Al. Some were carrying pieces of equipment: folding metal stands and what Anna thought was a gun.

Al spoke again to the man with the duffle bag and shook his hand. Now the men put on white jump suits that looked like space suits and helmets with large glass visors. They tightened some Velcro straps around their ankles and wrists and then lined up and one by one they went through the arch.

Al came out and Anna asked, "Al, who were those men?"

"They're going ahead of us to the moon. They're going to do a few things to hopefully help us when we get there."

"What are they taking?"

"Communications equipment. And a portable arch. We'll use that to get back from the moon."

"And they were wearing space suits."

"They don't know for sure where they'll come out. If inside they won't need the suits."

"They can't bring us back with this arch?"

"No." Al shook his head. "They can send us to the future with this arch but it can't bring us back."

Anna, Ben and Wolfie finished their coffee and had some eggs and were sitting and reading when someone knocked on the door. The door opened and Anna's mom walked in carrying a suitcase. She set her bag down and walked over to Anna and Ben, who were now standing.

"Mom?" Anna said.

"Anna. You came from the future?"

"Yes."

"Well. It's good to see you. I hope you're OK. I know you can't tell us anything."

Sam came in and ran over and hugged Anna.

"I know you're a different Anna but I'm glad to see you," he said.

The door opened again, and a man pushed Ben's mom in a wheelchair into the room and they stopped in front of Ben and Anna.

"Ben," she said and then looked away.

"Hi mom."

Ben looked at Al, and he motioned to one of the rooms and they took her into the room. Ben went in and they helped her get into bed. He sat with her for a few minutes, holding her hand and she fell asleep.

They sat down again and Sue asked when Anna and Ben would arrive.

"In about an hour," Al said.

There was another knock on the door and Al opened it. Stewart was standing there.

"Come in," Al said, and Stewart came in.

He looked at Anna and Ben anxiously. "Hi," he said.

Ben and Anna nodded.

"I know you can't tell me anything. About how it went in England. I hope it went well."

"I wish we could tell you more," Anna said and picked up two apples from the table and she and Ben went outside and walked over to the barn.

"It's weird seeing my mom," Anna said. "I want to tell her everything that happened, tell her everything is going to get better but I can't."

"I know," Ben said.

The three horses in their stalls started whinnying when they saw them and Anna gave them each some apple.

They heard some cars driving up over by the house and walked out and the three LTVs pulled up and stopped. Dust was swirling around the vehicles. Now the doors of the LTVs opened and Anna and Ben got out of one of them. Now Al got out and they started walking to the house. They stayed with the horses for a little while and when they went back into the house, Anna and Ben were resting. Stewart was sitting at the table and looked up at them when they walked in. Al was inside the arch room talking to the other Al and they were both looking at a display and making some calculations.

They sat down on the couch to read and a few minutes later Anna and Ben walked out of their room. They looked at Anna and Ben on the couch and raised their eyebrows. "Hi," Anna and Ben and Wolfie said, standing up.

"Wolfie, how are you?" Anna said, walking over.

"Good," he said. "And there's only one of me here," he added, grinning.

Al motioned for Anna and Ben to come sit at the table with Stewart who told them why they needed to go back. Anna and Ben sat on the couch and listened.

Anna's mom had gone into the kitchen to make some dinner and there was the sound of potatoes frying.

"That smells good," Wolfie said smiling at her.

There weren't enough chairs, and Anna went outside and brought some chairs in from the porch.

"Two of us means twice as many chairs," she said.

When they were finished eating, Anna and Ben came over and sat on some chairs near the couch.

"Has anyone said we can't play games?" Wolfie asked.

"I don't think so," Anna said.

Wolfie went over to the shelf and came back with Pictionary.

"This should be fun!" he said.

"I'll be on Anna's team," Anna said smiling and Ben went over to stand by Ben.

"That doesn't seem fair," Wolfie said. "But I'll be on the Ben team."

They put the board and cards out and Anna rolled.

"This is an action," she said, and started drawing.

She had drawn one line and Anna said, "Surfing!"

"That's right!" Anna said.

"Not fair," Wolfie said.

"OK," Ben said, drawing a card.

"This is a thing."

He drew two small circles and then Ben shouted, "Spaceship!"

"That's it," Ben said laughing.

"Incredible," Wolfie said, shaking his head.

When it was Wolfie's turn to draw, he had drawn a circle and then drew a line and both Ben's at once yelled "Newton's apple!"

Wolfie nodded slowly.

The game went on for a while, Anna and Ben guessing correctly every time with just a few marks drawn, and Anna's team won.

"Only because you went first," Ben said.

Wolfie shook his head. "Let's go outside," he said.

They went outside and to the barn.

"We rode the horses," Anna said walking over to the black horse to stroke its nose.

"I wish we had more time," Anna said.

Wolfie and the two Ben's walked to the end of the barn.

"I wish I knew what to expect going back to England," Anna said.

Anna nodded. "Nature never did betray the heart that loved her," she said.

Anna looked at her and nodded slowly and Wolfie and the two Bens came back and they went inside. Anna's mom had made a cake and put some plates on the table.

"Anyone want desert?" she said.

"Yes!" Wolfie said and they sat down.

When they had finished, Anna stood up and looked for Ben, who had taken off his hat. She looked from Ben to Ben for a few seconds, confused.

"Sorry," Ben said, putting his hat back on.

She and Ben walked out onto the porch and looked at the barn. They could hear the horses whinnying softly. The moon was visible just above the trees.

"Anna, I think we should get married," Ben said.

She looked at Ben. "I do too," she said. "But I want to marry all of you."

Ben laughed.

"When we get back. To our time," and they kissed.

The next morning, when they woke up, the other Anna and Ben were up and getting ready to go back to England. They had changed into the older clothing.

"We look pretty good!" Ben said.

They watched them go into the arch room and through the arch and Stewart looked over at them. Anna smiled and nodded.

"We'll be leaving soon too," Al said to Anna and Wolfie.

"This is getting confusing," Anna's mom said to no one in particular and went to sit down. She took a ball of yarn and some knitting needles out of her bag and Anna came over and sat down beside her.

"When did you start knitting?" Anna said.

"A week or so ago. I needed something to do while waiting for you to come back. Was trying not to think about you getting eaten by a dinosaur."

"What are you making?"

She held up a small knitted blue square. "A sweater maybe? Or a sock?" They both laughed.

"Mom. I guess now that we've left for England it won't matter. If I tell you something."

Anna's mom looked at her.

"Things get better."

"I know. Al told me."

Al walked in and looked at Anna and they smiled. Sam came in and sat down with Anna and Sue.

Anna wished she could tell him how much better things would be. That he would be in an orchestra. "Hang in there," Anna said.

Now she walked over to Stewart and said, "Thank you for your help."

Stewart smiled and nodded.

"We need to get going soon," Al said.

He handed her a backpack and then stood up and gave one to Wolfie. "You can put anything you want to take in here."

She and Wolfie went to their rooms and put a few things in their bags. When she came out Ben was waiting for her.

"I hope you can find me," he said giving her a hug. "I'll see you in a few days."

Now the other Al came in the room. "How long?" he asked.

"I'm not sure," Al said. "Maybe we should let you know after we get there and have a look around. We can send someone back to discuss."

"Let's go in here, we need to get ready," Al said looking into the arch room.

He handed them each a white jump suit like the men who went through earlier were wearing and a helmet. "We'll need these."

Anna looked at the white suit. Now that she held it, she could tell it was a thick, insulated fabric. It had lots of pockets and Velcro straps and there were gloves. Anna put the suit on over her jeans and T-shirt and Wolfie put his on and then they put on the helmets. Al checked to make sure everything was closed up on their suits and he touched a button in his helmet. "Can you hear me?" he said.

"Yes," Anna and Wolfie both said.

"OK," Al said. He nodded to a technician who turned on the arch, which started to glow blue between the two poles.

Anna looked back at her mom and Ben and then stood behind Al. Al walked through the arch and Anna and Wolfie followed.

They stepped out of the arch into a grassy area with trees. There was a small hill on their right.

"Anna, can you hear me?" Wolfie asked.

"Yes."

"Are we on the moon?"

"I'm not sure."

"Maybe we're inside a dome?"

"I don't see one."

Al took a small walkie talkie out of his bag and turned it on.

There were a few other people walking by and they weren't wearing jumpsuits or helmets.

Now they heard Al's voice. "It looks like we don't need these suits. Or masks. Let's take them off and put them in our bags. People are starting to stare."

They put their bags down and took off their helmets. They took a few small breaths.

"I can breathe OK," Wolfie said.

They took off their jump suits and put them in the bags and Al picked up his walkie talkie and pushed a button on the side of it.

"I think that's too big to be the moon," Anna said, pointing up at a sphere in the sky.

"It's not bright enough," Wolfie said.

"No. It's dark."

Now Al started talking into his walkie talkie and listening. "OK," he said. "I see," and he put his arm down to his side and looked over at them.

"Wolfie, Anna. That's the earth."

Chapter 49

"The earth?" Anna said. "In pictures I've seen it's blue and white. Water and clouds."

"It's not now."

"What? How?"

"Right now we need to go find my men. They'll explain."

They walked over the small hill and saw that they were in a city. They started walking on a sidewalk and on the other side of the street there were buildings and more people. They now saw that they had been in a park.

"Not to ask the obvious question," Wolfie said. "But if we're on the moon, how is it that we're breathing?"

"Not to mention the trees and grass," Anna said.

"Hopefully we'll find out soon," Al said.

At the corner, they crossed the street and started walking down a smaller street. A few people were coming in and out of stores and apartment buildings.

"Tennessee fried chicken," Wolfie read a sign out loud.

"I wonder how big the city is?" Anna said.

Al talked into his radio and then said, "This way," and they turned right. The buildings seemed to be made of a dark concrete.

"Here it is," Al said, and they walked up a few steps and knocked on a door.

The door opened and a man Anna recognized from the arch room yesterday was standing there.

"Al," he said, shaking Al's hand. "Come in."

There was one other man in the room.

"Jim and Dave," Al said to Anna and Wolfie.

"Anna."

"Wofie."

"Well," Jim said. "Have a seat."

"What's going on?" Al said.

"We've been able to find out quite a bit. As you can see, the moon is different."

Anna nodded slowly.

"And the earth."

"It looks dead," Anna said.

"It basically is. After the last two hundred years, in this future, earth is no longer able to support life."

"The temperature?" Anna asked.

"Yes. But mainly the carbon dioxide levels. It got above two thousand ppm, which also starts to affect physiology."

"So there's nothing left on earth alive?"

"No."

"No water?"

"No."

"So everyone had to leave?" Wolfie asked.

"Yes."

"How many people?"

"Well, there are two million here."

"Where did everyone else go?"

"There's not anyone else."

"You mean only two million people survived?" Anna asked.

"Yep."

"Jesus," Al said. "And this city?"

"Well, there used to be a moon colony, of course. In our time. And there were resources here. Regolith," he gestured to the walls. "Bricks basically made out of moon dust."

Anna ran her hand along the wall.

"And there's water." Jim said.

"But how is there an atmosphere?" Wolfie said.

"The moon used to have an atmosphere," Al said.

Yes, but not enough gravity to hold onto it, so it was lost."

"So they increased the gravity." Al said.

"Yes. Gravity seems to be one thing we can control."

Al nodded. "And an electromagnetic field?"

"They created one. Lots of wire, metal and electricity. To protect the atmosphere."

"Holy shit," Wolfie said.

"And water can be split to generate oxygen." Al said.

"They made the atmosphere they wanted."

"Only two million people," Anna said, shaking her head.

"But here's the craziest thing. Once they jump started the environment and the temperature started to go up, they found life."

"What?" Wolfie said.

"It was at the pole, where most of the water is, but dormant. Microbial. Once it woke up it started adding oxygen to the atmosphere."

"Photosynthetic bacteria. Like Cyanobacteria." Wolfie said.

"Well that's a big deal," Anna said. "I guess under normal circumstances that would have been the headline."

"And this timeline? Does it have anything to do with Ben being taken? Did we not go back to England?"

"I think that's right."

"I thought there would be more robots in the future," Wolfie said.

"Well there is at least one," Jim said. "Qweb."

"Qweb is a robot?" Al asked.

"Yes. We've seen him."

"What does he look like?"

"Those people you saw in the park?"

"Yes."

"He looks like that."

"You mean he looks just like a person?"

"Yes."

"So there could be more. We just don't know."

"Yes."

"How can we tell them apart? From people?"

"We haven't figured out a way yet."

"And there's one more thing. It seems like, what we thought before, that Ben may not look the same here."

"Anna," Al said, thinking. "Did it seem like that Pyrorapter back in the Cretaceous was friendly to you? Like it knew you?"

"Kind of. It seemed to recognize me."

"How, do you think?"

"Well first it saw me," She paused. "But when it got closer, it seemed to be sniffing me."

Al nodded. "I think we could use its help."

"You mean here?"

"Yes."

"You're going to bring a Pyrorapter. A dinosaur. To the moon?"

"I'd like to. Would you go back and see? To get it?"

"I guess so?"

"Where have you set up the arch?" Al asked.

Jim walked over to a table and unrolled a sheet of paper.

"This is a map we've made of the city. Based on what we've seen."

Al and the others walked over.

There was one central clump of buildings in the center of the city. And smaller clumps around it, like at the end of spokes.

"It's arranged like the underwater city," Anna said.

"Both designed by Qweb, we think," Jim said. "We're here," he said, pointing to the map. He pointed to one of the small peripheral clumps.

"How big is the city?" Al asked.

"Ten by ten. Kilometers."

"Is that the park where we were?" Wolfie asked.

"Yes."

"This is where we've set up the arch," Jim said, pointing to a building a little farther out.

Al nodded. "Have you tested it yet?"

"No one's gone through. But it's working."

"Do they have a command center?"

"We think here," Jim pointed to a building in the central cluster. "But we haven't seen anyone that looks like police. Or soldiers."

"So basically they've won," Anna said.

"People may just be happy to be here. And not up there," Jim said pointing up, towards earth.

"How do people get around?" Al asked.

"There are some cars. Pods that come and go regularly. People walk a lot."

"Can we get to the arch facility now?"

"Yes. We haven't had any trouble getting around."

"We can leave some things here," Al said to Anna and Wolfie.

"Take these," he said, giving each of them a walkie talkie after he had switched them on. "You can put them in these shoulder bags."

Anna and Wolfie took the bags and put the walkie talkies in them and put the bags over their shoulders.

"OK," Jim said. "Let's go." They walked out the door and onto the sidewalk.

"Has anyone seemed to notice you?"

"We've been trying to keep a low profile. So far no one has approached us."

They walked down the street and Wolfie said, "Do you think we could get a bite to eat?"

"Here," Jim said, and they went into a small store.

They went inside and Anna and Wolfie picked up sandwiches and some drinks and fruit. Al picked up a package of lunch meat and they went to the counter. Jim paid and they went outside.

"How did we pay for those?" Anna asked.

"We sold a couple of the things we brought with us. Not exactly black market but not exactly not."

They started walking again.

"It's so strange. Walking around on the moon like this," Anna said.

"The changes they made. They call it Lunaforming," Jim said.

"But the earth," she said, looking up.

"Do you have an idea where Ben might be?" Al said.

"We think probably the control center. We've been able to get into their monitoring system, but we haven't seen anyone that looks like him. That's why we think maybe he looks different."

"They probably aren't expecting us?"

"I don't think they think we could have come here."

Al nodded.

They passed an open area and Anna could see a farm in the distance. A large area with a green crop and she pointed at it.

"Corn," Jim said. "Here," he said pointing, and they turned and walked down a smaller street and stopped at a large building with no windows. It looked empty. Jim knocked on the door and another of the men from the arch room opened it and smiled at Al.

"Welcome to the moon," he said shaking Al's hand.

They went in and Al started talking to the man. When Al had finished talking, the man raised his eyebrows but didn't say anything.

Anna saw that a portable arch had been set up. It was like the one they had used to get back from England but smaller. The poles were extendable, like antennae, and had wires reaching from their tops to the floor.

"They keep getting smaller," Anna said.

"Have they made a pocket-sized one yet?" Wolfie asked.

"So just to make sure," Anna said. "We're going back to the Cretaceous. And we're going to try to bring back the Pyrorapter."

"Yes," Al said.

"To here."

"Yes. And he's going to help us find Ben."

Anna nodded slowly and looked at Wolfie.

"How are we going to get it to follow us? Through the arch," Anna said.

"Well, it's been through once. And it seems to know you."

"Uh-huh."

"Maybe with some food," Wolfie said.

"I wonder what Pyrorapters eat?"

"Maybe it would eat this," Al said holding up the package of lunch meat he bought at the store.

Anna took the package of meat and put it in her backpack. Al handed her a knife, which she also put in her backpack. Wolfie put a knife in his backpack.

"Do we have the right coordinates?" Anna asked.

"Yes," Al said. "For sending Wolfie back. We'll leave the arch open."

"For how long?"

"Well, it seems to live near there and found us pretty quickly the last time. Hopefully you won't need more than fifteen minutes or so. Ready?"

Anna and Wolfie walked over to the two antennae.

"Are you sure this thing works?" Anna said.

The man who let them in opened a laptop computer and typed something and a green arch formed between the antennae. "Yep," he said.

Anna looked at Wolfie and walked through and Wolfie followed. When they stepped out it was raining, and they were standing in water up to their ankles. Rain was dripping from the broad tree branches above them.

Anna looked over at Wolfie. His hair and beard were wet. "You look older Wolfie," she said.

"I feel older."

"You know. You could stay. With Suzan. We can probably do this."

Wolfie shook his head. "We need to finish this."

The rain had slowed, and the sun was starting to shine through the canopy. "I never noticed before," Anna said looking up. "They kind of look like giant Christmas trees."

There was a log near one of the tree trunks that wasn't too wet, and they sat down on it.

"This is near where you twisted your ankle," Anna said.

"I've been looking down a lot more," Wolfie said.

Behind them, the arch continued to glow. Anna noticed, for the first time, that it made a slight crackling sound.

Now they heard a rustling sound to their right. They stood up, and out of the broad leaves of the understory of plants, several heads appeared. Their gray noses first and then red heads. They moved slowly forward, crouching with their wings outspread, almost touching the ground. One of them hissed.

"Here we go," said Anna.

"Wolfie? Anna?"

They heard a voice behind them and turned their heads and saw Jim from the camp. He had a bow that was drawn and an arrow and was pointing it at the Pyroraptor.

"What are you doing here? Watch out!"

The Pyroraptor had stopped and lowered its head and started hissing.

"No! Don't shoot! We need the Pyroraptor!"

"What do you mean you need it?" Jim asked, still holding the bow. Two or three of the men with him also had their bows drawn.

"I mean we need to take it."

He lowered his bow and motioned for the others to lower theirs.

"Take it where?"

"To the moon. We can explain later."

He nodded slowly, his eyebrows raised, and started backing away and with his arms indicated for the others to move away also.

The Pyroraptor stopped hissing and raised its head slightly. Now it started moving forward slowly. The other Pyroraptors stayed near the bushes where they had appeared.

Now it was about three feet from Anna and lowered its head slightly.

"Anna," Wolfie said.

"Don't move," Anna said.

Now the Pyroraptor was close enough for her to touch.

She could see the holes in its beak and the reddish brown feathers on its head. She thought of a scarlet macaw she had seen once. Now it extended its neck and sniffed her and then looked up at her.

"Let's back slowly towards the arch," Anna said, and she took one step backwards.

Wolfie took a step back and the Pyrorapter turned its head quickly in his direction.

"Anna," he said.

"Keep walking slowly," she said.

They were close to the arch now but the Pyroraptor hadn't moved.

"Take the lunch meat out of my pack," Anna said.

Wolfie reached slowly into Anna's pack and took out the meat. The Pyroraptor raised its head slightly and started sniffing. It started moving forward slowly. They stopped just in front of the arch and now the Pyroraptor was right in front of them. Wolfie was holding the meat out in front of him.

"On three I'll slowly back through the arch, and then you follow," Anna said, and she took one step back and into the arch. She was back in the room now with Al who looked relieved to see her. Now Wolfie came backing through with his outstretched arm holding the meat. A few seconds passed and then the Pyroraptor's beak appeared and then its head. It paused, half in and half out of the arch, its head moving side to side. It sniffed as it turned its head and then continued moving slowly forward. Now wings appeared, stretched forward, and the body, with a long white stripe. It took one last step, and Anna noticed how long the claws on its hands and feet were and then it was in the room.

"Go ahead and give that to him," Anna said, and Wolfie tossed the meat to the ground in front of him. The Pyroraptor stretched out its neck and sniffed the package and then holding it with one claw, used its beak to tear open the package. It took a small bite of the meat, throwing its head back to swallow and then ate the rest in a few bites and looked around.

Al looked at the technician and nodded and the technician shut down the arch. When the humming behind it stopped, the Pyroraptor turned its head quickly behind him and then forward again. Then it stood still looking at Anna and then Wolfie.

"One Pyroraptor," Anna said to Al and they both smiled.

The Pyroraptor looked around. It walked to the antennae and reached out with its beak and pulled on the wire attaching the antennae to the floor. The technician stepped forward but then back again when the Pyroraptor quickly turned its head and looked at him. Now it walked over to a mirror and looked at its reflection, first with one eye then the other.

"We can't stay here," Al said. "We'll need to go back to the apartment. We should probably get going."

"Al," Anna said. "He'll need to come too." She looked over at the Pyroraptor who had its head inside a cabinet. Something startled it and it bumped its head when it turned around.

"Right. Jim, how often do those cars come around? Do they come here?"

"They do. Every hour or so."

Al looked at Anna who looked at the Pyroraptor who was pulling some stuffing out of a chair. Anna raised her eyebrows.

Al took a sandwich out of his backpack and handed it to Anna. "Anna, can you see if you can get him to come over to you with this?"

The Pyroraptor had gone into the office and Anna walked over to the door and held out the sandwich. The Pyroraptor looked up and walked over to her.

She turned to look at Al. "This was easier I think than getting him into a car is going to be."

"Maybe sit down over there and see if he'll come over," he said looking at the chair.

"Will this arch stay up?" Wolfie asked looking at the two antennae.

"Yes, we're keeping it up," Al said, and the technician nodded. "He'll stay here."

Anna went over to the chair and sat down, still holding the sandwich. The Pyroraptor walked over and stood beside the chair, and she dropped a piece of the sandwich on the floor. The Pyroraptor ate it and looked up at her. When she put the rest of the sandwich in her bag the Pyroraptor stayed.

"There aren't a lot of people around here," Al said. "Getting him into the car shouldn't be a problem. But the area by the apartment is more crowded."

"Maybe wait till it's dark?" Anna said.

"We could. I'd like to get back as soon as we can though."

"We'll just have to move as fast as we can, I guess. He can move pretty fast." She looked over at the Pyroraptor who was pulling at something under a table.

"There should be a car coming around in about ten minutes," Jim said looking at his watch.

They put a few things in their bags and Al went over to look out the window. Anna walked over too and the Pyroraptor followed her.

"When the car pulls up and stops, I'll go out first," Al said. "Anna, you come out next. Hopefully he will follow you," he said, looking at the Pyroraptor. "Wolfie, you and Jim come last."

Anna looked at Wolfie and nodded.

A few minutes later the car drove up and stopped. Al went out the door and opened the front passenger door and back door. Anna came out the door and looked back at the Pyroraptor. It looked at her and then stuck its head out the door. She started walking to the car and gestured to it with her arms. It hopped out the door and stopped. When it saw Anna get into the car, it jumped in after her and stood on the seat, stretching its neck to look in the front seat.

"Good," Al said, looking relieved, and got in the front seat. Jim got in the front seat on the other side and Wolfie got in the back seat trying to sit as far away from the Pyroraptor as he could. A few seconds later the car drove off.

"Will this car make any stops before it gets to the apartment?" Al asked.

"Probably not since it's full," Jim said, pointing to a few sensors inside the car and the car pulled away from the curb.

The car slowed down once at a stop where three people were standing. Wolfie and Anna moved closer to the Pyroraptor to try to conceal it and the car kept going. A few minutes later, the car pulled up in front of the apartment and stopped. Al got out and opened the back door. Wolfie got out and looked back in the car at Anna and the Pyroraptor. Al went up the steps and opened the door to the apartment.

"Let's get out," Anna said to the Pyroraptor and gently pushed against it with her shoulder. It hopped out and stood beside Wolfie. Anna quickly got out and ran up the steps to the open door and the Pyroraptor followed her in. Al looked up and down the street and breathed out, and he and Wolfie went in and they closed the door.

Anna went to the kitchen and opened the refrigerator. The Pyroraptor followed her and stuck his head into the refrigerator and quickly took it out again. Anna took out an apple and sat down.

"Anna, did you bring any clothes for Ben?" Al asked.

"Yes. A shirt and some jeans."

"Can you do me a favor and take out the shirt and leave the pants in the backpack and take the backpack and put it in a closet in one of the bedrooms?"

"OK," she said and took out the shirt. She stood up and carried the backpack into one of the bedrooms and put it in a closet and shut the door and went back out to the living room.

"Thanks. Now, show the Pyroraptor the shirt and give it a treat."

She held the shirt up to the Pyroraptor and it sniffed the shirt, and she gave it a piece of a sandwich.

"Great," Now put the shirt away and walk towards the bedroom.

She walked towards the bedroom and the Pyroraptor ran ahead of her. When she got to the bedroom, the Pyroraptor was standing in front of the closet scratching at the door with its claws.

Al came in and smiled.

In the living room, Jim and Wolfie were sitting in front of two computer screens. Anna and Al walked over.

"Video feeds from the monitoring system we hacked into," Jim said.

Each screen was divided into four displays showing interiors and exteriors of buildings: hallways, conference rooms and courtyards. The displays changed about every fifteen seconds.

"Anything yet?" Al asked.

"Not yet. We're looking," Jim said.

"Jim, have you been coming and going much?"

"Yeah. We haven't had any problems."

Al nodded. "I'm going to go have a look around," he said. "Anna?"

Anna looked up.

"Want to come along?"

"Sure," she said and stood up.

They walked out the door and turned left onto the sidewalk. They crossed the street and walked back to the park where they first arrived and sat on a bench.

They sat for a few minutes, not talking, and then Al said, "Anna, what do you think the most important things are to be happy?"

"Well. I think it's different for different people. For some people money. Or power. For me, friends and being with people I love."

Al nodded.

"I wonder how far the park goes," Anna said after a while, and they stood up and started walking. They walked through the park for about fifteen minutes and soon were the only people in the park. They walked up a hill, and at the top, they stopped. The grass stopped abruptly and beyond it were only grey dirt and rocks. Strange dark shadows on the dark surface. Farther off they could see rows of solar panels.

"I guess this is it," Anna said, staring at the expanse of nothingness.

"It takes a lot sometimes for people to stay in power," Al said.

Anna nodded and looked around then looked up at the dark earth. "Striving night and day with prodigious effort to scale the summit of wealth and secure power."

"Lucretius?" Al said.

"Yes. Epicurus."

"Simple pleasures."

"Getting and spending they lay waste their powers."

Al looked at her.

"Wordsworth," she said.

Al nodded. "I wonder where they'll go next?" he said.

"Maybe they've learned something."

"Anna, do you think you and Ben will get married?"

"Yes. When we get back."

"That's wonderful," he said and smiled at her.

They walked back through the park and to the street. In the distance, about two miles away, they could see the central complex with its mass of tall grey buildings. A car drove past them with two passengers in the back seat. In the distance, two cars in the sky flew towards the central complex. They stopped at a small store where they bought some things for dinner with money Jim had given them and then walked back to the apartment.

As soon as they were in, Jim looked up. "I think we have something," he said.

Al and Anna walked over. "What is it?" Anna asked.

"Here, in one of the buildings in the central complex. Area B we're calling it. In this corridor. Here." He held up a printed copy. "People keep coming and going through this corridor and there is always someone standing by this door." He pointed to a door off the corridor.

"A guard?"

"Looks like it."

"Have you seen anyone coming in or out?"

"Yeah, but they always talk to the guard on their way in and out."

"So there may be someone in there."

"That's what I'm thinking. We've managed to lock the feed onto that camera."

"Good," Al said. "Keep an eye on that door to see if anyone else goes out."

Wolfie took some meat from a package and put it in a frying pan. "What is this stuff?" he asked.

"I think basically what we eat at home. Soy protein." Jim said.

Wolfie boiled some water and added some pasta to the pot.

"Do people still settle I wonder?" Anna said.

"It doesn't seem like it," Jim said. "They have the one arch. That they used to get Ben. But I think this is it. I think they're here to stay."

Anna shook her head.

"I think we're ready to eat," Wofie said.

"Y'all go ahead. I'm going to look at this for a minute," Jim said.

They sat down with their plates and the Pyroraptor came over and sat down next to Anna.

"Hi," she said and got up and put some food on a plate and put it on the floor and the Pyroraptor started eating.

They were just about finished eating when Jim stood up. "I think I have something!" he said.

They all ran over.

"What?" Anna said.

"Here. They brought someone out. Two guards on either side and took him into another room. Here's a still."

The photograph showed a young man, maybe six feet tall with blond hair.

"It doesn't look like him," Wolfie said. "Not really."

"But there's something about the walk," Anna said. "And the eyes. There! When he looked up at the camera."

"I see it too," Wolfie said. "I think that might be him."

"OK," Al said and picked up his walkie talkie and started talking into it. "The others are going to meet us there," he said putting down the walkie talkie. "Jim, where is the rest of the stuff you brought?"

"There," Jim said pointing to two bags on the floor.

Al took out a gun and a few small, round discs and a few handheld controllers. He handed the gun to Jim and took another one out and put it on the table.

He put the things into a backpack and put the backpack on.

"Anna, where's the Pyroraptor?"

"He's in there," she said pointing to the bedroom just as it came walking in.

"Will he follow you?"

"I think so."

"Do you have Ben's clothes?"

"Yes," she said, putting on her backpack.

"OK, let's go," Al said, and they all went out the door and the Pyroraptor followed.

A van stopped in front of the apartment. There were already two people on it but when Anna and the Pyroraptor stepped on the two people got off.

"We have to go to a main terminal first and change cars," Jim said. "To take us into the central complex."

The van made two more stops but no one else got on and then stopped at the main terminal. They got off and walked across the terminal. People moved out of their way when they saw the Pyroraptor, who was walking upright and turning his head left and right. His claws made a clicking sound on the hard floor.

Above them, they saw a car land on a platform.

"Skycar!" Woflie said. "Can we take one of those?"

"We're going to have to," Jim said.

They went up an escalator and Jim looked at a display. "The next car will take us there," he said.

People were looking at Anna and the Pyroraptor and moving away.

"If they didn't know we were here, they probably do now," Jim said.

Now Al waved to three other people on the platform and they joined them and they looked at a map of the transportation system. Al handed them the backpack but took out his gun first and put it in his coat pocket.

"They're going to get off at the stop before ours," Al said, "and go in on foot. One of them will go to the roof of the building where there is a skycar pad. The other two will stay in the lobby."

"There's our car," Jim said as a car dropped to the pad and several people got off.

They all got on and the Pyroraptor looked out the window as they took off.

"Anna, can you show him Ben's clothes?" Al said and Anna took out a shirt and showed it to the Pyroraptor who started looking around.

As they got closer to the central complex, the buildings and cars became more dense.

"It's been light since we got here," Anna said. "How long are the days?"

"About thirty of our days," Jim said. "Daylight won't be a problem."

The car slowed and started to descend and then stopped and the three men got out.

"Good luck," they said as they left the car picking up the backpacks, and then the car rose again.

Now the car banked slightly right and rose. They were flying between tall buildings and the number of flying cars increased.

"That's it ahead," Jim said, pointing to a tall building. The car rose and was headed for a flat area about half way up the building. It started to descend and gently landed on the platform.

"That's us," Jim said, and they stood up. The car door opened and they got out. The car rose and another one was descending to land.

"Busy place," Al said.

"This way," Jim said.

Al and Wolfie followed.

"Anna," Al said.

"We're coming," she said, trying to get the attention of the Pyroraptor, who was looking over the edge of the landing platform. It was windy and they were about forty stories high, and when the Pyroraptor saw her, he ran to her and they followed Al and Wolfie into the building.

"What floor are we going to?" Al asked.

"The fiftieth," Jim said. "I think we'd better take the stairs."

The found an entrance to the stairwell and opened the door and went in. They started climbing the stairs and Anna saw that the Pyroraptor wasn't climbing.

"Anna, why isn't he following?" Al said.

"Probably never seen this many stairs before."

"Can you carry him?"

"Have you seen his claws?"

"Did you bring any food?"

Anna reached into her bag and brought out a bag with small pieces of meat in it. When the Pyroraptor saw it, he carefully took a step and was soon walking up the steps to her. She gave him a piece of the meat and then they both continued up the stairs.

After a minute, Jim said, "This is our floor."

"I think go ahead and show him Ben's clothes," Jim said and Anna took the shirt out of her backpack. She showed it to the Pyroraptor who put his head close to it and then looked at Anna.

"OK," Al said, "Let's go."

They opened the door and stepped out of the stairwell and a man was standing there. He was tall with blond hair and wearing a black suit.

"Colonel Paris," he said. "Good to see you again."

Al stood looking at the man for a few seconds. "Qweb," he said. "Last time I saw you, you were a bunch of wires in a hole in the ground at the bottom of the ocean."

"Yes, well, that was a long time ago. Congratulations on getting here. Finding us." He looked at the Pyroraptor. "And on bringing a dinosaur to the moon. I don't think anyone has ever done that."

The Pyroraptor walked slowly forward and stuck its beak out, almost touching Qweb. It cocked its head and looked back at Anna and then walked back to her.

"Doesn't like the way you smell, I guess," Al said.

Qweb smiled.

"Where is he?" Al said.

"Interesting question."

"Where is he?" Al said, now pointing the gun at Qweb.

"Colonel Paris, you know I am just as human as you."

"Good. So this gun can kill you same as me."

Now the Pyroraptor looked up suddenly and started running down the hallway, its claws slipping on the hard floor.

"I'll stay here. You all follow him," Jim said raising his gun and Al, Anna and Wolfie ran after the Pyroraptor.

The Pyroraptor was running ahead of them and skidded as it turned a corner. They turned and went after it. It ran up to a door and a man was standing beside the door. He took a couple of steps back when the Pyroraptor ran up. When they caught up to it, the Pyroraptor was scratching at the door.

"Open the door," Al said to the man. The man looked at him.

"Open the door," Al said again, this time pointing the gun at the man.

The man looked at him for a few seconds then looked at the Pyroraptor who was scratching at the door and entered some numbers on a keypad. The door opened and the man they had seen in the camera was standing there. The Pyroraptor ran up to him and then looked back excitedly at Anna.

He looked at the Pyroraptor for a few seconds and then at Anna and Wolfie.

"Anna! Wolfie!" he said.

"It's him," Wolfie said, and Anna ran to hug him.

"How did you get here? I have no idea what's going on. I don't look like myself."

"We'll have to explain later," Al said from the hallway. "We need to get going."

Ben looked at the Pyroraptor and then at Anna who said, "We'll explain that too, let's go."

They went back into the hallway and Al was still pointing the gun at the guard. The guard had a walkie talkie on his belt.

"Give me that," Al said, pointing at the walkie talkie and the man took it off his belt and handed it to him. They walked quickly back to the stairway and Jim was still there with his gun on Qweb.

They opened the door to the stairwell and went in, the Pyroraptor looking back at Qweb as he went in.

"How are we getting out?" Al said.

"There was a slight problem downstairs, so I think we're going up," Jim said. "There is a car waiting for us outside."

They started walking up the stairs and at the top they went through a door which led to the outside. A skycar was sitting on a pad and one of Al's men was standing beside it. They ran to the car and Al spoke to the man briefly and they got in.

"It's on manual," Jim said. "We're going straight to the arch."

The car rose from the platform and turned and flew in the direction from which they had come earlier. In the distance they could see the grey, rocky landscape outside of the city and above them the dark earth.

"Anna, what happened?" Ben said. "Why do I look like this?"

"Well, Qweb kidnapped you. Brought you here."

"OK."

"But also somehow to the past."

"To two places?"

"Yes."

"When in the past?"

"A few days before we went back to England."

"They wanted to stop us."

"Yes."

"So, I'm there and here at the same time?"

"Somehow, yes."

"You saw me? Did I look different?"

"No you looked the same. There. Then."

"But wait. I was already there. Waiting for you to get back from the Cretaceous."

"Yes."

"So there are actually two of me there. And one here." He thought for a few seconds. "There are three of me right now."

"Yes. Well, you and I went back to England."

The car started to descend and landed in the street near the building with the arch and everyone got out and the car rose again. The Pyroraptor watched it as it ascended and flew away.

They went inside and Al went into the room with the arch to talk to the technician.

"But why do I look like this?" Ben said to Anna and Wolfie.

"I don't think we know," Wolfie said. "But Al thought it was a possibility. You're somehow not complete."

Ben nodded and looked at the Pyroraptor.

"We brought him here to help us find you. We gave him your clothes to smell and he found the room where you were."

Ben nodded, looking again at the Pyroraptor who was standing next to Anna.

"And he's going back? To the Cretaceous?"

"Yes. With Wolfie."

Now Ben looked at Wolfie. "It's good to see you. Thanks. Again."

"Anytime."

Al came back in. "OK," he said. "Jim is going back first to make sure Ben from the past goes back to our time at the same time as Ben goes back." He nodded at Ben. "Then we'll send Wolfie back. To the Cretaceous. And the Pyroraptor." He looked at the Pyroraptor who had gotten up onto a couch.

"When the time comes, Ben will go back. At the same time as the other Ben. Then Anna. Then me."

Jim was standing in front of the arch. He and Al confirmed the time that both Ben's would be sent through the arches. Now he shook hands with Al and walked through.

Anna breathed out. "Anyone else getting tired of time travel?"

"When will I go?" Ben asked.

"In about thirty minutes," Al said.

"And me?" Wolfie said.

"Are you ready?"

"I think so." He turned to Ben and Anna. "I'll see you both again soon?"

Anna looked at Ben, who somehow knew that they had talked about getting married. "Yes," Ben said, and he put his arm around Anna.

Wolfie smiled and nodded. "OK," he said and turned to Al.

"Here," Anna said, handing Wolfie the package of treats for the Pyroraptor who looked up at Wolfie.

Wolfie took the bag and walked to the arch room. The technician had turned on the arch and was making some adjustments with his laptop.

"OK," he said to Al who gave the technician a thumbs up.

The technician looked up and nodded. Wolfie walked through the arch. His outline became indistinct and then he was gone. The Pyroraptor hopped through and disappeared.

They stood looking at the arch for a few seconds.

Al looked at his watch. "OK, we have about half an hour," he said and sat down. Ben and Anna sat down too.

"Anna," Al said, "what do you think about Qweb's claim to being human?"

"Well, I think it would be hard to define what it means to be human by looking at humanity."

Al nodded. "I think I see what you mean."

"Why do you think Qweb didn't try to stop us?"

"I think he was surprised we were here. He probably thinks we won't succeed. In getting both Ben's back."

"How do you think you would have felt? Shooting him."

"It's hard to imagine what it's like to be Qweb. His internal life. But he must have one. He certainly looked human."

"I guess like any of us he's all of his appearances," she said. "So when we go back, he won't exist anymore?"

"Not in our timeline."

Anna nodded.

"Five minutes," Al said, and Ben stood up. And then the lights went out.

"Damnit," Al said, and looked in at the arch, which was no longer glowing.

"I guess Qweb is not going to go gentle into that good night," Anna said.

The technician came in holding his hands up.

"Is there any other way to power the arch?" Al said.

"Well, there's that," he said, pointing to a battery near a pile of equipment.

"Is that enough?"

"There's a few more," he said pointing and walked over.

"We could connect them. In series," Ben said walking over and kneeling to look at them.

"There's wire here," the technician pointed to a box.

"Three minutes," Al said.

"Hurry," Ben said, and the technician handed him the wire and they carried it into the arch room. Anna ran over and picked up one of the batteries and carried it in and Ben took the other two.

"Heavy," Anna said, setting it down.

"Are there any wire cutters?" Ben said.

"Here," the technician handed him the wire cutters.

Ben cut some lengths of wire and turned nuts on top of each battery and connected the batteries together. "OK," he said. "That's it."

"One minute," Al said looking at his watch and shaking his head.

"Al," Anna said.

The technician hooked the batteries to the arch and turned it on. Nothing happened.

Ben looked at Anna and then the arch started to glow.

"Thank goodness," Anna said.

"Fifteen seconds."

Ben stood in front of the arch.

"Now," Al said, and Ben walked through.

"Did he make it?" Anna said after a few seconds.

“Let’s hope so. Are you ready?”

“Never more ready,” Anna said and walked through the arch.

She walked out into the arch room and saw Ben standing there and ran to hug him. His mother and Sue were standing near him smiling and Sue came and hugged Anna.

“Anna, you did it,” she said. “Again.”

Now Al came walking through and breathed out deeply when he saw them.

“How do I look,” Ben asked.

“Like you. Thank goodness,” Anna said. “How do you feel?”

“Tired. I need some sleep.” He and Anna went into one of the bedrooms.

A few hours later they came out and Beth and Sue were sitting at the table with Sam.

“We have some news we’d like to share,” Anna said.

“Oh?” Beth said.

“Ben and I are getting married!”

“That’s wonderful!” Beth said and Sue came over and hugged them.

“Also we’re going to go settle, live in the Cretaceous. With Wolfie and Suzan.”

“Where will you have the wedding?”

Anna and Ben looked at each other and smiled.

Chapter 50

Beth, Sue, Sam and Al stepped through the arch onto the wet ground.

Anna, Ben and Wolfie were waiting for them.

"Where are the dinosaurs?" Sam said excitedly.

"Yes, where are the dinosaurs," Sue asked, looking around nervously.

"You don't need to worry about the big ones," Anna said and laughed, and they started walking in the direction of the sea.

"Look!" Sam yelled, pointing at some Hadrosaurs raising their heads from the water, plants hanging from their mouths.

They could hear the surf and when they got to the beach, they turned right to walk to the camp. They walked up to the camp and Suzan ran out to hug Wolfie.

Mary walked out too to meet everyone. "You all are welcome to sleep in my cabin tonight," she said, and they put their bags in the cabin. Anna and Ben walked out to look at the ocean. "I think I'm going to like living here," Ben said. "Me too," Anna said, and they kissed.

That night they had a dinner and Settlers from the other camps came. After dinner, the Settlers with musical instruments played music and everyone danced.

The fires were dying down and Anna and Al walked down to the shore and sat on the pebbles, listening to the water come onto the beach and then pull away, throwing pebbles up the beach of the round earth's shore.

“What will happen to the Quantco CEO?” Anna said.

“I’m not sure,” Al said.

“Did he come back?”

“I think so. He can’t hurt us again. The safeguards.”

“Will he go to prison? He did try to kill us.”

“I don’t think so.”

“I guess maybe justice isn’t really about going to jail. It’s more about what’s right. I think doing what’s right is somehow good for you.”

“The just man has become a friend to himself,” Al said.

The wedding was the next afternoon on the beach. Al acted as the minister and Wolfie and Suzan stood up at the front with Ben and Anna. Just as they exchanged rings, the sun was setting behind them and two Pterosaurs flew up to their nests on the cliffs. Anna heard a rustling behind them and turned to see the head of the Pyroraptor looking at them from out of the bushes.

Acknowledgements

I want to thank my wife, Jami, for encouraging me to write. I acknowledge borrowing descriptions from Dorothy Wordsworth's journals and William Hazlitt's "My First Acquaintance with Poets" to provide descriptions of the Lake District, William Wordsworth and Samuel Taylor Coleridge.

www.ingramcontent.com/pod-product-compliance
Lightning Source LLC
Chambersburg PA
CBHW021149160726
47994CB00001B/122